DEEP WEB

by Ryan Wiley

Copyright © 2015 by Ryan Wiley
All rights reserved. This book or any portion thereof
may not be reproduced or used in any manner whatsoever
without the express written permission of the publisher
except for the use of brief quotations in a book review.

First Printing, 2015
Amazon Digital Services, Inc.

Ryan Wiley
Visit my website at www.RyanWiley.com

Disclaimer

Hidden on the Internet is a place called the Deep Web. It's easy to get to with the right software, and near-impossible to trace your activities on.

It's home to illegal activity such as credit card fraud, prostitution, buying and selling of drugs, and even hiring hitmen.

Bitcoins are the currency of choice for many of these offerings, a cyber-currency that isn't regulated or taxed by any government. It's also completely anonymous.

All of the above is REAL.

The characters and events are fiction.

Chapter 1

"You looking forward to date night with your sister?" Shane asked.

"It's not a date night. I haven't seen her in two weeks and wanted to catch up with her. It's not like I have anything better to do," Greg said.

"You could hang out with us sales guys instead. It's amateur night at Foxxxie's. It's fun watching them not have a fucking clue what they're doing. It somehow makes it better that way. Because they're more real, ya know? You get to laugh at them *and* get a big chub at the same time. Does it get any better?"

"Sounds romantic," Greg said.

"It is! You've gotta be about to burst. How long has it been since Carrie broke up with you? Six months?"

"Yeah."

"God, man. And I'm sure you haven't gotten any since then. Bet you're whacking off three times a day. Tell you what: you come tonight and I'll pay for the Asian special lap dance. You can't go all the way, but they do throb the knob and give you a happy ending."

"Well, as tempting as that sounds, Shane, I think I'll hang out with sis tonight."

"Fine. Be an incest homo. If you change your mind, let me know. You still golfing with us on Sunday? It's finally supposed to warm up and quit all this cold bullshit."

"Yeah, of course."

"Cool. Tee time is 9:30. My new Callaway driver came in yesterday. I can't wait to finally beat your ass."

"How much did that thing cost you? Four hundred?"

"Five. I had a custom shaft put in."

"When are you going to learn it's not about how far you drive it, but how well you chip and putt?"

"Yeah, yeah," Shane said, waving his hand in the air. You just make sure your wallet is stacked on Sunday."

"If you say so."

Greg accomplished nothing that afternoon. As a research analyst at Vinditec, he could easily get most of his work done in the morning and then slack off the rest of the day, as long as he pretended to work when his boss walked by.

Shane was in sales, and it was part of Greg's job to create fancy charts for him to take into pitches for prospecting clients. Greg liked to live vicariously through the sales guys, since he knew he'd never have the internal fortitude to sell to people. His personality was a far cry from the egotistical, alpha-male mindset that all of the sales guys had. But Shane had taken a liking to him from day one and had brought him along on their golfing excursions every Sunday. He figured they liked having one "normal" person with them, someone they could crack jokes at. Greg didn't mind.

On his way home from work, Greg thought about his sister. Being twins, they'd been through a lot together and were very close. It was much different than most other brother-sister relationships. All of his friends in school had hated their sisters.

But he and Jessica had always had a great relationship.

In elementary school, they had insisted that their parents place them in the same classes. And it wasn't until the fourth grade, when classes were divided into periods and subjects, that they were forced into different classes.

In middle and high school, they began to spend a little more time with their own friends, but both considered the other to be their best friend. Jessica set up almost all of Greg's dates for dances. Unlike her brother, she attracted a lot of attention from the opposite sex. Greg, like most brothers, was always extremely protective of her. Their only real arguments came when Jessica dated a guy that he didn't like or trust: mostly jocks that he knew were assholes from conversations he'd heard in locker rooms.

This had happened on two different occasions. Jessica would get mad at Greg's initial lecture. They'd yell at each other. But in the end, Jessica was always quick to forgive. She never said it, but he knew she was always grateful that she had him to look after her.

When college came, they both chose Ohio State. As close as they'd been, they never discussed which school they were planning on attending. He'd always been too scared to bring it up and figured Jessica had been the same way. But Greg had planned on walking on to the golf team, thinking he could eventually get a scholarship, which he did for the last two years. Jessica carried a perfect 4.0 grade point average in high school, was valedictorian, and was offered a full ride to Ohio State, essentially making her decision for her.

When their parents addressed concerns of them attending the same school, they argued that it was one of the largest campuses in the United States. They could be living miles away from each other and hardly ever see each other.

But that did not turn out to be the case. During their first two years, they had lived in adjacent dorms and ran into each other a lot. While they no longer took the same classes, they often found the time to have lunch and dinner together.

It was their way of coping with the major change of being in college. No longer living with their parents, they could still have a little piece of home each time they were together.

The first time that he began to feel as if they were growing apart was when she met James, late in their junior year. Greg liked him and thought he was a nice guy. Jessica stayed with him for the rest of college, and he thought that they'd get married. But three months after they graduated, James felt inspired to go to Africa to help those in need. Jessica had already started her job at Adriar Pharmaceuticals and stayed.

James fell in love with helping the people there and Jessica loved her job, so they both parted ways.

It was the saddest he'd ever seen her. His heart broke with hers when it happened.

Greg pulled into the driveway of his apartment in downtown Columbus. Jessica's place was within walking distance, just a few blocks down. Even though they weren't together much, he liked knowing she was close by. They'd promised each other that, at the end of each month, they'd take turns going to each other's apartment for a homemade dinner and quality hang out time.

That night, it was his turn to do the cooking, and he carried the heavy brown paper bag, full of ingredients, up the stairs. For dinner, he was making their mom's special pasta that they had grown up on. The family recipe had been passed down over three generations. Greg and Jessica both joked, saying that if they needed something to fall back on, they could start a spaghetti restaurant together.

He entertained the idea much more often than she did.

Greg started the prep work. It was 5:30, and he knew she'd be there any minute. Their entire family had always been punctual.

He was looking forward to catching up with her. He hadn't heard from her in two weeks, except for the text that she'd sent yesterday to confirm she was coming.

The pasta was boiling as he stirred the sauce. The sweet smell of marinara filled the room.

Greg couldn't wait to see her.

But little did he know, that night would be one he'd soon want to forget.

It would change his life forever.

Chapter 2

"So, sis, did you ever have a second date with Dan?"

"No. He was all right, but all he talked about was going to this place and that place. He was *super* into traveling. I even mentioned that I had a fear of flying, but he kept on rambling and ignoring anything I had to say."

"Ahh, that's too bad."

"Oh, it's fine. What about you?"

Greg sighed, "I'm still… you know."

"Can't get over Carrie?"

"Yeah."

"Come on, bro, you need to put yourself out there. You've probably got a subscription to a dozen porn sites by now, don't you?" Jessica said with a smile.

"No, I don't!" Greg said, defensively. "Everyone knows PornHub is the only one you need."

"I see. You know, I could set you up with one of my friends."

Greg laughed, "I'm still not ready to forgive you for setting me up on that date with Vicky."

"Fine. I'll admit she wasn't the best looking."

"Wasn't the best looking!? Jess, she reminded me of an owl. I mean, literally half of her face was made up of eyeballs."

Jessica paused. "She does have an unusual staring problem. But hey, she was skinny, right?"

"Yeah, but it was hard for me to tell since she was always sucking me into her crazy stare. I couldn't look away. And to make matters worse, she had a lazy eye."

"She does not!"

"She does! Her left eye. It's not a full-blown lazy eye, but there's something off about it. She could probably get away with it if her eyes weren't the size of basketballs."

Jessica started laughing. "Now that you mention it, I knew there was something a little off about her. All right, I messed up on that one. But Stacy? She's much better. Her eyeballs are perfectly average."

"That's good. What does she do?"

"She's…" Jessica paused. "I don't want to tell you."

"Oh great, what is it?"

"She works at the place that I get most of my groceries from."

"What, like a manager or something?"

Jessica looked down at her lap, afraid to say anything else.

Greg continued, "She works the checkout aisle, doesn't she? You're setting me up with a grocery bagger? I'm kinda looking to settle down here, Jess."

"It's not like that. She's a grad student at Capital. The grocery thing is just to help pay rent."

"What is she looking to do?"

"She's a journalism major. She wanted to do a story on my company for a school project, and she interviewed me. We hit it off. Then, when I was down at North Market the other day, I saw her there working. I asked if she was single and if she'd be interested in meeting you. That's about it."

"All right, so she doesn't work at a grocery store. She works at a little mom and pop place at North Market. That's a little better."

"Yeah, I think her parents own a farm. She doesn't work the checkout aisle at Wal-Mart or anything like that. I was buying some produce for my morning smoothies. She helped answer some questions I had about kale and spinach, like if it was still healthy if it wasn't cooked."

"Wait," Greg interrupted. "Now raw veggies aren't even healthy? Jess, you need to stop reading so much shit on the Internet."

"I don't read that much. You wouldn't understand; it's different for girls. You can chow down on plate after plate of pasta and not get fat. But for me, I'm already bursting out of my pants after eating this." She paused for a timely belch. Jessica had always been a tomboy like that. "And for the record, they are healthy. Stacy convinced me. There's something about oxalates that go away when you cook them. But Stacy told me that, as long as you buy dino kale and eat organic spinach, it would be all right."

"Of course she said that. My guess is that happened to be what they were selling that day."

"As it turns out, they were. But I believe what she said. Nevermind that, though. Do you want me to set you up or not?"

"I don't know. I appreciate it; I really do. I just don't know if I'm ready to start dating again. Carrie really broke my heart."

"I know she did. I was there. But sitting at home every night on your computer isn't going to make anything better. You need to get out there and at least try."

"Yeah, I know. I'm just scared. I don't want to feel that way ever again."

Jessica got up from the table and stood behind him,

massaging his shoulders to console him.

"Bro, I don't like seeing you like this. Tell you what: go on a date with Stacy. If it doesn't work out, then it doesn't work out. In fact, don't even expect anything good to happen. Just think of it as practice for when the right girl finally does come along."

"I've been practicing a lot, though, sis. Why do you think I'm on my computer so much!?" He turned and gave her a grin. She gave him a playful slap on the face.

"You're gross. Why do guys have to be so disgusting?"

"Well, why do girls have to be such heart-breaking, evil bitches?"

"We're our own worst enemy. No debate about that. We have everything we want right in front of us, and we refuse to grab it and make ourselves happy."

Greg wasn't sure if she was talking about James or if she was speaking in general terms to make conversation. He knew not to bring up James; it was a very sensitive topic. She had spent months crying and aching over the guy.

"Do you have a picture of her?" Greg asked.

"Yeah, we're Facebook friends."

They both walked over to the computer that was on his desk near a window. Jessica sat down and booted up his computer. Greg had never been as tech-savvy as she was. She also knew money was a lot tighter with him. He worked his ass off, but research jobs didn't pay as well as they should. She didn't need him to tell her about that; her company was the same way.

While they waited for the browser to load, she said, "How about I get you a Mac for Christmas? I promise you'll never look back."

"Oh, please! Macs are for people who want to pay twice as much to be able to do half of what a PC can do."

"That's not true! It can do anything a PC can, and the

second I flip open the lid, it boots up."

"Really?" Greg said, genuinely surprised.

"Really! You could have PornHub up and be done before this thing even loads a browser."

"You're disgusting, sis. I only go there to read the articles. What kind of person do you think I am?"

"Uh huh, sure."

Once the computer finally booted up, she logged into her Facebook account. They'd become friends last week, she explained while searching for Stacy Melendez.

Greg had expected to see a tan-skinned Latina, based on the name. But when her picture came up, he saw that she was fair-skinned. Black hair. Pretty smile. So far, he was impressed. She was cute.

Jessica scrolled through all of her previous profile pictures, and again, they only showed her face. He'd learned long ago that if a girl only posted pictures of her face online, the rest of her was usually a fat mess. Jessica then clicked on an album of her in college at Capital. He finally saw full body pictures of her with her friends at bars and clubs.

"Wow!" Greg said. "She's hot!"

"I told you! I thought she was cute."

"Yeah, but has she seen a picture of me? She's not going to want to date me."

Jessica turned around and punched him hard in the stomach. "Ow!"

"Stop being so stupid. You're a good-looking guy, Greg. You just have shit for confidence, which is what girls really go for."

"Fair enough. So you did show her a picture of me?"

"Yeah," Jessica said, but she didn't elaborate.

Greg could tell she was holding something back. They were, after all, twins, and they both always knew when the other had a secret.

"What picture did you show her, Jess? Be honest."

She looked at him, covering her hands over her face to hide her laughter.

"You did not!" Greg said. He knew what she'd done. In her purse, she kept a picture of him from the week he had dressed like a chicken and held up a sign at Cluck's Chicken. "You showed her me dressed as Clucky!? Why would you do that, Jess?"

"I love that picture. It shows your personality."

"Give me that picture back. I'm burning it right now!"

"No way! You'd have to take it from my cold, dead hands!"

"What did she do when you showed it to her? What did she say?"

"She loved it. She laughed and said you were cute."

"No, seriously, what did she *really* say?"

"She thought you looked funny and went on about how she loved guys with a sense of humor. I admit, the picture isn't the best one to win over a lot of girls, but it was the only one I had on me at the time."

"Well, I'll give you a replacement picture if you're going to keep showing it to a bunch of people. I have some golfing pictures from college."

"Yeah, like those would work to charm a girl. You should be happy; she said she wanted to meet you. I'm using that picture from now on until it stops working."

Greg didn't know what to say, so he let out a frustrated growl and flopped onto the couch.

"So do you want me to call her now and set you two up?"

Greg let out a long breath.

"I still don't know. What would we do? What do I say? It's been so long that I've forgotten how these things work."

"Just take her to a movie or something if you're so damn nervous about it. You won't even have to talk to her, then."

"Fine, do you have her email address? I haven't decided yet, but if I do, I'll email her."

Jessica stared at him, shaking her head. She knew he wouldn't contact her, even though it would be the best thing for him. Nevertheless, she opened up a new tab in his browser and logged into her email account. Her phone rang.

"Who is it? Is that her?" Greg asked.

"Relax. My company is anal about security. I have to enter a PIN code from my phone to get into my email."

She punched it in and found the girl's email address. After meeting Stacy at North Market last week, she had emailed her with a couple of health-related questions.

She copied Stacy's email address and pasted it in a new email to send to Greg. In the body of the email, she wrote a message:

Stacy's email is s_melendez200905@capital.edu. Don't be such a wimp and set up a date ASAP.

She hit send.

Jessica left the computer open. She knew he'd want to look at Stacy's pictures again, so she left her Facebook account open, trusting that he wouldn't snoop through her emails or post something stupid.

"I emailed you her contact info. Don't wait. She's a cute girl. They don't stay single for long."

"Fine, I'll email her after you leave."

"You better. I'm going to call tomorrow and check up on you. If you haven't done it by then, I'm scanning Clucky and posting it all over the Internet."

"You wouldn't!"

She gave him a 'you want to try me' look. He knew she was bluffing, but he still felt the added pressure.

Wanting to change subjects, Jessica asked, "So how is work going?"

"It sucks. As always."

"Are you golfing with Shane and the boys on Sunday?"

"Of course. It's the only thing in life that I look forward to," Greg said, looking down.

Jessica could tell this was more than his usual sarcasm. He seemed depressed.

"Don't say that! I know you're down right now, but things will get better."

"I know they will. I just feel like I'm in a rut. I've been at Vinditec for five years now. I've had the same job for the last four. I slave away, working shitty hours. Get paid shit. With my skill set, I really have no career options other than what I'm doing now. No girlfriend to keep me busy."

"Stop being so hard on yourself! I was starting to feel that way at Adriar, but then an opportunity came up about six months ago. I'm really excited about it. And I couldn't be happier."

Greg knew not to ask about it. Jessica's work was very secretive. He knew she'd tell him if he really wanted to know, because she trusted him, but she would feel uncomfortable saying anything, so he didn't ask.

"You know I'll always be here for you, too."

"I know. Not to be a sentimental dork or anything, but I'm glad I have you, sis. I don't know what I'd do without you. Don't ever leave Columbus."

"I don't plan on it. The company is headquartered here, so you're stuck with me," she teased, trying to lighten the mood in the room.

They spent the next few hours discussing less emotional topics. They were both Cleveland Browns fans. They got that from their father, who never missed a game. Complaining about Cleveland sports teams' roster decisions was a frequent topic of discussion in the family.

After that, they watched some TV. They both liked several of the same shows and neither had seen the latest episode of *The Walking Dead*, so they watched it together.

Jessica looked down at her watch and saw that it was getting late. She looked over at Greg, whose yawning was becoming more and more frequent. They were both morning people and rarely stayed up past eleven, even in college.

"I'm getting tired. Think I'm going to head out."

"All right, sis," Greg said, yawning again.

They both stood up and gave each other a hug.

"It was great seeing you and catching up."

"Yeah, thanks for having me. Dinner was excellent. I haven't had mom's pasta in forever."

"I know. That's what I was thinking, too."

Jessica grabbed her coat, and they walked to the door.

"Will you be all right? Do I need to walk you home?"

"I'm fine," Jessica said. "We live in Columbus, not Detroit."

"Still, you're a girl, and it's getting late. You've had a few glasses of wine. I know how guys can be."

"What are you saying? I can't defend myself? I've whooped your ass before."

"First off, no you haven't. You had me pinned down once, but I *so* could have gotten out of it if I'd wanted to. And second, that was in middle school."

"First off," Jessica said mockingly. "You were screaming for Mom to come save you, and this happened senior year of high school. I warned you not to mess with me."

"Well… whatever. I'm way tougher now."

"Are you?"

"No," he said, grinning. "But I *have* seen a couple kung fu movies since then."

Jessica looked at her brother and smiled. She gave him a playful pat on the cheek. "I'll be fine. I'll text you when I get back."

"Please do," he said. She then opened the door and left.

With Jessica gone, he gathered all the plates from the table and put them in the sink. Their rule for their get-togethers was that the cook also did the cleaning. The guest always got the full treatment.

Greg was a slob and had no intention of washing the dishes before he went to bed. The apartment didn't come with a dishwasher, which he hadn't thought would be an issue when he signed the lease, but he'd regretted that decision ever since. He rarely cooked at home and often brought fast food back, because it was easy to clean up.

Getting tired, he turned off the TV. He was about to flick off the lights and go to bed, but then he noticed that his laptop was still open. He'd promised Jessica that he'd email Stacy but was planning on putting it off. He did want to see if Jessica had left the pictures of Stacy open. When he sat down, he saw that she had.

As he clicked through, he noticed an album from an apparent spring break trip to Miami. A couple of the pictures were of her and her friends in bikinis.

"Damn!" Greg said to himself. She was *very* hot. An incredible body.

He was scared to set up a date; she was completely out of his league. He couldn't imagine how nervous he'd be if they went out. Greg kept reminding himself that Jessica had already showed her the worst picture of him. If she was willing to go on a date after seeing that, things could only go up from there. Of course, Stacy told Jessica that she liked a man with a sense of humor. Greg did like to make people laugh, but he imagined himself getting tongue-tied while talking to Stacy. Their date would have to be to the movies. Chances were slim that anything would work out with her, and a movie would be the best way to minimize his embarrassment. Plus, it would get Jessica off his back about dating again.

With those thoughts in mind, he opened a new tab to log into his email. He'd email Stacy and then go to bed. He knew if he wanted until the morning, he'd check his email every five seconds until she responded. Hopefully, if he did it tonight, she'd reply while he was asleep and he would find it waiting in the morning.

As he was typing in his login information, he heard a loud boom from outside. Thinking nothing of the sound, he logged into his account. After copy-pasting Stacy's email address into the recipient line of a new message, he stared blankly at the screen.

He thought about what he should put as a subject line. Should he be funny? Or was that trying too hard? He already knew it was going to take a long time to compose.

He figured it might be better to write it in the morning.

He put his laptop to sleep and was just getting ready to close the lid when he heard loud screams coming from outside. This time, he rose from his seat and peeked his head out the window.

Down the street, in the distance, there was a small crowd gathering. Something had captured their interest. As he looked closer, he saw that someone was lying on the ground.

His first thought was that someone must have had a heart attack. That, or they were already too drunk and had passed out. Then, Greg remembered the noise prior.

Did something happen?

He had to find out. He grabbed his coat, put on his shoes, and stepped out. There was an elevator down the hall, which, if he was going to work, he usually took. But that was because he was in no rush to get where he was going. The stairs were much faster, and they were right next to his room.

He ran down the stairs, wondering what had happened. It was cold outside. It usually started getting warmer in May, but the cold front that had through had brought record lows.

As he got closer, he heard a man with a phone in his hand shout to everyone nearby. "They said someone should be here any minute."

Greg could only assume that he meant an ambulance or the police. He tapped on the back of a woman, about forty years of age, and asked, "Hey, what's going on? What happened?" He looked over and saw that she was in hysterics.

She looked at him and sobbed, "It's horrible. Why would someone do such a thing?"

He fought through the crowd, which had piled up with even more people now. There was a lot of resistance. Everyone wanted a view of what had happened. With enough effort, he was finally able to break free.

The moment he saw her, his heart started beating uncontrollably. He fell to his knees.

"Hey man, get back," someone shouted, but Greg didn't pay any attention.

He was looking at Jessica's face. Her eyes were still open, but there was blood pooling around her neck and chest.

"Jessica?" he said as he put his arm under her back to lift her up. "Jessica!" he screamed, but her eyes remained frozen.

"No, no. Jessica!" he screamed again.

The guy that had told him to get back asked, "Hey man, do you know her?"

Again, Greg ignored him. He looked at the crowd and pleaded, "Somebody help. Is anyone a doctor?"

"Police are on their way. Should be here any minute," the guy said.

Greg gently lowered Jessica's body down to the ground. His hands and arms were covered in blood. He looked around and saw the pool of blood surrounding her body.

"Why? What happened? Did anyone see what happened?"

The same guy again spoke for the group, "Nah, man, no one saw nothin'. It was a drive-by. Some black car, but no one caught the license plate."

Greg turned away and closed his eyes. All he could see in his mind was all the blood.

He couldn't imagine all of it could be from Jessica.

But it was.

Chapter 3

The ambulance arrived five minutes later, but there was nothing they could do to save Jessica.

Greg called his parents.

His mom answered and didn't believe him when he told her, as if he would say something like that as a joke. Never in a million years. When he completely broke down and she could hear him crying through the phone, that's when she knew he was serious.

When Greg hung up and turned around, he saw that three police cars had arrived. Not long after that, another three came.

Someone from the crowd, who was speaking to one of the officers, pointed in Greg's direction. The officer came over.

"Hello, sir. I'm Captain Sloan." He took off his hat. "It's been brought to my attention that you knew the victim?"

Greg opened his mouth to speak but, again, started breaking down. The officer waited patiently for Greg to collect himself and speak.

"Yes, she's my twin sister."

"I'm sorry to hear that," the captain said and motioned for another officer to come over. "This was a travesty. Take all the time you need. Once you collect yourself, I'd like to ask you a few questions, okay? See if we can find out who did this."

Greg nodded.

The other officer, who wasn't much older than Greg, put his arm around him for comfort and walked him to his cruiser. He opened one of the back doors.

"Please, have a seat here," he said.

"Wait, am I in trouble?"

"No, of course not. The captain just wants to ask you a few questions, and I'm here to keep you safe in the meantime." He put out his hand. "I'm Detective Maxwell."

"Greg Anderson." They shook.

"So, that was your sister?"

"Yeah."

"Really sorry to hear that, man. Can't imagine what you're going through. We're going to find out who did this. I'm sure that's not what you're thinking about right now, though, huh?"

"I- I just can't believe something like this happened. She didn't have an enemy in the world that I knew of. She was the best twin a guy could ask for."

"You were twins?"

"Yep."

"My cousins are twins. They're real close, too. I really am sorry. Again, take all the time you need."

"Thanks."

Fifteen minutes passed, and Greg's mind went totally blank. He didn't want to think about what happened, because any thought would make it more real.

When the captain came up to him, Greg didn't even realize he was there. It wasn't until he spoke that he looked up.

"Son, is it all right if I ask you a few questions now?"

Greg calmly said, "Yeah, sure." He saw that Detective

Maxwell was still there, too. With a pen and paper in his hand to take notes.

"When did you last see Jessica?"

"Tonight. She was at my house. I made her dinner," he said, choked up again.

The captain didn't hesitate and said, "And about when did she get there?"

Greg wiped tears from his eyes, "Around six or so."

"Six. Did she say where she'd been before that?"

"She was at work. Went home. Got ready. Then came over."

"All right, and when she was at your place, did she say anything that was out of the ordinary? How was her mood?"

"She was fine. Everything was fine. We talked about me, mostly, and all my problems."

"Your problems?"

"Yeah, nothing serious. Just work and relationships and stuff." With his eyes still watering, he let out a brief laugh. "Pretty unimportant when something like this happens, huh?"

"Yeah, I suppose it is. I know this is hard. So, anything at all that stuck out in your conversation?"

"No, nothing."

"Did she have any enemies? Did she mention any arguments she'd had lately?"

"No, not at all. My sister was very likable. I can't recall her ever having someone not like her."

"What about any ex-boyfriends?"

"She had a date with a guy recently, but it was nothing serious. They decided not to see each other again, but she made it sound mutual."

"Do you know this person's name?"

"Again, I don't think this is the person that did this. But she said his name was Dan." Greg paused. "She didn't say his last name."

The captain waited for the detective to jot all the information down before continuing.

"And how did you find out what happened?"

"I was over at my computer looking something up, and I heard a loud bang. It didn't sound like a gun. More like something big had been dropped from a window. I didn't even bother to see what it was. Then, shortly after that, I heard screaming. That was what made me look out, and I saw the crowd of people."

"So you saw the crowd. Then what?"

"I came down to see what was going on."

"Did you know it was your sister that had been shot?"

"No, it didn't really even cross my mind. I was just curious to see what had happened."

"I see," the captain said. Again, he looked over at Detective Maxwell to make sure he was writing everything down.

Greg didn't like the demeanor of the captain. The inflection in his voice sounded accusatory, like Greg might be a potential suspect.

Greg broke the silence, "What have you learned so far? Do you have any idea about who might have done this?"

"It's still way too early to tell. We're gathering evidence now. Is there anything else you'd like to tell us? Anything that would help the investigation?"

Greg thought, but nothing at all came to mind. "I don't think so, officer. I'm still in shock."

"Completely understand. It would be for anyone. I have all I need from you for now. Tell you what," he said, pulling a pen and card out of his shirt pocket and writing something on it. "Here's my number. If anything jogs your memory, you let me know. If you think of anything at all, you don't hesitate to call.

You'd be surprised at how often the tiniest, most insignificant detail turns out to be the lead that cracks the case. I'm going to have Detective Maxwell here write down your information. We'll be in touch. Sound good?"

"Yes. Thank you, officer."

"No problem," he said. He gave Greg a pat on the shoulder and then walked away.

As he did, Greg was thinking how he didn't much care for the captain. He couldn't quite put his finger on why. Detective Maxwell was more to his liking. They talked for another ten minutes, and he provided all of his information. Greg was starting to calm down when he turned and saw his parents.

Both of them were bawling. Greg ran over and gave them a hug. Time stopped as the three of them stood there, saying nothing. After all, what was there to say?

They'd been dealt a crushing blow.

Things would never be the same.

Chapter 4

The viewing was on Sunday. Greg had immediately canceled his golfing plans. He and his parents were overwhelmed with support. From noon until four, there was a constant line out the door of people wanting to give their condolences. Greg guessed that at least a thousand people came by.

Several people from his office came. Most he knew worked with him because he recognized their faces, but he didn't know their names and rarely spoke to them.

Shane and the sales guys all came together. They had all pitched in to buy the biggest bouquet of flowers Greg had ever seen. Greg almost found the size annoying. It hardly fit through the door.

While he knew that many people couldn't stand the sales team for their rude and obnoxious behavior, Greg knew that they all had hearts of gold and were very generous people.

Greg got to see a lot of old friends from high school. At one point, around two in the afternoon, it felt like they were having a reunion. For whatever reason, the high school crowd was the one that asked the most questions about the investigation. "Do you know who did this?" "Do they have any leads?" "What evidence do they have?"

The answers to the questions were no, no, and none.

Neither he nor his family felt like talking about it. That wasn't what was important. They just wanted their Jessica back. Still, they knew there would come a time when they would need closure and more news on why it had happened.

Several people from Greg's fraternity and Jessica's sorority came. Most of them had moved far from Columbus since college and only made phone calls or sent letters, but the ones that still lived in Ohio were there.

If there was a surprise at the turnout for Jessica's viewing, it was from Jessica's coworkers. Only around six or ten of them came, which, for a company that employed five hundred in the Columbus headquarters alone, seemed like a very small attendance. Especially considering Jessica's friendly and outgoing personality. He'd never been to her work before, but if she was anything like she was in high school and college, she had to have had a lot of friends at work. But few of them came, and the ones that did didn't say much. It was as if they wanted to get in and get out without anyone seeing them or knowing they were there.

After a long day of shaking hands, giving hugs, and engaging in brief conversations next to Jessica's casket, Greg and his parents were exhausted both physically and mentally. He hadn't known it was possible to cry as much as they had in a day. His mom, in particular, was having a hard time keeping it together.

Greg was starting to go on autopilot after having had repeated the same conversation with hundreds of people.

"So sorry for your loss."
"Yes, thank you."
"It's such a terrible tragedy."
"It is."

"I just feel awful for you. Hang in there."
"Thanks."

Greg and his parents were finishing up a conversation with their old neighbors when he turned to his left and saw her.

It was Stacy.

Greg was taken off guard by how beautiful she looked. Even more beautiful than the pictures. She was wearing a long, sleeveless black dress. It was appropriate to wear to a viewing but sexy enough to wear to a bar.

"Hi," Greg said, reaching out to shake her hand. He looked down, too intimidated to stare at her face.

Her hand was soft and warm.

"So sorry for your loss. I'm Stacy. I met Jessica a couple of weeks ago."

"Thank you. Yeah, I recognized you. Jessica showed me your picture the night that… well, that it happened."

"Oh, you were with her that night?"

"Yeah."

"Oh, that's so terrible!" She reached in and gave him a hug. "It's just so sad. She was such a good, nice person."

Greg's mom had finished talking to the neighbor and turned her attention to the girl that was next in line.

"Greg, dear. Who's this?"

"Hi, I'm Stacy. I'm so sorry for your loss." She took a step in and gave Greg's mom a hug. "I was just telling Greg how I met Jessica only a couple weeks ago."

"Thank you, dear. Do you two know each other?" She pointed at Greg.

"No!" they both said together.

Greg was too shy to say anything further, but Stacy continued the conversation.

"Actually, I believe Jessica was looking to set us up on a date."

"Oh, really?" Greg's mom said. "Sweetie, why don't you two go over and talk? I think we can handle the line for awhile."

"I can stay, Mom. It's all right."

"Nonsense. You've been standing for four hours now. Take a break."

"Well, so have you."

"Yes, but I can handle it. Now go."

"Fine," he said a little more ungratefully than he'd intended.

As they walked away, a sickening feeling grew in Greg's stomach. His mind was telling him not to screw it up.

What was he going to say to her?

They found a couple of chairs in a secluded corner of the room. It wasn't total privacy, but it was a lot better than it would have been two hours before.

"Sorry, I didn't mean to take you away from your parents," Stacy said.

"It's okay. I'm so tired. Feels good to sit down."

"I can't imagine how hard this is on you."

"Yeah, I just don't understand any of it."

"It must be so awful. I have a little brother. Can't imagine what I'd do if anything happened to him."

Greg still didn't know what to say, so he remained quiet. Stacy again broke the silence.

"This may be none of my business, but do they have any idea who did it?"

"We really don't know yet. They say they're still gathering evidence, but who knows what's really going on?"

"Do you think it was just a random occurrence?"

"Could have been. I mean, I don't understand how anyone could do this to her. She was the most loving, caring person I ever knew."

"You're so sweet," she said.

Greg felt guilty scoring points with Stacy at his sister's expense. She put her hand on his knee, which he felt was pretty forward, considering they didn't even know each other. He wasn't about to complain, though.

"I really loved her. With all of my heart. We weren't like regular brothers and sisters. She was my best friend."

"Yes, Jessica was so kind. She was going to introduce me to some folks at her work after I graduate. Thought there might be a job opening for me there. I thought that was really nice of her, especially considering I didn't know her well."

"Yeah. Jessica was always a very generous person."

"Well, I can see she must have been well-liked. I waited in line here for a half hour."

"You should have seen it earlier. The line snaked outside as far as I could see."

"I can imagine. Not sure I've ever seen a viewing so busy."

"Hey, do you want to grab dinner or a cup of coffee some time?" Greg blurted out. The words came out before he even realized it.

"Yeah, of course. Obviously, I know you'll be busy for a while with the funeral and everything. Let me give you my number so you can call me."

As she was digging in her purse, a small part of him thought she was only agreeing because of what happened to his sister. But then he remembered she'd wanted to go on a date before any of it had happened.

She wrote her number on the back of a receipt. Greg stuck it in his pocket.

Now that it was out of the way, Greg loosened up. He asked about what she was doing in college. He already knew she was majoring in journalism but had her tell him anyways.

Turned out, she had a lot of really neat stories to tell. She talked about how, during the previous semester, she got to interview a student that was already a multimillionaire investor. Another had been on the singing show *The Voice*. Then she had the opportunity to dine at the dean of the school's house and discuss changes she thought needed made to the cafeterias.

"So are you wanting to be more of a journalist?"

"No, it was just for one of the classes I took. I've decided I'm mainly interested in PR. So I'm already going outside of my degree, but I was told there were a lot more opportunities, especially for graduates."

Listening to her speak, Greg could tell she was smart. There were some people that clearly just knew what they wanted and would end up being very successful, and Stacy was that type of person. Whoever ended up being with that girl, he thought, was going to be a lucky man. He was glad he would at least get to have one sympathy date with her.

"So what do you do?" she asked. "If I remember, Jessica said you worked at a tech company?"

"Yeah, Vinditech. I do research there. Mainly working with account managers and sales folks before they talk to clients."

"That's cool. Do you like it there?"

Greg had been asked that same question countless times over the past five years. It was usually the part where he'd say he loved it and talk a little more about what he did, making it sound way more important and exciting than it actually was. But this time he surprised himself again.

"I fucking hate it."

"Oh really? How come?"

"I'm buried behind spreadsheets, which often need finished on very tight deadlines. Especially for the account managers. The sales guys aren't quite as bad. I usually have a little more time to pull reports for them. They're also pretty cool guys, unlike the account managers, who are total dicks." He hadn't meant to come across so boldly, so he tried to ease the mood by saying, "I usually go golfing with the sales guys on Sundays."

"I love golf!" Stacy said, excited. "I'm not very good, but I like watching it on TV and stuff."

"Really?" he said. "No girl that I know likes watching it on TV."

"I do," she gleamed.

"I played at Ohio State for two years, so I'm okay."

"Wow, that's awesome. You *must* be good. I've always wanted to learn."

"Maybe we can go to the driving range or something sometime?"

"I'd *love* that," she said, genuinely enthused.

Greg was thinking that their conversation was going perfectly. He couldn't think of an easier first date than going golfing. Plus, he imagined that Stacy would look pretty damn good in a golfing outfit.

"Great! Maybe we can go next Sunday?"

"Sure. I don't want to rush you, though. If it's still too soon and you need to cancel, I totally understand."

"I appreciate that. I'll let you know, I guess. I could probably use something to take my mind off of things."

"Okay, cool."

Greg looked up and saw the last person he wanted to see talking with his parents.

"Ahh, man. My boss is here. I should probably go talk to him."

"Okay. Of course. I should probably get going."

They both stood up. Greg felt awkward, not knowing if he should give her a hug or if a handshake was more appropriate.

Fortunately, she stepped in and hugged him again. He got a whiff of her hair. It smelled like cherries. Very girly.

"Thanks for coming by."

"No problem. Call me sometime."

"I will," he said, patting the pocket he had stuck her number in.

She walked away, and Greg couldn't help but check her out. She was wearing heels, which accentuated her calves. Her body looked stunning in the dress. She was a ten. There was no other way to put it.

He rushed back in, hoping to talk to his boss while he was still with his parents. Unfortunately, their conversation had just ended when he got there.

Greg didn't hate his boss, at least not as much as he hated the account managers. Still, Bob Valentine wasn't someone he'd hang out with on a Friday night. Or ever.

"Greg! Hey there. So sorry for your loss."

Greg went back into sad mode. Stacy was a brief, pleasant distraction from the reality of the situation. The conversation with Bob was a firm stake back into the real world.

They talked for ten minutes. It was a very formal conversation, the kind a person would have when they were making small talk with a relative they rarely saw. Not usually the kind of conversation they'd have with someone they had worked with and spoken to every day for five years. Greg was now realizing that 99% of their communication was Bob giving him orders or following up on what was being done. For those last ten minutes, they'd spoken more non-work related words than they'd had in a year. It was uncomfortable for both of them.

As he was talking with Bob, he reached in to feel the receipt with Stacy's number, making sure it was still there.

He thought he could still smell the cherry scent from her hair.

Two days later was the funeral. It was the hardest thing Greg had ever gone through in his life.

Unlike the viewing, they tried to reserve the burial for just family and the closest of friends. Several people offered to come, and although it was appreciated, the Anderson family needed some quiet time to themselves. This was challenging enough for all of them.

As the pastor gave his sermon on the warm, partly cloudy Thursday afternoon, the only other thing that could be heard was sobbing. It was as if even the birds kept quiet to pay their respects to a girl that didn't deserve to die so soon.

Life was taken away, and for what?

That was the burning question that lingered in Greg's mind after they walked away from burying his sister.

Chapter 5

Captain Sloan stopped by Greg's parents' house on Friday evening to give them an update. He told them there had been no eyewitnesses of the shooting.

At the diner across the street, everyone had heard the shots being fired. When a woman by the window screamed, it caused everyone in the diner to panic. Most of them rushed outside to see what was going on.

The street was full of people after Jessica was gunned down, but no one could identify the car that drove away. Because of that, police could only go off the evidence surrounding her body.

"We know, based on the trajectory of the bullet, that it came from a passing car."

This alone was too much for Greg's mother to hear. She scurried out of the room, wiping the tears from her face. Greg and his father stayed, wanting to learn what else had been discovered.

"As I was saying, the path of the bullet suggests that the gunman was facing Jessica when he fired. Now, that might mean he was aiming for her or it might not. With a drive by, a shot to the side or back of the head often implies a random occurrence." The captain paused to let the new information sink in. "We found fragments of the bullet. We know it came from a pistol——a Glock 9mm——which we've gathered from the ballistic fingerprinting." The captain hesitated. "I've asked before, but have you thought of anyone that Jessica didn't get along with? Anything you remember now that you may have forgotten before?"

"You knew her better than anyone, son," Greg's father said.

"I told you. No one. She went on a date with a guy, Dan, but it didn't sound like it was serious at all. Jessica was always the popular girl growing up and everyone always liked her," Greg said, choking up.

"Still, if there's any way you can find out more about who he is, we'd like to speak with him," Captain Sloan said.

"Sure. Although, I'm not sure how much I'll be able to help."

Captain Sloan gave him a look that he didn't appreciate. It was accusatory. "Do your best. And call me if you think of anything."

After fifteen additional minutes of discussing all of the things that the police *weren't* doing, the captain said once more to call if *they* found anything. It took everything Greg had to not scream at the man. Based on all that he'd heard, their investigation was a half-assed effort at best. It was as if they had several other cases to go through and they were just going through the motions in order to say that they tried.

If Jessica's murderer was going to be found, it was going to take a lot more than that.

Someone needed to get their hands dirty.

On Saturday, Greg went back to his apartment for the first time in nearly a week. He had stopped by for only a few minutes the previous Sunday to get some clothes for the funeral.

Being there brought back painful memories of Jessica. As soon as he closed the door behind him and looked around at his apartment, he began to cry. Her last precious moments on Earth had been spent in that room. The last time she laughed. Her final meal. The final words she ever spoke were to him at this door.

It was too much for him to think about.

He collapsed on the couch and let it all out. He felt, for the first time since it had happened, that he could mourn in solitude. That was the only way he thought he could really recover, spending night after night thinking about it, taking it one day at a time. One cry after another, thinking of every last memory they had shared in their twenty-nine years together. Being twins, it felt to Greg like half of him had died. He'd never be the same person he was. Not even close.

Jessica had been more than a sister. Way more. She was his other half, always there for him when he needed her. She could help him with his problems because she was wired the same way he was, only in female form. She knew what he was thinking and could say the right thing at the perfect time to get him to see reason.

After four hours of moping on the couch, he realized it was two in the afternoon and that he hadn't had lunch yet. For breakfast, he hadn't eaten much, pushing aside the scrambled eggs his mom had made him.

He finally snapped out of his daze enough to get up and pour himself a bowl of cereal. He checked the milk and saw it had expired several days before. He took a whiff. It was sour, but that didn't stop him from pouring it in his bowl. Nothing could make him feel worse than he already did. Getting sick might actually be a good thing, he thought. It would be something to take the attention away from Jessica.

As he ate his cereal, he thought about Stacy. He hadn't communicated with her since the funeral, not even a text message. He'd said he would take her to the driving range, and at the time, he had really been looking forward to it.

They'd only talked briefly, but he really liked her. She was very comforting, once he got over his initial fears. She had great empathy for what he was going through.

He really wanted to go on that date, but he wondered if it was too soon. Stacy had said that it would be okay if he changed his mind, that she'd understand. She must have known that he was going to have a much harder time processing Jessica's death than he thought.

He pulled out his phone, thinking he needed to at least send her a text to let her know that he wasn't blowing her off. He remembered Jessica telling him that pretty girls like her didn't stay single for long. Greg had to cancel their date but wondered if this would be his only chance. Would postponing it by a week be too long? Would she move on to someone else?

It was possible, but it was a chance he'd have to take.

He took her number out of his pocket and began punching it in. He thought about what he wanted to say and how he should say it.

Just be honest, Greg said to himself. *She's an understanding person.* He started typing the first thing that came to mind.

Hey Stacy, it's Greg. I know I said I'd take you to the driving range tomorrow, but I don't quite think I'm ready to do that yet. I'm still in shock over what happened to Jessica. I'd love to take you next Saturday, though, if that's all right?

***

He pressed send and waited, staring at his phone in suspense. An agonizing minute went by. He re-read his message, wondering if he should have said something different.

He sat up and waited for her reply.

That's completely fine. I totally understand. Besides, I think it's supposed to rain all day tomorrow. Get in touch with me next week? We can go to the driving range, see a movie, go out to dinner... whatever you want. Or if you're still not ready, that's fine too. :)

Without thinking, Greg sent a message back.

Thanks for understanding. I'll get in touch next week.

The moment he pressed send, he wondered if he should have said more. But she responded within seconds:

Sounds good!

Now he was glad he'd kept it short and sweet. He had a date with Stacy and more time to get himself together.

He already had the following week off. Company policy allotted two full weeks of bereavement leave for immediate family. He remembered seeing that when he first started working there, but he never considered that it would be something he'd have to use.

On Sunday and Monday, Greg spent most of his time sitting around and watching television. All of his meals had been purchased from a burger place within walking distance.

It wasn't until Tuesday that he finally went to the grocery store. He mostly did it so that he wouldn't have to keep going outside. With a few days of groceries in the fridge, he wouldn't have to shower or put on fresh clothes.

He got a few calls on Wednesday. One was from Shane, who was calling to see how he was doing. Again, Shane rubbed many people the wrong way with his arrogance and entitlement, but Greg knew deep down how caring he was. Shane was the kind of guy you could count on as a friend.

Greg's mom also called, just to check up on how he was doing. He told her he was lousy, because he was. She didn't have to say anything for him to know that she was the same. The crying did that for her.

The entire time he had been at his parents' house, his mom hadn't had any interest in the investigation. She just wanted her daughter back. That's why it surprised him when she brought it up. She seemed quite upset that the captain hadn't called back with an update.

"They're doing everything they can, Mom. There just isn't much news to go off of."

"But you'd think they'd have the decency to call and tell us that. Don't we deserve that much? It's like they're not doing anything down there."

"They have a lot of cases that they have to go through, I'm sure."

Truth was, Greg didn't believe that. He was trying to comfort her, and talking about how infuriated he was at the police wouldn't help. Just as his mom had said, he felt like they'd hardly done anything with the investigation. They knew what kind of gun was used. Were they even looking into that lead? Didn't they have some kind of surveillance that captured the image of the car? Surely they could have been doing a lot more than what they were.

When Thursday came, Greg didn't feel any better than he had on Monday. The only difference was the added stress of needing to contact Stacy. He wanted to cancel again. He was sure she'd be understanding and polite about it. However, he soon changed his mind. He figured that a distraction from his thoughts might be the best thing for him.

He checked the weather before calling and saw that it was supposed to be perfect all weekend. He didn't have that excuse to fall back on. He needed to make something happen or he might as well say goodbye to Stacy forever.

His palms were sweating as he dialed her number. When she answered, all the happy memories from their previous conversation came back.

If there was anyone that could help him pick up the pieces in his life, it was her.

Chapter 6

One Month Later

"So you fuckin' golfing with us on Sunday or what?" Shane asked.

"I can't. I'm taking Stacy to the par-3 course. It's her first time."

"Ahh, nice. You tappin' that yet?"

"Umm, that's none of your business!" Greg said with a smile.

"You dirty dog, you! I'll bet you've put it in her from all directions by now. You sly son-of-a-bitch!"

Greg didn't say anything, but the grin remained on his face.

"All right, you don't wanna kiss and tell. I respect that. Can you at least show me a picture of her? Just so I know that 'Stacy' isn't the name of some sex toy you bought."

"She's real! Hold on."

Greg opened up the browser on Shane's computer. He shook his head at the bikini-clad girl being used as the wallpaper on his desktop. Greg logged into his Facebook account and pulled up some of her graduation pictures. He did it as quickly as he could, preventing Shane from spotting the photos from Miami.

"Holy shit, dude! She's fuckin' hot! I'd totally hit that."

Greg swelled with pride. Sure, Shane would have sex with anything that had breasts, but he still liked the compliment.

Their relationship had recently become Facebook official. Stacy was like an angel sent from God to help him get through the most troubling time in his life.

They had really hit it off when they went on their first date to the driving range. She seemed genuinely interested in learning to play, and Greg loved to teach golf, whether it was to his 62-year-old neighbor Bob or to someone as beautiful as Stacy.

During their first time at the range, their focus was mostly on the basic fundamentals like how to hold the club, perfect a stance, and aim. She had a good enough time that she seemed eager to set up their second lesson. They had met up the following Saturday and then gone out again on Sunday. For a while, Greg wasn't sure if they were entering into a relationship or if they'd just become friends who shared a hobby. That all changed when she called him that Monday and requested they go out for dinner the following Friday.

That date couldn't have gone better. Talking to Stacy was effortless. She knew Greg was still picking up the pieces from losing Jessica, but she didn't bring it up unless he wanted to talk about it.

Things were going really well. She'd even spent the night the previous Saturday. It was already the best relationship that Greg had ever been in. He was emotionally attached. The good thing was that she seemed equally into him. Greg made her laugh often, and they had a lot of the same interests. They even liked watching many of the same television shows.

In a sometimes-creepy kind of way, her personality reminded him a lot of Jessica.

"Hey," Shane said, snapping his fingers in front of Greg's

face. "You with me?"

"Oh, yeah, sorry."

"Good. Can you wipe your drool off my keyboard?"

Greg looked down. Shane was only kidding.

He minimized his browser, which brought back the bikini-clad girl on the screen.

"Is she a friend of yours?" Greg asked.

"Yeah, I wish! I'd do unforgivable things to that chick if I ever met her."

Greg laughed. He looked back at the screen and noticed a minimized program at the bottom that he didn't recognize. Since he was in research, he knew just about every program the company used.

"What's this Tor thing?"

"Oh, that's nothing!" Shane said, quickly taking the mouse from him.

Greg looked at him and could tell that Shane wished he hadn't seen it.

"Come on. We're friends. I'm not going to tell anyone. Is it some kind of game or something?"

"No, it's not a game. It's… nothing," Shane said.

Greg looked him in the eye and saw that Shane was studying him, contemplating whether or not to tell the truth.

"All right, you really wanna know?" he asked.

"Yeah, but I mean, if you don't want to tell me, it's cool."

"Nah, just promise you'll keep it between us." Shane went to close his door. The sales folk were the only people that got their own offices. Greg and his research team were all stuck in cubicles.

"I promise I'm not going to say anything."

"All right." Shane reached over and took control of the mouse, opening up Tor. A web browser expanded onto the screen.

"Oh, so it's just a website? It's porn, isn't it?"

Shane laughed. "No, it's not a website. It's a web browser. And not just any browser. On here, everything you do is completely anonymous."

"Yeah, so what? What good does that do?"

"Think about it."

Greg did. He let it sink in, but he still couldn't figure out what the big deal was.

"So... you use it to spy on competitors or something?"

"You could. Some people use it for that. Personally, I don't really give a shit if they know I'm checking out their websites. I'll still outsell their asses."

Greg was still confused. Complete anonymity. What good would that do?

"Are you looking at kiddie porn or something?" Greg said, teasing. He was trying to ease some of the tension that was building in the room.

"No, man. Do I seem like that kinda guy? Porn is fucking great and all, but I'd prefer watching a couple chicks going at it. Adult chicks. And I don't watch that shit on this. As you'll see, things load pretty slowly on it. I'd just use my regular browser for that."

Greg was about to make another guess——one that would no doubt be wrong——when Shane interrupted.

"Here, let me show you."

He typed a phrase into the search box: "onion directory." As he did so, he said, "They recommend that you don't use Google because of privacy and shit. Apparently Google tracks everything you do and will give that information to the government at the drop of a hat."

"Really? I didn't know that."

"Yeah, Google is an evil little company. StartPage or DuckDuckGo are all I use now."

After searching, he clicked the first link, which pulled up a directory of websites. The page was very basic, as if it had been created a decade ago.

Greg scanned through the sites.

"This is a list of websites that most people have probably never heard of. You can only get to them if you're using this browser."

"I can't just type the URL into a regular browser?"

"No. It'll just give you an error. I've tried. If you use Tor, though, it'll take you to the website. The way it works is, by using Tor, it connects you to hundreds of computers throughout the world. When you go to a page, it sends your signal across several of them, disguising your location and shit. No one can figure out where the original signal came from, not even our big brother government. In fact, they're the ones who actually created this."

"Really?" Greg said, genuinely surprised.

"Well, they funded a lot of it. The military uses it when they're spying on enemies and stuff."

"This is crazy. So what are all of these sites for?"

Shane was giddy with excitement. "You're not going to believe this shit."

He clicked on the first link.

"This site lists all the stolen credit cards that people are selling. They have gift cards, too. Sometimes they just post the numbers up here and it's first come, first serve until the funds run out or the credit card overdraws."

"Oh my god." Greg was starting to get very uncomfortable. Just looking at the stuff felt illegal, but he wanted to see more.

Shane went back to the directory and clicked another link.

The screen was black with white letters.

"As you can see, these guys claim they'll steal anything you want. You just gotta pay them half the value of it."

Greg took the mouse from Shane. He wanted to scroll and read the page for himself. "This is just fucking crazy. I've never heard of this before."

"I know, right? I couldn't believe it, either. Trust me, this is not even the tip of the iceberg. There's some crazy shit on here."

After reading the entire page, he clicked back to the directory. Greg scanned down, noticing that the websites were organized by category.

"So what are you on here for? Just to look?"

"Well..." Shane said, looking at Greg.

"Relax, I'm not going to tell anyone. I'm just curious."

"Fine." Shane took the mouse back. He scrolled up, looking for a specific page. He was having trouble finding it. "Ahh, here it is." He clicked the link.

Greg didn't catch what the site was called. When the page loaded, it showed an FBI warning.

"Oh shit!" Greg said.

"Ha. Don't let that scare you. The FBI logo is kind of a tease. The original site got taken down because the FBI figured out who the owner of the site was. But about a month later, someone else put the site right back up. Now it's pretty much invincible."

Shane punched in his login details.

Once he was in, Greg saw the site's name: *The Silk Road*. It didn't take him long to realize it was a place to buy drugs.

"They sell anything you could possibly imagine on here."

Greg looked at the navigation bar, which offered categories like ecstasy, opioids, and psychedelics. Shane clicked on the cannabis tab, bringing up a page that neatly displayed pictures of different types of marijuana.

"Every drug you could ever want, shipped right to your doorstep."

"What?" Greg said in disbelief.

"It's true, man. The fucking United States post office knocks on my door and hands it to me."

"Are they in on it or something? I don't understand."

"Nah, man. Big brother doesn't have a clue. Think about it: the post office only knows it's a package, but they don't know what's inside. It's not like they open them up to find out what they contain. I read that, occasionally, they may get drug dogs to come in, but that happens very rarely."

"Won't you get in deep shit, though, if you get caught?"

"Most likely no. Again, think about it. If a package full of drugs gets shipped to your door, there's still no evidence that you were the one who bought it. I could go on here and buy drugs and have them sent to Aunt Edna in Omaha, and there's nothing she could do to stop it." Shane laughed. "Speaking of which, how fuckin' funny would it be to send a pound of grass to some random old lady?"

"Yeah, but if they find out that you have drugs shipped to your house regularly, doesn't that make it pretty obvious that you're the one buying it?"

"Probably. But like I said, they can't prove it in court. I protect myself, too. Once I get it delivered to my house, I take it over to Sebastian's and we blaze over there. I figure if the cops come, they'll search my apartment. They won't find anything, so my tracks are covered."

"Yeah, but what about your bank records? Can't they look at those and see where you've been buying stuff?"

"Ahh, yes. Forgot to mention!" Shane was really getting

excited now. He turned Greg's attention back to the computer. "See the prices?"

Greg realized that they weren't in U.S. dollars. In fact, the symbol next to the amount was something he'd never seen before.

"Everything is sold in something called bitcoin. Completely untraceable." Shane opened up a new tab and entered in an address.

Greg now understood what Shane was talking about when he mentioned slow loading. It took forever for the page to appear. When it did, the title read "How to Buy Bitcoin."

"You buy bitcoins here. You do use your regular bank account for that. But once you have the electronic currency, you can buy and sell whatever you want and no government has any clue."

"Wouldn't it be obvious, though, if the government saw you bought bitcoin and then drugs were shipped to your door? Couldn't they put two and two together?"

"I'm sure they could. But again, it wouldn't hold up in court. They can assume all they want, but they don't have solid enough proof. Keep in mind something else: it's not like everyone who buys bitcoin are doing illegal shit. Some people see it as an investment. Some people just want money that they can use to buy stuff without being taxed. As much as the government probably hates it, it's a totally legit and legal currency to own."

Shane clicked back to the directory and went to a site called Toys4Coins. Here they were selling toys, each price listed in bitcoin.

"See? This site sells legitimate stuff. This crypto-currency stuff, man, is the future. I mean, how cool is it that you can buy and sell stuff anonymously and not have to pay taxes on it?

"As far as investments go, the famous story is that one of the first times bitcoin was used, it was by a guy that posted in a forum that he wanted a pizza delivered to his house and that he'd pay in the currency. So some other guy saw it, bought a pizza with real cash and had it delivered it to his house. The recipient electronically delivered him a payment in bitcoin. A few years later, the value of the bitcoins he had sent the delivery guy was worth several hundred thousand dollars!"

"Are you serious? How did they become worth so much?"

"Supply and demand, man. At the time, bitcoins were just starting out, and people didn't know what to do with them. Everyone in the forum was probably thinking that the guy who bought the pizza lost out on twenty bucks. But then people found some great use for the currency. It took off, and because everyone wanted them, they became worth a lot more.

"The value of bitcoin is pretty volatile. But every day that it becomes more popular, it becomes a little more stable."

"Yeah, I can't believe all of this. So how many times have you used it?"

Shane lowered his voice, "Four. I was scared shitless the first time I did it, but I'm pretty confident in it now. I mean, it's probably safer than buying weed from a dealer. There are loads of undercover cops selling on the streets these days. And the ones that are legit——what's stopping them from pulling a gun and robbing your ass? You shop online, right? Isn't that so much better than going to a store and dealing with lines and paying more? That's kinda what it's like buying weed online. You can read reviews of the dealers and comparison shop on prices. People say buying it online makes it a lot safer, too. It keeps people off the streets."

"I don't know. I could never do something like that. Then again, I'm not a big drug person either."

"I understand. The habit is not for everybody. Weed calms me the fuck down. And I was reading some shit about how it's not all that bad for you. That's why some states are legalizing it."

Greg respectfully disagreed but didn't mention that. "So how do you get to all of this, again? I want to check this out later."

Shane smiled. "It's real easy. If you just search Tor, T-O-R, in a search engine, it should come up. It's just like downloading anything else. Once you get it installed, you open it up. From there, it connects you to the Tor network where it hides your location and ensures that you're anonymous. Once it's connected, you can do pretty much anything you want and no one will be any wiser. They say not to check your email or anything like that while you're in there. And don't have any plugins installed, because sometimes those can trace where you're at when you log in. But all of those are just safety precautions. There's virtually no chance that anyone is going to find out what you're doing once you're on there. The people behind Tor are super intense when it comes to security. Again, our military uses it, and they're dealing with the biggest hackers on the planet who are trying to get in and steal our secrets."

"Sounds cool. I'm definitely going to check this out when I get home. I can't believe you do this from work, though."

"They don't give a shit what we do. As long as I'm making my sales figures, I could have sex slaves coming in and out if I wanted. Which reminds me, that's something else you can get on Tor. Never done it, though. Brian said he was thinking of trying it. I told him if I made a six figure month, I'd order girls for everyone on the sales team."

Shane closed the browser.

"Again, man. Don't tell anyone about this."

"Yeah, I won't."

Greg thought Shane was absolutely crazy for being involved in this.

But, at the same time, he couldn't wait to get home and explore it for himself.

Chapter 7

The first thing he did upon arriving home was to search for Tor on Google. Immediately after doing so, he remembered what Shane had said about how Google tracked everything. He already felt like he was getting himself into trouble just searching for Tor, but it was too late.

He went to the site and saw the logo, a white and purple onion. He began the download. As he waited, he read what was on the page. It seemed to sum up everything that Shane had already told him. They made it sound like a noble, useful tool. Not something people downloaded so that they could perform illegal activities.

Greg wasn't a computer expert, but he knew how to install programs. In less than five minutes, the Tor browser was open on his screen.

He momentarily forgot what to search for in order to find all the websites. Luckily, he had written it down in his notebook: "onion directory." It made sense since the Tor logo was an onion.

Greg clicked to a website called TorDir. It wasn't the same one that Shane had showed him, but it said "Deep Web Directory," so he had to be in the right place.

The first thing he noticed were financial services websites that offered bitcoin. He clicked on the first and waited. Everything on here was frustratingly slow to Greg. Eventually, a new page came up that said "Unable to Connect." He clicked back and attempted to go to another bitcoin-purchasing page but got the same results.

He decided to skip the financials since he wasn't interested in purchasing. It was then that he saw a page entitled "Become a REAL U.S. Citizen." Greg wasn't interested in the offer but found it intriguing nonetheless.

The link worked, and he was taken to a page that said:

"Want to become a U.S. Citizen? We can help, guaranteed! How? That's our dirty little secret. We can grant you citizenship, a passport, a SSN, a driver's license, and a birth certificate. Just provide us with your preferred name and a photo."

Greg noticed that the going rate was ten thousand dollars. He couldn't believe that any sane person would hire such a service. Especially not through such a website. Still, he was fascinated that such a service was offered.

He went back to TorDir and saw other pages offering both American and British passports. Others were offering fake driver's licenses from any U.S. state for only two hundred dollars. Greg understood that better, as every teenage kid in America wanted a fake ID in order to buy alcohol.

The next category offered hacking services. Just by reading the descriptions, Greg learned that there were websites that taught the art of hacking while others allowed users to hire professionals to do the hacking for them. He clicked on the page for hiring.

The homepage was written in poor English and claimed that the hackers could be "legit making 100 euros an hour if they wanted to." But apparently they didn't want to work for "the man," so they opted to work illegally instead. There were two payment options. For a hundred euros, a person could get any account hacked, from email accounts to bank accounts. For only a hundred euros more, the person was offering to "ruin someone," saying they'd completely corrupt a person's imagine, to the point where they could be arrested for looking like a "child predator."

Greg had seen enough. The idea was even worse than the U.S. citizenship service.

He scrolled down through TorDir again. There was a section for various porn and sex sites. One in particular caught his eye: "Sex Workers—escorts, exotics, massage." He found the "massage" part particularly funny, but he didn't click it.

Scrolling down further, there were sites that offered a variety of services. Lifetime HBO and Netflix accounts. Books on how to cash out stolen credit cards without getting caught. Lots of drug-related products. It was every bad and illegal thing that one could possibly imagine, all right there at his fingertips.

Then he saw the worst one yet. "You've got to be kidding me," he muttered to himself.

It read "Hitman Network." There were four websites offering such services. The link to the first one was broken, but the next one worked.

"We are trained assassins. You want someone gone, we'll take care of it. All we need is the name and any other information you are able to provide. Our only rules: no one under 16 and no politicians."

"How noble of you," Greg muttered.

The cost to have someone killed in the United States was only ten thousand dollars. It bumped up to twelve thousand in the UK. *Apparently British lives are worth more.* The site had a referral page, where previous members got a 1% discount for each person they sent to the site to use their services.

Hitman services seemed like the top of the horrific pinnacle to Greg. He hated the thought that the site might actually work.

The next site made a similar claim:

"We don't know you, and you don't know us. Guaranteed hit or your money back. Photo and video evidence sent to you upon completion."

At this site, politicians weren't off the table. It was one hundred thousand dollars to kill them, excluding presidents and other high-ranking leaders (they were priced closer to a million dollars).

This website also had the decency of a "no children" rule, but it seemed a lot nastier than the previous site he'd been to. This service seemed promising, whereas the last site looked as though they might take the money and run.

Greg leaned back in his chair. Seeing all of this was beginning to frighten him. All of this was out there, easily obtainable. He could access it within fifteen minutes. Shane had introduced him to the website where he could buy bitcoin, which was as easy as setting up an eBay account. If he wanted to, twenty minutes from now, he could have unlimited access to drugs, prostitutes, and hitmen-for-hire. People were *really* using this stuff every day. Shane said he was buying drugs with it, and Greg believed him.

He'd seen enough. He clicked back to TorDir. There was one more link at the very bottom of the page, another hitman service. Curious to see what kind of services this one offered, he clicked it. He told himself this was the last site he'd be going to, now and forever. He was planning to uninstall Tor as soon as he was finished and prayed to God the police didn't find out that he'd even looked at this stuff.

The site was entitled *American Hitmen.*

"We're your friends and neighbors. The guys you see at the bar on a Friday night. The people you went to school with. But on the weekends, we kill.

It's our secret little hobby. We just can't get enough of it. If you've seen *Dexter*, then you understand what it's like for us. We're sociopaths who have urges we can't control. Let us take care of someone for you, while we scratch our itch at the same time.

It's a win-win for us both. We'll kill people whether you hire us or not, so we might as well help you out at the same time."

Greg scrolled down to see the pricing, but couldn't find it. Instead, there was a contact form and the following message:

"Our services are FREE. That's right, no catch whatsoever.

All you have to do is fill out the form below, telling us who you want killed and why. We get a lot of requests, so be sure to make your reason compelling. We prefer to kill people who've done wrong in the world and deserve to be punished. It makes us feel all warm and fuzzy inside to know that what we do makes the world a better place."

There were two fields: one for the name of the potential victim and another box for a reason.

Like the previous site, it gave Greg a wary feeling in the pit of his stomach. This was real. After all, they weren't even asking for payment. He supposed it could be a site set up by the police. That would be pretty clever, actually. They could immediately protect those whose names were submitted and ask them questions regarding any enemies they had. Greg didn't think that's what it was, but the uncertainty was reason enough for him to avoid ever entering the name of even his worst enemy. He supposed most people would never consider that it could be a fake website, though. This was just another place to get oneself into trouble. It was convincing, sure, but he was beginning to doubt if it was real.

He scrolled back to the top of the page and was about to exit Tor when he saw a link entitled "Proof," which took him to a page with the headline, "Previous Submissions Completed." Below it, there was a picture of a man in his forties. He had glasses and a scruffy beard. It looked like it could have been a mugshot. Underneath the picture was his name, Charles Taft. To the right was another picture, which appeared to be from a crime scene. It was a body wrapped in a white bag. There was blood surrounding it on the pavement. Below the picture, in small letters, it said, "deceased, for crimes of pedophilia."

Greg scrolled down further. The next picture was a woman in her late thirties named Trixie Davis. The left picture was her walking out of a mini mart. The picture on the right made Greg sick to his stomach. He hadn't felt this uneasy looking at something online since he watched the Saddam Hussein hanging. The picture was a close-up of her pale face, eyes closed. Beneath it, it said "deceased, for crimes of filth and prostitution."

The next was another male in his twenties. The left picture looked like it was taken out of a yearbook. The one on the right wasn't a picture from the crime scene. Instead, it was a scanned picture from the newspaper and said, "Andy Jones: Dead at Age 21" Beneath it, in small letters, "deceased, for crimes of drug dealing and addiction."

Greg saw that he was nearing the bottom of the page. There was only one more picture.

As he reached the bottom, his first reaction was that of confusion.

For the briefest moment, he forgot what website he was on. It didn't make sense. Why would this picture be on a website like this?

A picture of someone so close to him.

It was a picture of Jessica.

Chapter 8

Greg recognized the picture on the left from a family vacation to Myrtle Beach that they had taken the summer after graduating from high school. It was a beautiful picture of Jessica; she was standing out on the balcony of the condo they were staying at. She'd just come from the pool, and her brunette hair was wet and flapping in the wind. The ocean was in the background. Greg had taken the picture, and everyone in the family agreed that it looked like the work of a professional photographer.

How did this website get this picture? Greg wondered.

Then he remembered how easy it was to get pictures of people off of Facebook, even for those who weren't friends. Jessica had used it as her profile picture for almost a full year before changing it. It was a great picture; she looked so happy.

The picture on the right was unsettling. It looked like someone standing in the street had taken it on the night she had been shot. There was the huge crowd around the body, but Jessica's frame couldn't be seen. Greg looked closely to see if he could find himself among the mass but couldn't. He had been in the middle of the crowd for most of the ordeal, and the crowd would have blocked him from view if the picture had been taken from the street.

Greg looked around for other clues or people he recognized. He recognized the woman he'd spoken to briefly before he'd learned that the victim was his sister. She was in disbelief at what had happened. Seeing her only reaffirmed his belief that the picture was authentic.

But that was the only thing noteworthy. It wasn't the best quality of picture. If he had to guess the time that it had been taken, he'd say it was either right before he got to the scene or when he was at his sister's side, right before the police got there. It had to have been one of those two time frames. Greg didn't try too hard to figure it out. What did it matter when the picture was taken?

There were other real questions. Had the person taking the picture been in the drive-by car? Did the police have some kind of surveillance system? If so, it was a terrific lead.

He sat back in his chair, realizing that by sheer luck, he'd found the people that had murdered his sister. No, he didn't know who it was exactly, but he knew that the person who pulled the trigger wasn't the only guilty person. The police also needed to find whoever had filled out the request form. Whoever did that was more to blame for his sister's death than the actual killer. That was the person who actually knew Jessica and, for whatever reason, wanted her dead.

That reminded him. He looked beneath the picture and read, "deceased, for crimes of dishonesty."

Dishonesty? Greg thought. What did that mean? It was so vague. Who was she dishonest to? That could be anyone. Hell, it probably even made *him* a suspect.

He scrolled down the rest of the page, but there was nothing else. The bottom just had a link that said "Hire us today," which linked to the submission form.

Greg leaned back in his chair, taking in all of this newfound information. It was the miracle of all miracles that he'd stumbled onto the page. Never in a million years would he have seen it if it hadn't been for Shane mentioning his new way of acquiring drugs. Greg had never heard of the Deep Web before.

He had to call the police, but what would he say? The first question they'd ask him was why he was on the Deep Web in the first place.

He opened a new tab in his browser. He made sure to use Google, because he wanted to make sure that his search could be tracked, and typed in "deep web."

The first hit was a Wikipedia article. Below it, there was a news article about "Dread Pirate Roberts," the figure that Shane had mentioned as the founder of *The Silk Road* website where he bought his drugs. This guy had been arrested, and the article discussed how the FBI had found him.

It was the perfect reason. It was his excuse as to why he had been on the Deep Web. He could tell Captain Sloan that he'd stumbled across the article in Google News, read about it, and became curious. Then, he'd say that he installed Tor and found the hitman site after doing some exploring. Most of that was the truth, and it left Shane out of it. The last thing that Greg wanted was for the police to start asking Shane questions. He hadn't said anything, but Greg thought Shane's drug purchasing was a ticking time bomb. It sounded like Shane had thought it through, but there was no way that it was as simple as it sounded. Sooner or later, he was going to get into trouble.

He took Captain Sloan's number out of his wallet and dialed.

There wasn't an answer. His voicemail came up, but Greg

didn't even think about leaving a message and hung up.

He wasn't sure what to do, but then he remembered that Detective Maxwell had provided his number as well. He liked the detective much more than the captain. He felt that Captain Sloan was just there to oversee things while Maxwell was more ambitious when it came to finding out who'd done this.

Greg didn't bother trying to call the captain again. He tried to reach the detective.

It only rang once before the man picked up.

"Hello."

"Detective Maxwell? It's Greg, the brother of Jessica Anderson."

"Greg! How's it going? What can I do for you?"

"I've found something. Something big that you're going to want to see."

"Are you at your apartment?"

"Yes."

"Third floor at Rivers Commons?"

"Yeah, room 301."

"I'm on my way.

While Greg was waiting on the detective to arrive, he thought more about what he was going to say. He was relieved that he was going to first explain this to the detective instead of the captain. Detective Maxwell wouldn't ask him those accusatory questions that Sloan liked to ask. He felt as though the detective was more on his side.

There was a knock on the door twenty minutes later, and Greg opened it. It was Maxwell.

"You really should be more careful who you open the door for, Greg. I know you didn't even look through your peephole, so you didn't even know it was me. What if I was someone that dropped by because I was a little afraid that you knew too much about the investigation?"

"I never thought of that. Good point," Greg said. "Officer, I think I do have something that will hopefully allow us to catch the person that killed her."

"Great. Let's hear it."

"It's on my computer. Come here and I'll show you."

Greg grabbed a chair from the kitchen table and set it down next to the computer. He'd intentionally left the article about Dread Pirate Roberts open. He wasn't going to come out and tell the detective everything he knew. He'd gauge his temperament first and see how it went.

"Did you hear about this story?" Greg asked casually.

Detective Maxwell looked closely at the screen. He grabbed the mouse and scanned through the article.

"I believe so. Is this the online guy that they caught?"

"Umm, yeah, sort of."

"I vaguely remember some guys at the department talking about it. Wasn't he selling drugs or something?"

"Yes, that's exactly right."

"I don't get it. Is this your lead?"

"Oh no, of course not. Well, maybe… but I highly doubt it." Greg fidgeted in his chair. "So, officer, do you understand the technology he was using to create his anonymity?"

"I do not. I investigate murders, Greg. Which, in Columbus, isn't a lot, but it's enough to keep me busy. I don't keep up with cyber crimes."

"Well, let me explain it to you then."

Greg gave Detective Maxwell the introductory overview of the Tor browser. He went to the site and explained how it was something that one would use if they wanted to be anonymous. He went on to give him the story about how he had downloaded it because he was curious after reading the articles about Dread Pirate Roberts. Then Greg took him to TorDir and explained how a lot of illegal activity was being conducted through it. The detective, again, took over the mouse and began scanning the page.

"Ahh, yes. I remember getting briefed on this. Someone from the DEA came in and gave us an overview. I thought this was mostly about drugs?"

"No. It's got *way* more stuff than drugs."

Greg let the detective click around to a few sites. All of them went to broken links except for the U.S. passport site he'd seen before. Detective Maxwell was only on the site for a moment before he clicked back. *Did that mean he was disinterested?*

"Can I show you what I found?"

"Please do," he said, letting go of the mouse.

Greg began to get anxious. He took a deep breath through his nose to try and calm himself down. His hand trembled as he scrolled down to the link at the bottom of the page. *What was the detective going to say or think?* He clicked on the link.

"There are a few sites that claim to offer hitman services. A couple of them look like they're just scams, but not this one." He scrolled to the form. "This is where people can submit an application of sorts, explaining who they want to be murdered and why. The site owners claim to offer their service free of charge because they're sociopaths and want to kill people. They select who to kill based on how evil they think they are."

Greg wanted to cry again and probably would have if the detective hadn't been there. He scrolled back up to the top of the page.

"I'll show you why I think this site is legit and also why I wanted you to come over and see this." He clicked to the proof section. "These people are arrogant enough to show pictures of their victims."

"Oh my God! I can't believe this."

"Pretty crazy, huh?"

"I didn't know stuff like this was out there on the web."

"Well it's hidden, like I said. You have to have this Tor browser to get to it."

"Still, you'd think the department would be more aware of this and provide more than a five-minute presentation on it to detectives."

Greg scrolled down to the bottom of the page. "Here's my sister. These are the people that killed her!"

Detective Maxwell grabbed the mouse back from Greg, which seemed pointless because he didn't even use it; he kept the screen where it was. He studied the picture from the crime scene, just as Greg had done.

"This picture was taken right as we got there," Maxwell said. "I didn't see anyone taking pictures, otherwise I would have confiscated them."

"Is there any kind of surveillance? Something to find the person that way?"

"I'll certainly look into it. As far as the street, no, there's nothing like that. We've checked with all the local stores to see if they had a camera with a view out onto the street, but there weren't any."

Detective Maxwell grabbed a pen and paper out of his back pocket. Greg peeked over to see what he was writing down. At the top, he wrote the address of the website they were on, which was an obscure combination of letters and numbers. Then, he wrote "Tor Browser" beneath it.

"How did you find this page, again? What was that site with all the links?"

"TorDir."

He wrote that down. "And where did you find and learn about all of this? What was the name of the guy in the article you were reading?"

"Dread Pirate Roberts."

"Right." He wrote down the name. Detective Maxwell then pulled the notepad closer to his chest so that Greg couldn't see what he was writing down. He jotted something down and put the notepad back into his back pocket.

"Greg, this is a great find——really terrific! I'm going to go back and show this to the Captain. I'll let you know how that goes. In the meantime, now that you have this information, does it ring any bells? Can you think of enemies or someone that would want to submit your sister's name?"

"The captain asked us that a million times. No, it doesn't, unfortunately. Like I said before, everyone liked Jessica. It makes no sense why this happened."

"All right, let me know if that changes. Even if it doesn't seem like a big deal. You never know with these cases."

"Will do. I hope this helps you out, detective. It has to, right?"

"Let's hope. It certainly gives me a lot of things to look further into. Like I said, I'll call you in a day or two and let you know how it's going."

"Great. I very much look forward to hearing back."

They both got up and walked to the door.

"You take care of yourself, Greg. Remember, we still don't know who put in that request. I don't want you to feel alarmed, but just watch your back, will ya?"

"Yes, officer. I have been, for the most part."

When Detective Maxwell left, Greg couldn't help but think that something positive was going to come out of the investigation.

Deep Web

Chapter 9

Greg decided to tell his parents what he'd found. He didn't want to but figured they'd hear about it the next time the police updated them. Greg's dad would be furious if he kept something like that from him.

He left out as many details of the Deep Web as he could, like how one could hire prostitutes and buy copious amounts of drugs.

It was uncomfortable enough just talking to his parents about it.

Greg's mom, again, was disinterested. It seemed to be her way of dealing with the situation: pretending as if she didn't care. His dad was more engaged in the investigation, but with each day, his attention was fading.

For Greg, it was the opposite. Each day, each hour, each passing minute that the people responsible were getting away with Jessica's murder, he grew more infuriated.

He wouldn't stop.

It would be his lifelong missions if it had to be, but he'd find out who did this.

His mind was racing, and he didn't feel like being alone that night, so he called Stacy.

"Hey, sweetie. How's it going?"

"Alright. It's been an insanely crazy day. Want to come over and stay the night? I'll tell you all about it."

"Sure, I'll be right over."

Stacy listened and followed his story. He could tell she really cared for him. They made love that night, which only eased Greg's mind even more. He still couldn't believe such a beautiful, smart girl was interested in him. Maybe it was the age difference. Now that he was getting close to his thirties, maybe he was finally becoming more attractive to the opposite sex.

Whatever it was, he wasn't complaining. He hadn't gotten laid since Carrie. Jessica had finally hooked him up with a great girl.

They decided to go golfing on Saturday instead of Sunday. She knew Sundays were usually reserved for golfing with Shane and the sales team. He'd already ditched them a few times so that he could be with her.

"Don't let me keep you from your friends. I don't want to be clingy. You should have time to yourself."

It was a beautiful spring afternoon. The sun was warm, but the light breeze provided the perfect relief. They walked nine holes together, and for her first time out on a real golf course instead of just the range, she wasn't bad.

Greg had never believed someone could have a natural talent for golf, but Stacy was proving to be the exception. She shot a forty-eight, which was amazing. Already she might have been able to beat Shane and was certainly better than Brian, who was a normal part of their foursome.

When they were in the clubhouse eating dinner, which consisted of two chili hot dogs each and a shared bag of potato chips, he looked into her eyes and smiled. Nothing was sexier than having her here, even with the bit of sauce hanging onto the edge of her lip. He wiped it off with his napkin. She gave a cute grin and kissed him.

"I really, really like you," Greg said.

"Well I really, really like you, too."

They went back to his place. He wanted her to stay the night again, but she insisted on leaving.

"You're not going to sleep well knowing that you have to play host in the morning. When is your tee time with Shane?"

"Nine."

"Exactly. By the time you wake up, get ready, have breakfast… you'll be out the door. Then you'll feel guilty that you didn't spend much time with me. You'll worry that I'll be upset, because that's what girls do. You won't play well because you'll be worried. How 'bout we skip the usual boyfriend/girlfriend drama? I'll go home now, and you can call me after your round some time and tell me how it went."

She was right. He wouldn't have much time to talk with her in the morning. Especially considering they were going to a new course that was an hour away. Still, she was completely naked in his bed.

He really didn't want her to leave.

"I want you to stay, though. I'll miss you."

"And I'll miss you, too." She put her hand on his cheek and kissed him. Her hand was so delicate. He was ready for round two until she stopped him. "But we'll have plenty more opportunities to spend time together."

She got up and started putting her clothes on, which Greg enjoyed watching from his bed.

"Promise you'll call tomorrow night some time?"

"I promise."
She kissed him goodbye and left.

"You should see the girl this guy's boning," Shane said to Brian and Kyle. "Show 'em the picture, Greg."

The four of them were waiting on the thirteenth tee box, a par three over water that every golfer in front of them must have hit into because they were all searching for balls by the edge of the pond.

He reluctantly took the picture out and handed it to Brian.

"Damn, dude. She's bangable for sure," Brian said.

"Oh my God! Isn't this the same girl that was at Foxxxie's the other night? The one that gave you that lap dance, Shane?" Kyle asked.

Greg had a sinking feeling in his stomach. No way it could be true. Was Stacy a stripper?

There was a long pause between the four of them. They all looked at Greg to see his reaction.

"Are you serious? Was she really there?" He tried playing it off like it wasn't a big deal.

The three of them burst out laughing at the same time.

"Relax, Greg. He's just fucking with you!" Shane said.

Greg let out a breath of relief. He'd completely fallen for the joke. He should have known. It got him thinking, though. How well did he know Stacy? They'd been dating for a month and had moved fast in the relationship from a physical standpoint. They talked a lot when they were around together, but as far as her life was concerned, there was still a lot he had to learn.

"Man, these fuckers are taking forever," Shane said. "I want to go over and fucking stab them with my three iron."

"I'd love to see that!" Brian said. "Although, you should probably use a nine iron. I saw that whiff back on seven."

"Shit. Whatever. I was under a fucking tree. Hit it on my downswing."

"That's not how I saw it. Greg, you were standing right there. What did *you* see?"

He turned to look over at Brian, who was sitting in his cart; Kyle was sitting next to him, rolling up a joint. It took Greg off guard, but he didn't say anything. He knew they all smoked, but he'd never actually seen them do it. The sight of it made him very uncomfortable. He looked over at Shane and grinned. "I don't remember your club coming anywhere close to that tree."

Brian and Kyle let out their biggest laugh yet.

"Stop it. Stop it! You're gonna make me spill my chronic," Kyle said.

"Hurry up with that. I need to mellow out or I seriously might go over there and attack those old fuckers," Shane said. He then turned to Greg, "This is that online weed I was talking to you about."

"You told him about that?" Kyle said, glaring at Shane.

"Relax, bro. Greg's cool. You're not gonna say anything, are ya, bud?"

"No. I don't care."

"Still…" Brian said. "Can we keep this shit quiet? I really don't feel like getting arrested again."

"You're fucking blazing in the middle of a golf course. Don't give me that shit about keeping things quiet."

Brian lit up the joint and inhaled. He blew it hard in the direction of Shane. "Fair point." He took another puff and passed it over to Kyle, who took a couple puffs before passing it to Shane.

Seeing Shane smoke weed seemed strange, like he was being let in on a secret side of him that Greg had never seen before.

"You want a hit?" Shane said, holding out the weed towards

Greg.

"I'm good." He tried to sound cool, like he'd smoked weed a million times but didn't feel like doing it this particular time. Truth was, he'd only tried it once in college, at a party his sophomore year. It was different, but he didn't like it any better than drinking alcohol, so he never bothered with it again. His honest opinion was that weed was something you tried when you were young and dumb. At some point as an adult, one needed to grow up.

As Shane continued to smoke, he said, "So what did you and Victoria do after we left the bar Friday?"

"We ended up going to her place 'cause it was closer. That girl likes it rough. For a moment, I thought she was going to start hitting me!" Kyle said.

"Yeah, some girls are like that. You goin' out with her again?" Shane said.

"Fuck no. That quest has been conquered. Time to move on to greener pastures."

The three of them continued with talks of their most recent lays. Greg turned away, watching the people in front of them continue to look for their balls. He'd never felt so out of place around Shane and his friends. He'd always known that he didn't quite fit in with them but always put up with their absurd conversations, but smoking weed around him was a bit too much. He didn't feel like getting arrested for something that he took no part in.

He thought about Stacy and how he could replace his Sunday golf days with her. Shane and the guys could easily find someone to replace him for a while. However, Greg would miss the income. He was up two hundred bucks today already, and since he was competing with people that were high, that number would likely only increase.

One of the guys in front of them waved his hand towards Greg, signaling that they could pass them.

"Hey guys, they're telling us to go ahead and hit."

Greg saw that Kyle had the joint now and kept it in his mouth as he went to hit his ball. When they drove up to the green, Kyle continued to keep the joint between his lips while he chipped on and putted. Greg couldn't believe he had the arrogance not to hide it. The other group had to have smelled the distinct scent. Greg hurried to putt his ball. He couldn't bear to glance over at anyone from the other group. Who knew what they were thinking? Greg thought for sure they'd be arrested by the time they made it to the next tee box.

The four of them finished up the hole. When Greg and Shane got to their cart, Greg asked, "Is it a good idea to be smoking weed right next to those guys? What if they call the police?"

"Relax, bro. What are you so worried about? They're not going to say anything."

"How do you know?"

"Because that's not what guys do. Whatever happens on the golf course, stays out here."

For the rest of their round, things didn't go well for Greg. He was still too nervous of getting caught, and it showed. He played some of his worst golf in months. And surprisingly, being a little high had made all three of them play exceptionally better. Several jokes were made that weed was the secret to better golf.

Great, this will only encourage them more.

After the round, they went to the clubhouse for a beer, like they always did. Usually it was just one, maybe two if they were in a particularly good mood after the round. Today, though, the three of them each had six. On top of that, they each had a burger and fries.

After they were done, they walked to the car. They'd all driven together in Brian's Escalade. Greg didn't think any of them were in good enough shape to drive. He knew he'd have to but was afraid to say so, because who knew what confrontation would ensure?

Fortunately, Shane stood up for him. "Hey Brian, man, why don't you let sober boy drive?"

"No way, man. Nobody fuckin' drives the Escalade."

"I get that, but if you want it in one piece, maybe you oughta rethink that this one time."

"I'm fine. No worries." He pulled the keys out of his pocket but immediately dropped them. When he reached down to pick them up, he fell over, hitting his face on the pavement.

Shane and Kyle busted out laughing. Greg was thinking about how he was going to die if he got in the car with Brian behind the wheel. He'd made up his mind that he wasn't going to. He'd have his parents or Stacy pick him up, or pay for a cab if he had to, but he wasn't going to die today.

"You sure, man? Just let Greg drive; he's not going to hurt your baby."

Brian got up and unlocked the doors. "I told you, no one drives the fuckin' Escalade."

Greg opened his mouth to say he was going to find an alternative ride home when Brian continued.

"Just this once." He threw the keys at Greg's chest.

"You made a good choice," Shane said, patting Brian on the back. Shane and Kyle got in the car.

Brian stayed outside the car with Greg, staring him down and saying, "You get even a little scratch on this thing, I'll fucking kill you."

As Greg looked at Brian, he realized that he wasn't blinking.

He could tell Brian was really drunk and high, and wondered if he might try to attack him if something went wrong on the way home.

He didn't want to drive them, because he knew how much they'd carry on in the car. It would be hard enough to drive with all the distractions; adding a death threat to the mix wouldn't make things any easier.

If something did happen, he knew Shane would have his back. So he got in the car and drove away.

The hour-long drive wasn't as bad as Greg thought it would be. He had to make two gas station stops so that they could go to the bathroom, but they had the decency to refrain from smoking anymore.

They finally got to the office parking lot, where they'd all met up. Greg got his clubs out and put them in his car. He left, hardly saying goodbye before driving away. He wanted to get as far away from the three of them as he could.

Now that he was driving back, safe from them, he felt much more relaxed. He could still smell the hint of weed on his shirt from being around them. He'd have to wash his clothes as soon as he got home.

He thought of Stacy again. What would she think about his round of golf with three potheads? He honestly had no idea if she'd find it funny or appalling. Maybe he shouldn't even tell her about it. He didn't know what the best thing to say was.

He'd planned on calling her as soon as he got back.

But when he got home, something else happened that made him forget all about his horrible day of golf.

He got a phone call with some very bad news.

Chapter 10

"Hey, Greg. It's Detective Maxwell."

"Hey! How's it going?"

"Well... I'm afraid I can't say things are going great, to be honest."

"Why? What's wrong?"

"I showed the captain what you had shown me. He wasn't nearly as interested in the findings as I was."

Anger boiled up inside of him. That captain was a fucking worthless piece of shit. An image flashed in his mind of the man sitting at his desk, feet propped up, stuffing a cheeseburger into his fat mouth.

"Anyway, I went ahead and checked through the surveillance videos again. We really didn't have anything close to where Jessica or our mystery cameraman was. I'm sorry."

Greg didn't say anything. He couldn't understand why this incredible discovery was getting them nowhere.

"So what are you saying, officer? That's it?"

"I'm afraid so. The captain told me that the website doesn't give us any solid proof that the person taking the picture committed the murders."

"But didn't you see all the other pictures? There's no way

they could be faking this."

"I hear you, and I've forwarded the information on to the lead detectives on the other cases, but as for the picture of your sister, anyone could have snapped that photograph."

"There has to be something else you can do."

"Perhaps, but…"

"But what?" Greg said, getting even angrier.

"This was the main reason for my call, Greg. I wanted to tell you that I've been reassigned."

"What? What does that mean?"

"Basically, it means Captain Sloan has decided to make the case cold, barring any new evidence. Personally, I think it's quite premature, given what you found. But unfortunately, I don't call the shots or make the rules." After a brief pause, he said, "Between you and me, I don't think the captain wants to get involved in the Deep Web stuff you showed me."

"Who gives a shit what the captain wants? I thought you were on my side. I thought you wanted to find who did this to Jessica."

"I do, Greg. How dare you accuse me otherwise! Reality is, there have been fifteen homicides since Jessica was murdered and resources have to be put into those as well. I know that must be frustrating for you to hear, Greg. This stuff doesn't work the way it does on TV. We have very limited resources, and we do the best we can with them. I want to find your sister's killer; I truly do. But… it's out of my hands."

"So, you're giving up?" Greg said, trying to make the officer feel bad.

"Again, I'm sorry. There's nothing I can do. All the evidence thus far has gotten us nowhere. We can only get so much information from a bullet. No one got a look at the vehicle. You live near downtown, so there were a lot of cars on the roads that night. Your website helps paint a better picture, but we've already interviewed her coworkers, friends, and your family numerous times. There's just nothing we can go on."

"I just don't believe that. Surely there must be something else you can do? Even if you do have to work on other cases."

"I'm afraid not. This is it for now."

"Well I'm not stopping. I hope you know that. I'm going to find out who did this to my sister. And I'll do it with or without your help."

"Don't do anything foolish, Greg. You're only going to get yourself in trouble. As far as that website you found, these are not people you want to mess with. You could get yourself killed!"

"Well maybe they deserve to die. Maybe it's me that should kill them." Greg knew that he'd gone too far when he said that. He was so angry with Deputy Maxwell, Captain Sloan, and the entire Columbus police department.

"I'll pretend like you didn't say that. Listen, I'm gonna check in once a month, if you'd like, so we can catch up. I'll do my best to squeeze in an hour or two to revisit the case and see if my fresh eyes overlooked something from before."

"Thanks, but why bother? We both know you're not going to do anything. Good luck on your other cases. I'm sure those murderers will get away, too."

"Greg..."

By the time the word was out of his mouth, Greg had already hung up. He screamed as loudly as he could, which he followed with excessive crying. He went over to the couch and buried his face into a pillow, screaming into it.

There was a knock on the door. He looked up, wondering if Detective Maxwell had come already. He got up to see who it was. He was about to open the door when he remembered what the detective had said about looking through the peephole first. He did and saw it was his neighbor, Mr. Peters. Most of the people on his floor were younger, but the man that lived right next to him was a nice, older gentleman that Greg occasionally bumped into in the hallway.

"What do you want, Mr. Peters?" Greg asked through the door.

"Are you all right, son? I heard screaming."

"Yeah, I'm fine. Everything's fine. Go back to your room."

"Are you sure?"

Greg wiped some tears from his face and then opened the door. He saw Mr. Peters standing there with a very worried look on his face.

"Mr. Peters, really, I'm fine. I've just been thinking about my sister and heard some bad news about the investigation."

"That's terrible, son. Heard about it in the papers. Do you want someone to talk to about it? I've got hot chocolate over at my place... even got the big marshmallows."

"That sounds nice, Mr. Peters. It really does. I think I just want to be alone right now, though."

"All right. You take care of yourself. I heard the screaming, and I just got worried that—"

"I appreciate it." Greg interrupted. "You're a good man. I don't care what our other floormates say about you," Greg said, forcing a grin.

Mr. Peters looked like he didn't know what to say. He took a step forward and put his hand on Greg's shoulder. "It's going to get better, son."

Greg could feel Mr. Peters transferring his positive energy into him. It made him want to cry. It was comforting.

"I hope."

Mr. Peters stared at Greg for a few more seconds before

letting go and walking away.

Greg closed the door, thinking about what a good man Mr. Peters was. He'd always found him a bit mysterious, though. Why was someone at his age living there? He'd asked him before, and he'd given him some wisecrack to deflect the question like, "This is where all the good-lookin' young ladies are."

Greg figured the real reason was sadder and more depressing, but he never asked him again.

Greg's mom called twenty minutes later. Apparently, and adding to Greg's frustration, Detective Maxwell had called his parents to update them on the case as well as tell them about their son's recent outburst.

"Are you doing all right, Greg?"

"No, Mom. You heard what he said. They're giving up on the case." He got choked up, "They're never going to find out who did this."

"Karma has a way of taking care of itself. That's what I've learned. I'm sure whoever has done this will have it coming to them, in this life or the next."

"I don't believe in karma, Mom. That doesn't make me feel any better. I want them to pay for this, and I want it to happen in this life. Especially the person who ordered the hit."

"You don't know for sure that's what happened, Greg. Do not, I repeat, do *not* get yourself involved with this. Jessica is dead." She stopped herself to cry. She could barely get her words out. "She's dead, and there's nothing you or I can do about it."

Greg didn't say anything. He sat and listened to his mom cry through the phone, and it made him cry, too. It was awkward, having a phone call where two people were doing nothing but crying.

They finally collected themselves.

"Promise me. Promise me you won't get involved with this. I've already lost my only daughter; I don't want to lose my only son."

"I promise," Greg said, lying to comfort her.

"Okay. Do you want to come over? Your father is cooking steak tonight."

"That sounds good. I'm fine, though. I'm supposed to be doing something with Stacy tonight.

"How are you two doing?" She seemed glad the conversation had switched to something happier.

"Good. She's really great, Mom. I *really* like her."

"That's good. What are you doing tonight?"

"I'm not sure." It was the truth. He hadn't even talked to her yet and was unsure if they were actually doing anything. "I just know that I like being around her. She helps me get through the days."

"I'm glad to hear that. When do I get to have her over for dinner?"

"Whoa, easy there, Mom. Not yet. We've only been dating for a month."

"I know. You know how I get excited whenever you or your sister get into a relationship."

"Yeah, and I also know how heartbroken you were when James moved to Africa. Maybe it's best that you don't get so attached. It only makes it harder if things don't work out."

"Perhaps," she said, disappointment in her voice. "I'm sorry. I won't ask again. You have her over whenever you're ready."

Greg had never been as open about his relationships as Jessica had been with their mom. He didn't know if that was a mother-son thing, or if it was because of his less open personality. Either way, while it was true he hadn't been in nearly as many relationships as Jessica, he hadn't had his heart broken as often either, which was fine with him.

"I'm going to hang up now, if that's all right," Greg said.

"Of course, dear. I should probably get started with dinner. You sure you don't want to come over?"

"I'm sure. Thanks."

"All right. Call me tomorrow after you get off work."

"Will do." Greg, sensing his mom was worried, said, "I'm all right, Mom. I can take care of myself. You don't have to worry about me."

"Okay. Have fun tonight. I love you."

"Love you, too."

As soon as he got off the phone, he called Stacy. As it connected, her picture came up on the screen and he was reminded of how beautiful, sweet, and kind she was.

"Hey!" she said. "How was golf?"

"Good. Actually… that's a lie. It was horrible. It feels like so long ago that I almost forgot all that happened. Can you come over?"

"Of course. I'd love to."

"Cool. I was thinking I could make mom's famous pasta."

"Ohhh, I like the sound of that. Is that what it says on the TV dinner label? 'Mom's favorite pasta.'"

"Funny. But no. My mom has this incredible recipe that she made from scratch. Jessica and I lived off of it growing up."

Greg always felt awkward when he brought up Jessica. He knew talking about his dead sister was probably the last thing a girl wanted to hear about, except for maybe stories of ex-girlfriends. He couldn't help himself, though. So much of his life had involved Jessica, and so most of his stories involved her in some way. He didn't know how to get around that.

Fortunately, Stacy didn't seem to mind. In fact, she almost seemed to enjoy hearing more about Jessica. Greg wasn't entirely sure if it was genuine or if it was because Stacy had a kind heart. For now, he'd just have to count on it being genuine.

"Well, mom's favorite pasta sounds delightful. I can't wait to try it. Do I need to pick up supplies on the way? Or do you have everything?"

"Actually, I do need oregano and two roma tomatoes. Do you like mushrooms? If so, get those, too, and I'll pay you back."

"I *love* mushrooms. I think I have some in the fridge. I know I have the tomatoes. They're organic, too. Does mom's favorite pasta require a special brand of oregano? I have Organics oregano. I get all my seasonings from them. But if you need a special kind, I'm happy to get it."

"No, not really. At least, I don't think it requires anything special. You sound like you know what you're doing. I'm getting the sense that you like to cook."

"Just a little," she said, unable to hide her enthusiasm. "Growing up on a farm, food is pretty much a way of life."

"Ahh, well, that's just great," he said sarcastically. "I didn't think about that. Now the pressure is on!"

"Oh, stop it! I'm sure I'll love it."

"All right, if you say so. I'm still feelin' the pressure."

"Well trust me, I've eaten some of my little brother's prepared meals before, so I've experienced all ends of the food spectrum before. I can eat and enjoy almost anything."

"I didn't know you had a little brother!"

"Really? I haven't told you that? Yeah, he just started at Ohio State this year."

"There's so much I don't know about you. I was thinking about that today, actually. Tonight, I want to hear about your childhood."

"Well I'm not sure it's all that exciting, but if you want to suffer through listening to it, I'll tell."

"I do. I truly do. Kyle had me convinced you were a stripper."

"What!? How did he do that?"

"It's all part of a day of golfing hell. I'll tell the story when you get here."

"Okay, I'm on my way. I *have* to hear this story."

"See you soon."

Chapter 11

Stacy got to Greg's apartment thirty minutes later. She had a reusable bag with all the ingredients he'd asked for.

She had a thin bandanna wrapped around her head. Any time Greg had seen people wearing them, he'd stereotyped them as being hippies. The girls wearing them usually walked around without makeup and looked like they hadn't showered in a few days or shaved in months. It caught Greg off guard the first time he had seen Stacy wearing one, but he had to admit that she looked really cute in it.

She did have a lot of the hippie traits. Loved organic foods. Believed in peace and love. Supported liberal government policies (especially gay marriage and abortion rights). As far as his views went, he was fine with gay people getting married and women getting abortions. But he'd never go down to a rally and hold up a sign. He wasn't *that* passionate about it.

Stacy seemed the type, though.

And opposites attract.

"So, what can I do?" Stacy said.

"You can pop open a bottle of wine for us. Then you can find your way over to the couch and make yourself comfortable."

"I think I can handle that."

"Good. The wine, FYI, is so my food will taste better. The more you drink, the better it'll be."

"I figured that much. But why do I have to sit over there? Can I sit at the counter and watch? Do you not love me? Don't you want to be around me?" she said in perfect imitation of a needy girl.

Greg laughed. Every time she did that, he couldn't help but think of Carrie. She had been the classic, clingy girl that Stacy always made fun of. He'd told Stacy about Carrie, again unsure if it was a good idea to discuss ex-girlfriends, but he'd thought Stacy would think it was funny, and she had.

"Yes, the couch is so I can have my privacy. I can just imagine you cringing at my cooking methods. I'm already nervous enough cooking for a master chef."

She giggled, something that she often did and that Greg adored. "I'm hardly an expert cook. And like I said, I'll love your food no matter what. I think it's really sweet that you're cooking for me. Not many guys are willing to do that."

"Well, I don't claim to be like most guys."

"I know that. To reiterate something else I said earlier, if I can survive my brother's meat loaf——which he decided to put curry, cinnamon, and carrots in——I think I can get by with mom's famous pasta."

"Curry, cinnamon, and carrots?"

"Yeah, it was horrible. Our dogs, who literally eat everything you could possible imagine, wouldn't even touch the stuff."

"I can imagine. That sounds disgusting, cinnamon in meatloaf."

"I had nightmares for months," she laughed as she pulled two wine glasses from the shelf.

"Well, hopefully I can do better."

***

As Greg was cooking, he glanced over occasionally and saw that Stacy had gone through two glasses of wine. She talked about life on the farm. He still couldn't imagine someone as beautiful as Stacy milking cows and shoveling horse dung for hours on end.

She also talked about her brother, with whom she had a love-hate relationship. It was similar to what many people felt for their siblings. He didn't bother telling Stacy, again, the kind of relationship that he'd had with his sister. She already knew theirs was much different.

As soon as dinner was prepared, he scooped the pasta onto two plates and brought them over to the kitchen table.

"Is it ready?"

"It is indeed. Pour plenty of sauce on it. And if you can, please at least pretend to like it."

"I'm sure I won't have to pretend. It looks amazing!"

Greg loved the compliment. He was nervous for her to try it and was glad that she at least seemed to like the way it looked. It wasn't a total disaster thus far.

He watched as she poured a heaping spoonful of sauce onto her plate. Then he did the same.

As he was sprinkling on his Parmesan cheese, he stared intently at her. She was about to take her first bite. She looked up at him, and he quickly turned his head away.

"You're not going to watch me the entire time, are you?"

"Sorry. I just really want you to like it."

"Greg, it's going to be fine. Relax."

He looked down at his plate, stirring the Parmesan in. It was only a few seconds before he had to glance up again. When he did, he saw that Stacy was still looking at him.

"I knew you wouldn't be able to control yourself!" She

laughed.

"All right, all right. I'm not looking. Now will you please start eating before I have a panic attack?"

She put the fork up to her mouth, aware that he was looking at her intently. She stared right into his eyes as she started chewing. Then, she made a disgusted face. She covered her mouth with her hand.

"Oh my god. Get a napkin."

Greg rushed over to the counter where there was a stack of napkins. He grabbed all of them and turned around, ready to hand them to her. When he looked up, he saw that she had a huge smile on her face.

"It's delicious," she said.

Greg let out a sigh and sat back in his chair. "You little…" He didn't finish his sentence. "You got me!"

"You have to admit, you deserved it."

"You're right. I did. So you like it?"

"I do. It's really great! If I ever get to meet your mom, I can't wait to tell her. I presume the recipe is top secret?"

"Colonel Sanders' chicken recipe isn't even as guarded as this is."

"Okay, I won't guess then. I can pick up five or six ingredients right away. There's something, though, I can't quite put my finger on. "

Greg figured it was probably the stevia. "My lips are sealed. You'll have to get it out of my mom somehow."

"Oh, I plan to. I know exactly how to get a girl to spill all her secrets."

"Yeah, what's that?"

"Do you *really* think I'm going to tell you?"

Greg smiled. He looked into her eyes and, again, thought of how beautiful and perfect she was. When she smirked, she had little dimples in her cheeks. It made Greg want to get up from the table and kiss them——kiss her. He poured himself another glass of wine. He was hoping the dinner would earn him a reward in the bedroom.

"Now, before I forget, tell me why you wondered if I was a stripper?"

Greg recounted his day with the three stoners. He'd been worried before of what she would think, but she found the story hilarious.

"So… have you ever been to that strip club before?" Stacy said, accusatory.

Greg didn't want to answer. The truth was that he had been a couple times with Shane and the sales guys. He didn't want to lie to her and was about to admit it when she interrupted.

"I have. You should take me some time."

This was the last thing that he expected her to say. "Are you serious?"

"Yeah. In college, about eight of us went one time."

"All girls?"

"No, it was girls and guys. The guys even pitched in and got me a lap dance."

Greg was speechless. He had a hard time believing the story. "So… I don't understand. Are you…?" He didn't want to finish the sentence.

"What? Batting for both teams?"

"Yeah," he said, glad she guessed what he was thinking.

"Wouldn't you like that!" she said, giving him a playful pinch in his side.

"Ouch," he said, smiling. He knew his cheeks must be bright red from blushing.

"No, I'm not bisexual. Although, I have kissed several girls

——not that it's surprising, really. A lot of girls go through that little phase in college."

"Yeah, I saw my sister kiss a few before." Again, it slipped out without him thinking. Why did he have to always bring up Jessica?

The smile edged from Stacy's face. "You really miss her, don't you?"

"Sorry, I didn't mean to bring her up again."

"It's more than fine, Greg. I understand. I mean, my god, it was your sister. *Twin* sister. And it was so unexpected." She put her hand on top of his. "Have you heard any more news about the investigation?"

"Well, that was the other thing that I wanted to talk to you about." Greg had temporarily forgotten about Maxwell's call. That was why he loved having Stacy around. She could make him forget about everything that was going on. "Detective Maxwell, the one that was assigned to the case, called and said he'd been reassigned."

Stacy studied Greg's face and then said, "I take it that's bad?"

"Very bad. He told me the chief is filing the case away, barring any new evidence. They've given up."

"But what about the website you showed them? Can't they figure out who created that site and go after them? I did a Google search and saw you could look that up. I can't remember the name, but I wrote it down. It was some kind of initials or acronym."

"WHOIS?"

"That was it!"

"That's only for regular websites——not for these hidden, illegal sites. I looked that up, too."

"Oh, that's too bad."

Greg thought it was really cute that Stacy had been doing her own detective work. It meant a lot to him that she really cared so much about him.

"Anyway, he called and told me that they had looked through the surveillance again and didn't see any views from the street, so no one that took the picture."

"Well, did they interview people again? Maybe someone there saw him."

"Ya know, that's a good question. He didn't say whether they did or didn't. Honestly, though, I got the impression that the chief didn't want anything to do with the case. Detective Maxwell was kinda on our side for a while, but my guess is that he got a lot of pressure internally about Jessica's case once I told him about that website, and he basically was forced to quit the case. I don't think he wanted to. He said he'd look into it a little off and on, but it sounded like he'd be doing it behind the chief's back." Greg beat his fist down on the table. "I knew there was something about the chief that I hated!"

Stacy got up and put her arms around Greg. It felt good to have her comforting him.

"I'm sorry. I feel *so* bad. So what are you going to do?"

"I told my mom that I was going to start taking things into my own hands. I'm not sure what that will involve yet, but there has to be something that can be done." Greg was starting to get choked up now. "The person that ordered the hit out on Jessica is still out there. Now, maybe they weren't sure if the site was real, but it was, and it happened. But more importantly, whoever created the site is going to kill again and again. Someone needs to stop them."

"It's such a shame. Why don't the police see that?"

"You'd have to ask them. Detective Maxwell said this sort of thing gets handled at the federal level."

"Well, it doesn't look like they're doing a very good job."

"No, it doesn't," Greg agreed.

"So what are you going to do, exactly? I don't want to see you get hurt."

"I haven't figured that out yet, but I think if I uncover something else——something big——then maybe that'll help re-open the case. Depending on what I find, I may just look into it myself. I really don't know yet. There's a good chance I may never find anything. I got lucky, stumbling onto the website. I wasn't even thinking about Jessica when I clicked on the hitman site."

"I'm sure that if you really put your mind to it, you could figure something out. I know how hard this has been on you. Do you think it would help if you found the killer?"

"It would help *so* much. I can't get this image out of my head: the killer and the person who submitted the request sitting at home at this very moment, smoking a cigar, maybe watching some TV, probably laughing to themselves at how they got away with doing this. Those thoughts are what drive me crazy. I can't have it be this way. They need to pay for what they've done. I don't think I'll ever be able to get through life until I know they have."

"Well, if there's anything I can do to help, you let me know."

Greg looked at her and brushed some of her brown hair off of the corner of her eye. He reached over and gave her a kiss. He almost slipped up and told her that he loved her, but he caught himself. Instead, he said, "I... you're so beautiful." He put his hand on her cheek and kissed her again. "I appreciate you caring. I really do. You don't need to get involved in all of this."

"I want to, though. Like you said, whoever created that site is going to do it again. Who knows? The next person to have their name on a form could be my brother, or me… or you."

"You're right. Speaking of which, Detective Maxwell got on me about opening the door without looking through the peephole first. He said I should be a little more precautious in case the killer goes after me. I'm sure he was saying that to be overprotective, but it might be a good idea for you to look over your shoulder every once in a while, too."

The rest of the night didn't go as Greg had initially hoped.

Talking about the investigation ended up being quite the mood killer.

He had to go into work the next day, but he had been planning on Stacy staying the night since she didn't have any classes until the afternoon. But after watching some TV and snuggling, they both decided it was best that she go home.

He kissed her goodbye and watched her disappear down the hallway. He couldn't help but wonder what was going through her head. Was she really okay with his new obsession with the investigation? Or would she leave him because of it?

Greg didn't know, but he did know that he *really* liked her. He liked her more every time they were together. He still couldn't figure out why someone that smart and beautiful was with him, an unconfident nobody with major baggage. Was she just with him because she felt so much sympathy for him? Greg didn't want her to be with him for a reason like that. He wanted her to like him for who he was before Jessica's murder took place.

He imagined the three of them——he, Stacy and Jessica ——sitting around his apartment, eating mom's famous pasta. Maybe Jessica would eventually bring a new boyfriend over for a double date. It would've been the perfect life, where he could still have his sister, who would forever be his best friend, and also have Stacy.

He didn't dwell on it too much, because he knew it would never happen. He knew he'd have to move on, otherwise Stacy would get tired of putting up with him. He wasn't sure how long that would be, but he knew it would happen eventually.

The only way he could begin to pick up the pieces of his shattered life was to find the people responsible and make them pay for what they did.

But he was tired and ready for bed. Tomorrow, though, was a new beginning.

Tomorrow, he'd begin searching for the bastards that ruined his life.

Chapter 12

Greg woke up at five, as he often did. He didn't have to leave for work until eight, and it only took him an hour to get ready.

Between five and seven, he'd normally sit on the couch and watch SportsCenter. His mind would drift in and out as he'd think about his workday and all that he needed to get done. Dreading his day wasn't healthy, and he knew that. Almost always, the work tasks that he plagued his mind turned out to be far less painful when he actually got around to them. Still, he'd been following the same routine for so long that it was hard to change.

But today was a new beginning.

He picked up the remote, ready to turn on the TV, when he remembered the commitment that he'd made to himself while lying in bed the previous night. He was going to find the people who killed Jessica. He didn't know how, but he knew the more time he spent looking, the better his chances would be.

He put the remote down and walked over to his computer. Greg hadn't had the thing on in the morning since the day he'd bought it. He waited for it to boot up and remembered what Jessica had told him about getting a Mac. He'd dismissed the idea at the time, because he didn't use his computer for much except for porn. If he was going to find Jessica's killers, though, then maybe it was time for an upgrade. He was due for one anyway.

His computer finally booted up and he signed into the Tor network. When the homepage loaded, it gave him a message:

You are using an outdated version of Tor. Please upgrade by downloading the newest version here.

"Great," he muttered to himself. He was tempted to just go on and continue using the old version, but he was worried that the upgrade might be a security fix that would prevent someone from figuring out his identity. He clicked the download link and let it run.

While he waited, he went into the kitchen and got his bowl of cereal. He always woke up starving. Jessica had told him that it was because of all the wheat he ate. She swore up and down that wheat was the root evil of all health problems in America, and that if he'd cut it out of his diet, he wouldn't be so hungry all the time. He poured his breakfast cereal anyway, because she, after all, was the same person that said spinach was bad. If he followed all of her diet recommendations, he wouldn't be allowed to eat anything.

He took his bowl back over to his computer and clicked the install button.

He was able to eat most of his cereal in the time it took to finish installing and booting up. Once it did, the browser opened again and informed him that he was successfully connected to the Tor network.

First, he went to the *American Hitmen* site and checked to see if there were any new victims posted, but there weren't.

Just being on the site made him clench his hands in anger.

The black background with white letters was so creepy. None of the text had changed, from what he recalled, and the contact form was still at the bottom. He tried to imagine himself, both as the site creator and as someone coming to the site with a vendetta. Shane had told him the key to selling was to really put oneself in the buyer's shoes and figure out what made them tick. Greg thought if he could imagine himself as the person who set up the site, then maybe he could think of something that might help him identify the person.

But it was leading him nowhere.

His mind kept telling him how stupid it was. That there wasn't any way he could figure out who was behind everything and that he should stop wasting his time. He took a pen that was sitting on his desk and chucked it across the room.

He wanted to scream, but instead, he stared at the contact form sitting in the middle of his screen. Maybe he should use it. It wouldn't hurt. But what would he say? *Hey, you murdered my sister. Can you please tell me who you are so I can rip your head off?*

He said it to himself as a joke, but the more he thought about it, the more he was convinced that it might not be a bad idea. There was a small chance that they'd respond back, given how arrogant they were. Greg thought it was highly unlikely that these people responded to emails, but if he could get some kind of message back, even if it just told him to fuck off, then maybe it could bring him some kind of clue.

Greg had read the article about Dread Pirate Roberts and how he had eventually been caught running the *Silk Road* website. He was dumb enough to use his actual name for an email address. The FBI then watched him closely and eventually figured out that it was he who was involved.

He couldn't assume that these hitmen would be that dumb, but if he could see the email address, then maybe he could piece together some clues as to who they were.

He clicked on the "Name of person to be killed" field. That one was easy——he typed in "You, motherfucker." He then saw the "Reason why" field. He needed to put in some contact information; otherwise, what was the point?

He went back to the TorDir page and looked for an email service. As it turned out, there were several listed. The first two he clicked went to dead pages. However, the third one, *Anonymail - The Deep Web's home of anonymous email,* loaded right away.

Greg opened an account. He didn't have to use any personal information——just the email name and password he wanted. He made sure to use a different password than he'd ever used before. The email name was abc214@anonymail.com: abc to be completely random while 214 had been the garage door pass code from their old house.

With his account finally set up, he hit "Compose" and wrote a test message to see if it worked. He entered his fake address in the recipient field and "hi" on the subject line before sending it. He had to wait fifteen seconds before he was notified that a new message had arrived in his inbox. It worked exactly like a regular email account. Greg wasn't sure of this, thinking that the sender email may be disguised somehow, but it wasn't. This was a good thing.

He went back to the *American Hitmen* tab to finish his submission. He'd realized it wasn't a good idea to mention his sister in any way. That would defeat the purpose of doing all of his work anonymously. It would take them five seconds to figure out who he was and where he lived.

Back at the "Reason why" field, he watched the cursor blink on and off. His mind raced as he figured out what exactly he wanted to say and how he should word it. It had to be something that would stick out and play to their adventurous side enough that they'd want to reply back.

He checked the clock. There was still plenty of time before he had to start getting ready for work.

He wanted to say just the right thing. At first, he told himself that he only had one chance at this. But then he realized that wasn't true. Far from it. He could easily set up a new email address and try again. And again. Maybe he could pretend to be one of the other victim's brother or sister. Yes, that was what he would do. He put his hands on the keyboard with a newfound confidence that whatever he sent didn't have to be perfect. He typed:

Hey you... why don't you tell me who you are so I can spoon out your eyeballs and have them for breakfast? Reply back to abc214@anonymail.com.

Short and sweet. It wouldn't win any awards in journalism, but he thought that there was a good chance of getting a reply. His only worry was that they might read it and know it was someone related to one of the posted victims. There were only four people listed on the *Proof* page, so that wasn't a huge list. Then Greg thought about it more and decided that they wouldn't necessarily assume a friend of a victim would write that. The site owner probably got lots of feedback, both negative and positive.

Without any more thought, he hit the send button. The moment he did, he wished he hadn't. He quickly moved his mouse up to hit the back button, but it was too late. A message appeared on the screen:

Your hit request has been received. If we feel the person is a twisted fuck that deserves to die, we'll happily take care of it for you. If a few months have passed and they're still standing, then maybe you oughta consider doing it yourself. Trust us, it's SO much fun!

Greg read this a few times. He tried, again, to get in the mindset of the site creator, but it wasn't getting him anywhere. The part that said they wouldn't notify the person was discouraging, but maybe they'd make an exception since he provided an email address. They were, after all, pretty arrogant; they had the audacity to post a *Proof* section on the site.

He clicked back to the main page. He wanted to see the pictures of his sister again, no matter how much they upset him.

At the top, there was a picture again of Charles Taft, the heavyset, middle-aged man. It was tragic. Greg didn't know if this man was really guilty of pedophilia, as the website said. Chances were, the man probably was. After all, how could one make something like that up about a person? Whoever sent the hit in could have put Charles' name in by mistake, but that seemed unlikely. Still, Greg thought Charles should have the decency of a trial in a court to sort that out instead of having some online thug come up to him, unsuspecting, and murder him.

Before Greg could scroll down anything further, an idea popped into his head. He opened up a new tab in the *Tor* browser and did a search for Charles Taft.

As one would expect, many results came up. There were many people named Charles Taft in the world. He did another search——"Charles Taft pedophile"—— to see if that would help narrow his search. It didn't.

Greg then did the *one* thing that would make Shane cringe.

He tried searching Google, hoping for better results, but they were the same.

He clicked back to *American Hitmen* and scrolled down. He'd forgotten the name of the second victim, but saw that it was Trixie Davis, the supposed prostitute. Based on the picture, she looked like a heavy drug user. Her face had several disgusting red craters on it. He'd seen druggies portrayed on TV and knew that using meth for an extended period made a person's face look that way.

But again, Greg didn't feel that the fact gave anyone the right to murder this woman. She needed rehab and the opportunity for a second chance.

He and Jessica had seen the effects of drug use tear someone apart firsthand. Their uncle, Bobby, who was their favorite fun-loving uncle growing up, got mixed up with the wrong crowd. Greg's parents never told them what drug it was, but they did say he'd stolen from them and other family members on numerous occasions. They forced him to go to rehab, but he didn't last a week. He ended up getting arrested for armed robbery at a gas station and did five full years in prison. He'd been released four years before, right when Greg and Jessica were graduating from college. Bobby moved to Colorado, and to Greg's knowledge, no one in the family had seen or heard from him since. A perfectly normal man with a life destroyed by drugs.

He clicked back to Google and typed: "trixie davis prostitute."

The results that came up were nowhere close to related. There was a Trixie Davis who was a former senator. He browsed through the images, but it was filled with pictures of the senator Trixie. Not Trixie the prostitute.

After thinking about it, he doubted Trixie the prostitute

would be online much. Hookers usually didn't have their own websites or Facebook accounts.

Greg then got excited, having completely forgotten about the ability to look people up on Facebook. That mad it easier to browse and find people.

He went to go sign in but stopped himself. If he used his own account to do searches on the three victims, it might send up red flags somewhere if Facebook was tracking users' searching behavior. After listening to Shane, Greg assumed that nearly every site was spying on his activities. The last thing he wanted was to do something that would make it look like *he* was the one involved in these crimes. He imagined the police breaking down his door, seizing his computer, and seeing that he had Tor installed.

That reeked of suspicion.

Still, Facebook was a good thing to look into. He made a mental note to open a random account later and to do it on Tor so that it would disguise his IP address. From that account, he could stalk whoever he wanted without the fear of someone tracing the searches back to him.

He went back to *American Hitmen.* Before he went to research Andy Jones, he noticed that his sister was still the last person listed, and he kept it on the screen.

The picture on the left made him choke up again. She'd had such a long life ahead of her. She would have gotten married. Had several kids. He would have loved being an uncle. They'd already kidded about how they were going to corrupt each other's children, teaching them swear words when they were four years old. He'd imagined big family Christmases with both sets of kids, watching them play together.

Then the picture on the right brought him back into the real world, knowing that the vision would never become a reality.

That crime scene picture was filled with so many questions but no answers.

He studied the picture, thinking that there was something peculiar about it. The more he looked at it, though, the less convinced he was there was anything revealing.

He couldn't bear to look at it anymore, but he knew he'd come back to it later.

He went back to StartPage and typed in "Andy Jones drug dealer."

To his surprise, there were several relevant results that popped up. The first result came from gallia-times-herald.com. He clicked, and it brought up a local newspaper article. It used the exact same picture that was posted on *American Hitmen*.

Greg's interest piqued, and he focused intently on reading through the article. It said that Andy Jones had been pulled over late on a Friday night for a broken taillight. His car had been searched and heroine, cocaine, and methamphetamine had been discovered. The article was dated seven years before. His court hearing had been the following Monday at 9 AM.

Greg clicked back to the search results and saw that Andy Jones had seemed like a regular kid. He had a Facebook and a Twitter account, neither of which had been updated since his death. The Twitter account had only been used on occasion. His tweets weren't anything out of the ordinary. In fact, he had quite a sense of humor.

The same was true with his Facebook account. There he had posted more pictures of him and his friends. Greg thought Andy's friends looked completely normal.

If Andy Jones was a drug dealer, which seemed believable with his arrest, it didn't show.

He scrolled down further to see how Andy's posts had changed before and after his arrest. There was one post, dated six years before. It read:

Finally out of prison. I'm free at last!!!

It had 182 likes and 52 comments. Greg did a quick glance through the comments to see if they were hateful or congratulatory in nature. It turned out to be the latter. People were really happy for him.

He couldn't remember the exact date of his arrest but saw that Andy had opened up his Facebook account six years before. He scrolled through the posts and, again, wouldn't have been able to tell that Andy was a drug dealer. The only change was that there were fewer pictures and more text posts. That could have been because the smartphone revolution had just started to take off. Before that, it hadn't been as easy to snap a picture and post it online.

Greg went back to the Google results to see if he could find anything more on his jail sentence and release. He couldn't find an article in the results, but he figured it was posted online somewhere. He knew that one could dig up that kind of information on government sites, because they had done a lot of searching on those sites when Uncle Bobby had been arrested.

Greg, again, chalked that up as something to explore later. He was unsure of what he was hoping to get out of that information. Perhaps to see if he could figure out if ol' Andy went back to his drug dealing ways.

Running out of things to do, he went back to *American Hitmen*. He'd explored all the victims on the site except for Jessica. It never occurred to him until now, but what would come up if he Googled her name? For that matter, what would come up if he Googled his own name?

He went to find out, first typing in 'greg anderson.' As he'd expected, there were a lot of hits for Greg Anderson out there, so he narrowed them down by searching for 'greg anderson ohio state.' Golfing-related articles came up. Seeing them gave him a sense of pride, but it was also depressing at the same time. He loved that he'd worked hard to be an excellent golfer. But that had been a long time ago, and he'd accomplished nothing since. There was no *Forbes* "Billionaire's Under 30" article with his name on it. His bank account was barely into four figures.

He'd done enough research to remind him that he wasn't doing anything with his life, so he typed 'jessica Anderson ohio state' in.

After seeing the results, he wished he'd done it a long time ago, because he couldn't believe what he was seeing.

Chapter 13

Greg always knew that his sister was intelligent. She was also much more successful than he was. In college, she was always leading groups in her business and marketing classes. She was a natural leader, whether she liked it or not.

He knew that she loved to work, but the details of what she did were rarely discussed when they were together. In a way, Greg thought that he was her escape outlet into enjoying something that didn't involve work. He knew she was putting in long hours when she wasn't with him. He'd asked her how many hours she worked a week, and she had responded, "Usually I keep it in double digits."

Still, despite her high IQ and work ethic, he never imagined she'd be the VP of Marketing at Adriar Pharmaceuticals.

Why had she never told him that? And why had he never heard or figured it out before? Did his parents know?

The first result was linked to the Adriar Pharmaceuticals site. The title said, "Jessica Anderson - VP of Marketing at Adriar Pharmaceuticals." He clicked it.

Sure enough, the page took him to a website where there was a professional photograph of her in a gray button-up shirt and black pants. Growing up, Jessica hadn't been the type of girl that spent a long time getting ready. It was weird seeing her this glamorized.

To the right of her picture was a short bio. It said that she was a graduate of Ohio State, where she'd received a 3.9 GPA. This was true, and he remembered how upset she was when she'd been given a B+ in a philosophy class. Jessica had described the teacher as a 'quack.'

She was angry for months but then said she decided that being valedictorian wasn't something she wanted and that it was for the best. He wasn't convinced that she truly believed it.

The rest of her bio was where things began to get interesting. It was like he was discovering his sister's work life for the first time. It listed her crowning achievements since working at Adriar Pharmaceuticals. Apparently, she'd started at the bottom, which Greg already knew. She then was promoted to Marketing Assistant and then Marketing Director. Then finally, six months ago, she became VP of Marketing.

He clicked "Back to Corporate Profiles." This took him to a page with other higher-up people in the company, starting with the CEO, Daniel Kavern. Beneath him was David Henderson, CFO. Then Susan Coughlin, CIO, and then Jessica, VP of Marketing. He scrolled down and saw that there were only eight people listed on the page.

Greg knew that Adriar Pharmaceuticals was a multi-billion-dollar company and employed a few thousand people in Columbus alone. Jessica's name was on a list of the top eight people in the company, which must have meant that her salary was well into six figures, maybe even seven. Yet Jessica had never mentioned any promotions to him before, and she never flashed around her money. He knew that she made a lot more than him, but she was still living in a two-bedroom apartment downtown where the rent had to be no more than a thirteen hundred dollars a month.

But then he remembered that her will didn't show that she had exorbitant wealth. Her assets were as Greg would have guessed——a little better than his but certainly not 'vice president of a billion dollar company' assets.

Something didn't add up.

He went back to the search box and typed 'jessica anderson vp of marketing adriar pharmaceuticals.' The first result in his search was from a site PRweb.com, which Greg knew was a press release site from his research at work. He went to it and saw that Adriar Pharmaceuticals had formally announced Jessica's promotion. Greg read through it and found the news article very uneventful. It had the same corporate, way-too-professional tone to it. The only sentence that had an ounce of human touch was a quote from Daniel, the CEO: "Jessica has demonstrated great tenacity in her marketing efforts at Adriar Pharmaceuticals during her time here. She's revolutionized the way we reach our target audience, and I have been grateful to work closely alongside her. It only made sense that she be promoted to VP of Marketing and be provided with all the tools that she needs to expand her unique approach to a wider area of the company."

She'd had this job for six months.

He thought back to six months ago and tried to remember if there had been anything out of the ordinary with Jessica. Perhaps an above-average mood. But he couldn't think of anything. Granted, he had a hard time remembering things that happened even a week ago. Six months was plenty of time to forget details.

He did some more searches related to Jessica, but most of what he found were articles regarding the murder, which he had no interest in reading. He knew ten times more than what was published in the papers.

He was making news, not reading it.

He checked the time and saw that it was well past when he usually started getting ready for work. He'd lost track of time and needed to rush if he was going to avoid being late.

The thought of work, though, didn't interest him in the slightest, especially not today. He didn't hesitate to do what he (and most people in the company) did a few times a year.

Call in sick.

Corporate policy was two weeks paid vacation and three sick days. The sick days were "use 'em or lose 'em," and Greg hadn't truly been sick in two years. He usually waited until summer to develop an unexpected illness, and then he'd drive far out of town and spend the whole day golfing. But he had to make an exception to his annual tradition, which wasn't hard for him to do. He'd usually go on a weeklong family vacation and rarely had much use for the other five days he was allotted. They forced him to take the rest of his days at the end of December.

He called Bob Valentine, his boss, to give him the news. Greg wished that he could send him a text message, but ol' Bob hadn't entered the 21st century yet. It made him cringe, watching Bob use a computer. Right-clicking instead of left-clicking. Staring blankly at a screen. Wondering what to do next.

While Bob was a technological idiot, it could have been worse. Bob always accepted his sick days and vacation time, and he rarely asked any questions. That was what made the call so easy.

"Hey Bob, I can't come in today. I'm not feeling too well."

"All right, partner. Thanks for letting me know. You hang in there."

"Will do." He thought about saying "See you tomorrow," but he caught himself. He didn't want to make it sound like his illness barely qualified him to call off.

"Well, all right. Bye," Bob said.

"Bye."

Greg put his phone down on the table and relief poured over him. He was going to stop by Jessica's office, the big secret headquarters that Jessica was never allowed to talk to him about. Being around town on a day that he was supposed to be sick was like being on a roller-coaster ride. He rarely had much adventure in his life.

He was going to walk through those doors and demand to learn more about his sister and all the work she'd done there.

Considering that she was recently murdered, secrets were unacceptable. He needed to know anything and everything there was to know about her life. He'd need more pieces in order to put together the puzzle.

And he hoped Adriar Pharmaceuticals was a big piece.

Chapter 14

Greg waited until ten to leave his apartment.

As he drove over, he realized he'd never been to Jessica's office by himself. In fact, he'd only seen the place once, when she'd first accepted the job. She had been so excited that she took him and their parents over to see the place. It was a large building, just on the outskirts of downtown. It sat away from other buildings and had a beautiful pond next to the parking lot.

They hadn't been allowed inside. At least, that's what Jessica had told them. Greg didn't think that was true; he figured she just didn't want to ruffle any feathers during her first week.

Greg remembered feeling demoralized at the time. He was still looking for a job, and Jessica had already landed a position at a large company. It was ultimately what inspired him to direct his job searching efforts to bigger corporations. He thought it would be cool to work for a big company, too.

In retrospect, he realized that bigger companies had way more cons than pros.

When he saw the Adriar Pharmaceuticals building in the distance, the memories came flooding back. Something about the sight of the structure made a distaste form in his mouth. He had no reason to like this place, and on top of it all was the fact that only a few of the employees there had the decency to go to Jessica's viewing. He was still bitter about it.

He pulled into the large parking lot, which was quiet during this part of the day. It was filled with cars, but no one was coming or going.

He had to park in the very last row, which faced the pond. He got out and made the walk to the front of the building. It had just occurred to him that he should have been more considerate when choosing his wardrobe. He was in blue jeans and a collared shirt. That sort of attire wasn't accepted at his office, except for on casual Fridays. Even though he was only a guest here, he wished he'd worn something more appropriate.

As he got closer, he thought about what he was going to say and do. He started fidgeting with his keys. He was going to demand to talk to the CEO. While a normal person requesting this might get laughed at, he thought that they would take his request more seriously when he said he was the brother of Jessica Anderson.

He opened the front door and saw that it wasn't anything like he'd imagined, wasn't a good thing. First, standing two steps from the door was a security guard. He was wearing plain, light brown clothes from top to bottom, including his hat. He could almost pass as a UPS delivery person, if not for the black belt that was equipped with a gun and a big black baton that fitted down his leg.

Greg hadn't even had taken the time to look up when the guard said, "Excuse me, sir. Name and reason for visit?"

"Sure," he began nervously. "I'm here to speak with Daniel Kavern."

"Do you have an appointment?"

"No, I had some questions regarding my sister that I'd like to ask him. Her name was Jessica, and she was murdered a month ago."

"Sorry, sir, only scheduled guests are allowed onto the premises," he said without empathy. "Unless you have an appointment, I'm going to have to ask you to leave."

The look on the guards face meant business.

"Please, I only need five minutes of his time. I don't want any confrontation, I just have a couple questions to ask."

"Can't do. If you don't have an appointment, you'll have to come back later." He held out his hand, ready to guide Greg out the door.

He looked up and saw a fancy wooden desk with the Adriar Pharmaceuticals logo carved into it, a light illuminating it. There was a pretty, young blonde woman sitting behind it; she was looking down.

The front room was quite small, considering the massive size of the building. He tried to look around to see what else it featured, but by then, the officer had already made contact with Greg to lead him away.

A million things ran through his mind on what he could say or do that would cause him to at least get past the guard so that he could speak to the receptionist, but nothing was coming out of his mouth. The guard had opened the door for Greg and was following closely behind. Finally, Greg was able to blurt out, "Please, sir. If he just hears who I am, I'm sure he'll want to talk to me. My sister was the VP of Marketing here, and—"

"If he wants to speak with you, he'll set up a meeting. Good day, sir. Please don't return until something is scheduled."

Greg turned around, ready to say something, but the door slammed closed. He didn't even get the chance to have one last look at the guard.

Standing outside, he felt humiliated and embarrassed. He

had thought, in the worst case, he'd talk to a receptionist. She'd call Daniel, and he'd say he was busy. He never imagined that a security guard would make it impossible for him to even get to a receptionist.

All the energy was sucked from his body. The guard had left him feeling weak and pathetic. He didn't dare go back in to see if he could reason with the man. Greg thought that if he did, he might get to find out what that the guard's club felt like.

Other ideas passed through his mind. Perhaps there was another entrance to the building? Or maybe, if he stood outside and called their headquarters, he could make an appointment while he was still there.

After thinking it over, finding another entrance could lead him into big trouble. Calling the headquarters wasn't a bad idea, but he felt so defeated that he decided to give up and come back another time.

Embarrassment turned to anger, as he couldn't believe what a complete asshole the guard had been. Greg hadn't been rude in the slightest. He simply wanted to ask someone a couple questions. The request was met with such animosity that the guard felt he needed to put his hands on him to make sure that he would exit the door and not cause a scene.

Greg wasn't about to give up. Adriar Pharmaceuticals had a piece to the puzzle of finding Jessica; that much he was sure of. He'd come back, and when he did, he'd be much more prepared.

On his way home, he picked up lunch at Wendy's. He tried to convince himself that Jessica's company wasn't involved but couldn't.

He wanted to find out more about the CEO. Daniel Kavern may not have put the hit out on Jessica, but Greg was convinced that he probably had some kind of valuable information——a clue that would help with his search. He just felt it to be true.

After he had lunch, relaxed, and watched a little TV, it was already one o'clock. He'd often imagined before what it would be like to sit around all day and do nothing. How long the days would feel. He now knew the answer to that question: they flew by!

He paced around his apartment, thinking he needed to be doing something productive. He wouldn't have another weekday like this where he could look into her case.

Greg went to his computer and used StartPage to search for Daniel Kavern; he wouldn't be surprised if Adriar Pharmaceuticals was spying on him already.

The first result that came up was Daniel's bio page. He clicked and read it. Stanford Law? Check. Harvard MBA? Check. Advisory board of two Fortune 500 companies? Check.

He had a work resume that would land him a top management position for any company in America. It made Greg sick. *How does one person get to be so smart and successful?* He thought about his own career path. If he worked hard, in another ten or fifteen years, he *might* be able to get Bob's job. After another ten years, he might get Bill's job. Tack on yet another ten years, and then (and only then) would he even be in the running for vice president. By then he'd be at least sixty and almost ready to retire, but by God, he'd be a VP. Greg had no interest in doing this, of course. To work his ass off for thirty more years just to enjoy a few years of being one of the top dogs? No, thank you! At this rate and with his work ethic, he'd be lucky to ever get Bob's job, and if he did, he would probably quit the first year.

Daniel Kavern, though, had been a majority stockholder of

a Fortune 500 company by the time he was thirty. From there, it had been nothing but absurd success.

Greg didn't fully understand why he was so suspicious of the man, but he was. He'd learned long ago to follow his intuition, and right now, it was screaming at him to find out everything there was to know about Daniel fucking Kavern.

For the next hour, he armed himself with as much information as he could. His first company was a payment security processing company, XPay, which he and a friend had started in the mid-90s when the Internet was first taking off. It'd been acquired to the tune of fifty million dollars, which they'd split between the two of them. From there, he'd used his XPay funds to start another company. It was an investment company, which he only operated for a few years before selling. It sounded like he'd only made a measly twenty million on that venture. For the next five years, he was CEO of Jetco, Inc. before moving onto Adriar Pharmaceuticals, where he'd been for about six years.

All of this was fascinating to Greg, but it didn't help him get any closer to finding Jessica's murderer. He didn't know what else to do, as he felt he'd read most of the information that was available about Daniel online. The articles he was reading now just rehashed news from the articles he'd already read. He was stuck.

Then he remembered something——an idea, or at least the potential for an idea. He opened up Tor and scrolled down to a category he'd mostly scanned past before.

Hacking.

The first link took him to a page where, for two hundred euros, one could "ruin someone" by making them look like a child predator.

Greg had no intentions of doing that. Judging by the

sketchiness of the site, he thought the chances of his money being stolen were high.

The next three sites were all broken links. Why did the Deep Web have so many goddamn broken pages? Didn't these sites get updated?

He finally got to a site that he hadn't been to before. The site was much more professional than most of the Deep Web sites he'd been on. This one and *Silk Road* were the only two that looked like regular websites, with navigation bars and general user-friendliness. All the others looked like they'd been made in the '90s, which made Greg wonder how long the Deep Web had been around.

The site was called *Hacking4Hire*. Their services were straightforward:

150 USD – email account (ex. Gmail, Yahoo, Hotmail, etc.)
150 USD - social media accounts (ex. Facebook, Twitter, etc.)
250 USD - other non-financial account not mentioned above (please contact before ordering)
500 USD - Paypal or other financial institution

The service offered something that Greg hadn't seen from any other Deep Web site: an escrow service.

Greg needed a refresher on what escrow meant. At first, he had it confused with "escort service" and smiled at his stupidity. He read their explanation, just to make sure he was dealing with the same thing.

Deep Escrow, if it actually worked like it said, would protect his purchase by not allowing *Hacking4Hire* to receive his money until he confirmed that they had done their job. But at the same time, it protected them, too, as the disclaimer pointed out:

Hopefully you're not thinking, "I'll just receive my login and not release the funds." This is stupid for two reasons: 1) Reminder, you won't be able to get your money back unless we send it back to you through Deep Escrow. 2) Do you really want to upset a team of hackers? I didn't think so. :-)

Greg read through the information again, trying to absorb it all and looking for holes in the process where people could get scammed. He couldn't think of any, provided the *Deep Escrow* company was legitimate and not some fake third-party service that *Hacking4Hire* set up.

He spent the next thirty minutes researching both *Deep Escrow* and *Hacking4Hire* on forums. The more he read, the more convinced he was that it was all very real and legitimate. The only negative feedback he saw dealt with *Hacking4Hire's* inability to gain access to an account. There were three posts like this, but all three admitted that their funds were promptly returned to them.

Greg couldn't believe that he was considering doing such a thing, but he was confident enough to use the service if he needed to. He didn't have the audacity to have them break into Daniel Kavern's email account. Not yet, anyway. But he'd love to see what kind of communication he'd previously had with his sister.

Then it occurred to him: he didn't need to break into Daniel's account. He could have them break into his sister's account!

That wouldn't land him in nearly as much trouble as breaking into the CEO's account. He'd probably get more useful information, too, seeing who Jessica had interacted with and what about. Worst-case scenario, he could lie and say she told him her username and password.

Jessica had logged into her email the night that she'd died. That was the only way he knew the address to get to her email. Unfortunately, it was set to log out automatically, as was her Facebook account.

He went back to the *Hacking4Hire* website and clicked the button to order. It said:

Hiring us is easy. First, click this link and submit your payment at Deep Escrow. Upon completion, you'll be redirected back to our site where you can complete a simple form, describing what it is you need hacked.

Should you have questions, don't hesitate to ask us on our contact page.

Deep Escrow had only one payment option, and it was the first big snag in the process:

Payments are made in bitcoin. We've included below the USD equivalent, along with its bitcoin conversion equivalent (updated daily).

Greg had completely forgotten about bitcoins. He was ready to order until this setback arose. He was still unsure about buying the currency. Despite what Shane said, Greg thought having them wasn't as safe as he made it out to be. If he bought a hundred dollars worth of bitcoins and Jessica's account was hacked, couldn't they put two and two together? He thought they could. He reminded himself, though, that no one could trace what sites he was going to as long as he was on Tor. No one had any way of telling that he went to a hacking site. And no one, supposedly, could trace where his Bitcoins were going.

It wasn't the safest thing in the world to do, but he kept

thinking and figured the odds of having solid proof that he did it were pretty low.

He went back to TorDir and scanned through the financial section, looking for the bitcoin-purchasing service that Shane had mentioned. He couldn't begin to remember the name, but he knew he'd recognize it if it came up.

Greg opened six different tabs with sites that had the word "bitcoin" in the title. He walked to the kitchen to grab a glass of milk. He knew it would take a couple of minutes for all of those sites to load or (more likely) to figure out they were now dead sites. Greg was beginning to like the idea of complete anonymity, but using Tor was way too frustrating to use on a regular basis. It was only for conducting his gray-area detective work.

While he was up, he grabbed his wallet, which he always put on the coffee table when he got home. He sat back down at the computer and saw that only two of the six sites had loaded. The others sites gave error messages. Greg wasn't sure if this meant that these sites were really gone or if there was just a glitch in accessing them through Tor. Either way, it was really annoying that most of the sites he tried to visit were broken.

The first site, Bitxchange, gave an explanation:

Bitxchange is temporarily down.

Our bank accounts have been frozen, and we are in the process of migrating to a new offshore account. We hope to have this completely fixed within the next several months.

Seeing that made him question whether the whole bitcoin

thing was a good idea. The odds of being scammed, or a site shutting down and losing its money, seemed more and more likely.

He told himself, though, that it was only one hundred dollars that he planned on spending. Yes, that was a full day's pay after taxes, but it wasn't enough to put him in financial ruin. If he wanted to find out who murdered Jessica, he'd have to do some things that were unconventional. Detective Maxwell had done a thorough investigation of all of the obvious things to look for. Greg would need to do the things that the detective was either unwilling or unable to do.

Greg visited the other site. As soon as he saw the name, *Bitbase*, he recognized it as the site that Shane used. That was something else that brought his confidence back. Shane said he'd bought drugs at least five times, so there was no doubt that *Bitbase* worked.

The signup form was right on the home page. He didn't read any further on the site before beginning to sign up. He registered with his anonymail.com account, which he had to verify before being able to purchase bitcoins. He did and was taken to the form, where he had to enter his credit card information. He had second thoughts, but posted on the site were statements like "Your information is 100% secure" and "Completely anonymous."

He entered his information before he had the time to second-guess himself. Maybe he'd regret it later, but for now, he was starting to get more curious about the Deep Web and all its mysteries.

He got to the field where he had to enter the number of bitcoins that he wanted to purchase. One bitcoin was worth $134 USD at the current exchange rate. He could select how many bitcoins or what fraction of a bitcoin that he wanted, with the minimum purchase being a hundred dollars. Either way, there was a 6% fee for using *Bitbase*. Normally, something like this would upset Greg. He hadn't used Ticketmaster since they charged him three dollars just to have tickets emailed to him.

He wasn't as upset with *Bitbase*, though. He felt that he was already blowing money away, so what was another ten dollars?

He opted to buy an entire bitcoin, figuring there may be fees for using *Deep Escrow* and *Hacking4Hire*, which he hoped the additional thirty-four dollars would cover.

Greg's mouse hovered over the purchase button, and he took a deep breath.

"All right, this is it," he muttered to himself as he clicked. Greg waited for what felt like eternity as the page processed until, finally, he was redirected to a new page.

Thank you for your purchase! One bitcoin has been added to your Bitbase wallet. Happy shopping!

For more information on how to use your Bitbase wallet, please click here.

He read through the information, surprised that he hadn't read it before purchasing. Fortunately, it sounded very straightforward. It reminded him a lot of using his Paypal account. The concepts behind the two were similar.

Now that he officially owned a bitcoin, there was a new level of excitement. He'd officially become a member of the Deep Web.

It was the place where Shane, Brian, Kyle, Dread Pirate Roberts, and now Greg lived.

Not wasting any time, he went back to *Hacking4Hire* and clicked the order link, which took him to *Deep Escrow*. He selected the 100 USD option, chose *Bitbase* as his account option, and then made his order, which took him back to the *Hacking4Hire* website where there was a form to fill out.

Greg stopped for a moment. He couldn't believe how professional the site was. Part of his job was viewing the websites of his company's competitors to see what they did well. If *Hacking4Hire* was a competitor, then he'd suggest to Bob that they mimic the way the site provided just the right information at any given time to ease consumers' minds as they made purchases.

The form was pretty simple. He had been worried about what kind of questions he'd need to answer before he purchased, but those worries were put aside when he saw that there were just two fields:

Account needed hacked:
Any additional information (optional):

He entered in Jessica's email address. Under additional information, he thought about letting them know that Jessica had to enter a six-digit PIN code but decided not to. First off, if the security of the site was ever breached, knowing that information would make a detective's search substantially easier. Second, he thought that if he told them about the phone verification, they might not bother trying to hack into her account in the first place. If they went through all the trouble of figuring out her username and password, then maybe they'd take the time to find a workaround for the phone issue.

He pressed submit and after a few seconds, a message below the form appeared:

* * *

Thank you. Your service information has been received. Expect delivered work within 1-2 business days.

Greg sat back in his chair, thinking about what he'd just done. He had no idea how much trouble he'd get into if someone found out what he'd done. He didn't think it was enough to go to prison, but then again, he'd heard of people being locked up for less.

He reminded himself again that he'd done everything through a secure server, using money that was completely anonymous. He made another mental note to check his bank account later. He was scared of what the charge might be. *Bitbase* said $142.04, but who knew if they'd tack on something else? There was nothing that he could do about it if they did.

He checked the time to find that it was a little past three. His sick day was almost over. He felt good at all that he'd accomplished. He didn't get nearly as much done as he thought he could in one day, but he'd learned a lot about the Deep Web and had even begun taking part in it.

Greg knew he'd drive himself crazy by checking his email every five minutes if he stayed at his apartment. He knew *Hacking4Hire* wouldn't get back to him for at least a day.

He called Stacy to see what she was up to and ask if she wanted to go out to dinner or something, but she didn't answer. He then remembered she was working.

He wanted to get out of the house, unafraid now of Bob or his other coworkers seeing him. If they did, he could simply say that he was feeling better. He couldn't decide, though, on where he wanted to eat, so he ordered a pizza. Mondays were usually pizza night, anyway.

He unplugged his computer and hid it in his closet. He

hoped that would take away the temptation to check his email. That and a marathon of *Prison Break*.

The combination worked to distract his attention for a few hours. He thought about continuing his research, but he was too exhausted. He'd put more effort into investigating Jessica's murder in one day than he'd done in the previous two weeks at Vinditech.

He made it until eight o'clock before he couldn't take it anymore; he had to check his email. Taking his computer out of the closet, he found that Tor was running especially slow. It took twenty minutes to finally load his Anonymail account. When it finally appeared, there weren't any new emails. It was disappointing but expected.

As he lay in bed that night, he felt like there was something big that he was missing——something he should have been thinking more about.

Then he realized that there were a lot of things he was probably missing. He hoped his subconscious would have it all figured out when he woke up in the morning.

However, it didn't quite work out that way.

When Greg woke up the next morning, it wasn't his brain that helped him realize what he'd forgotten.

His email inbox had done it for him.

Chapter 15

Greg had rolled out of bed and gone straight to his computer. He logged in and waited for his email to load. He was determined not to leave until he had at least confirmed that they hadn't replied. Greg shuffled his eyes from the clock to his computer. He'd slept in and was way behind schedule for work.

A minute passed.

Then another.

Thinking something was wrong, he pushed the stop button and entered his login information again. This time, thirty seconds passed before he was directed to his account.

When he got there, his eyes bulged at the site of not one but two emails!

The first was from asf89dbv32@anonymail789.onion. The subject was "Order Completed."

The second one was from manicsocio009@jkvn32nm49s.onion. There was no subject.

Without thinking, Greg clicked the second email. When it came up, he saw a simple emoticon:

:-)

***

He had no idea who it was from. *Was it spam?* He scrolled down and saw a familiar message.

It was the message he'd sent to *American Hitmen*.

That was what he had forgotten about the night before.

He'd been so wrapped up in his run-in with the security guard that it had slipped his mind that he'd sent the test email to the hitmen to see if he could get a reaction out of them.

"That's it?" he said to himself. "That's all you have to say?" The message angered him. His mind raced for a response. He wanted to throw in every curse word there was.

But before he could say anything that he'd regret, he reminded himself that he accomplished what he'd set out to do. He now had their email, manicsocio009@jkvn32nm49s.onion. There was virtually no chance he'd be able to figure out who was registered to the encrypted account. He'd wanted the username, and he got it: manicsocio009. That was the key he was looking for. He could now dig through all of the Deep Web forums and see if that username had been used anywhere else.

That's what the FBI had done to uncover Dread Pirate Roberts identity.

That's what he would do.

He opened up the second email, the one from *Hacking4Hire*, which said:

We have the login details for the account you requested. However, we were unable to gain access because of a phone verification system. Please obtain access to the phone and login with the details below.

janderson@adriar.com
Tw!nbr0gr3g

Please release funds at your earliest convenience.

Greg stared at her password for a moment, trying to make sense of its meaning. He vaguely recalled a flyer that his company had once passed out about making secure passwords. One of the suggestions was to mix in capital letters and replace some letters with symbols.

Then he broke down the words. Tw!n br0 gr3g stood for her twin bro, Greg. *He* was her password. It made him smile.

Greg checked the time and realized that he needed to be leaving soon if he was going to work. He opened up a new tab and typed in the URL of the email system that Jessica had used when she was on his computer. It was a blank screen with only the logo of Adriar Pharmaceuticals at the top and two fields for an email and password. He copied them in from the *Hacking4Hire* email and pushed submit. Greg waited, hoping it didn't ask for a PIN as it had when Jessica was there. He was optimistic, but when the next page loaded, it prompted him to enter a six-digit PIN. Greg slammed his fist down on the table.

His parents had Jessica's phone, along with her other possessions. They'd put everything in her old bedroom until they decided what they should do with it. Greg's dad was in charge of canceling her cable, water, and other contracts. He'd probably gotten around to canceling her phone service, too.

Which meant getting into Jessica's email account was impossible now.

Greg realized that he'd just wasted a hundred dollars. If *Hacking4Hire* had been a regular company, he would've contacted their customer support to see if he could get a refund. However, since it was a team of hackers that he was dealing with, he thought it unwise. He remembered the *"Do you really want to upset a team of hackers? I didn't think so."* line and agreed; it was the last thing he wanted to do. They'd given him her account login. He knew about the phone verification and hadn't told them. Before completely giving up, he replied back to their email:

Do you know of any workaround for the phone verification? I can't get to the person's phone.

Then he hit send. He didn't expect much but decided, regardless of what they said, to release the funds. Although the phone verification roadblock was a letdown, he had to take a step back and think about how incredible it was that he'd just done the unthinkable. He'd purchased bitcoins. Used them. Obtained someone's email login information.

And if what Shane said was true, he'd done it all completely anonymously.

It worked, and it worked fairly easily. It made him feel uneasy, wondering what else would really work on the Deep Web.

He checked the clock again. He needed to leave immediately for work. If traffic was non-existent and he made it through every light, he'd be able to get there on time. But realistically, he'd be ten or fifteen minutes late at best, and for Greg, that was unacceptable. Besides, he had vacation time to use. It wouldn't hurt to take one more day off.

Without hesitation, he called Bob.

The phone rang once… twice… three times…

"You've reached Bob McDougall. I can't come to the phone right now so if you can leave your name and number after the beep, I'll get back to you." Beep.

"Hey Bob, it's Greg." He coughed. "Still not feelin' so hot.

Don't think I'll make it in today. Hopefully see you tomorrow. Bye."

Greg hung up the phone, thinking that it was the most convincing sick call in history. The little cough in the middle wasn't even planned; it was completely spur of the moment.

He really hadn't planned on calling in sick. He liked having something to take his mind off of things. But he'd already made the call, so it was completely out of the question.

He had a mental list of things he wanted to do, and thought it would be wise to write them all down before he forgot. Before that, though, he went to his computer. There was something he wanted to check before he did anything else: his online bank account.

With his regular browser, he logged in and saw his bank balance of $932.83, which seemed about right. There was a pending transaction from *BitBase* for $107.63.

They hadn't stolen all his money yet, so that was good.

He went back to his Anonymail email to reply back to the bastards that had murdered his sister. He didn't know what he was going to say, but he couldn't let it go without seeing if he could get them to say more. Whatever reply he received, he thought it could only help in finding who or where they were.

Greg had read an article online once that explained how there was software available that, if one submitted one chapter from an unpublished book, it could predict the author with incredible accuracy. It did it by matching the frequency of words and other phrases.

He was probably reaching, but if he could get this person to carry on a lengthy email conversation with him, then maybe ——just maybe——he could look into using that software.

Tor had disconnected, so he closed it and tried to restart it. While he waited, doubt began to creep in at what he was doing.

For two full vacation days, he could certainly find something more fun to do, especially with the warm weather finally arriving. Was he wasting his time with all of this? Even his best ideas had a slim chance of working.

When he finally got to his email, he wasn't expecting any new messages. However, *Hacking4Hire* had already responded:

Unfortunately, phone verification is a tough system to crack. While it's not impossible, it's not something that we do. If you must have access, we can negotiate pricing but I'll warn you, it will be very high.

Your best bet would be to gain access to the phone. I'm assuming you know this person or at least their location. If, for whatever reason, they cancel their phone, you could attempt to register a new phone service and grab their phone number. There are online services that allow you to obtain free phone numbers. As always, make sure you're taking precautions in protecting your identity.

With that said, we feel we've kept up with our end of the bargain. Please release the funds at your earliest convenience.

Greg read the email again, amazed at the level of professionalism in the response. He considered the different options that they suggested. Paying them to hack the phone would be silly. All he had to do was go to his parents' house and get access to Jessica's phone, hoping that his dad hadn't cancelled the service yet. But before he did that, he wondered if he could check online to see if the phone number was available to register.

He opened Tor and did some research. What he learned was

something that *Hacking4Hire* alluded to. It was really easy to get an available phone number for free. The most popular service to do that was Google Voice.

Greg then spent the next twenty minutes attempting to do just that. He registered a new Google account using Tor and using information that he'd never used to sign up for anything before.

When he finally got to the screen where he could select his phone number, he looked up Jessica's number, which he'd never taken the time to memorize, in his phone and typed it in.

This phone number is unavailable. Please consider the below alternative suggestions.

He thought, *All right, so that plan didn't work.*

That would have been too easy, and no part of finding Jessica's killer was going to be simple.

Before he forgot, he logged into his *Deep Escrow* account and released the funds.

He went back to his email and opened up the one from *American Hitmen*. He stared at that taunting response, which was centered on his screen. Greg wasn't sure how long he sat there, staring and thinking. Somewhere on the planet, the person who pulled the trigger, killing his sister, had typed those very characters on a keyboard and sent them to him. The more he stared at the smiley face, the more it angered him.

What he wouldn't give to have the murderers alone in a room somewhere.

He had to get to them, and he had to do it soon. The more time that passed, the more Greg felt that he'd never be able to find them.

The clock was ticking.

He thought about what he could say back. What would generate a lengthy response?

The more he thought about it, the more he figured that there was nothing he could say. His best chance was to open up a new email account and take the opposite approach: praise what they were doing. Maybe they'd give a lengthier response to a friend instead of a foe.

That was something he wanted to try, but then an idea came to him. Something that was better than back and forth emails from the fake accounts he could set up. It would be better if he could have access to all of the emails that *American Hitmen* had sent out.

To accomplish that, he'd need login access to their email.

And he knew just who to go to for that.

Chapter 16

Greg went back to the *Hacking4Hire* website. He reviewed the services section of the site again. He read thought it, looking to see if there were any additional charges for a Deep Web email account. All he could find was that it cost 150 USD to hack into an email account. He assumed that Anonymail fell under this classification.

He had doubts as to whether they'd be able to hack into the *American Hitmen* email account, but if they could, Greg could only imagine what kind of information it would bring him. Assuming they didn't delete emails and assuming the contact form on the website was tied to the same email address, he'd be able to find out exactly what was said when Jessica was nominated.

Greg reminded himself not to think too far ahead. He didn't feel like wasting another hundred dollars, but he remembered how the website had said that if they were unable to deliver, they'd refund his money. So, worst case, they'd hack into the account and all of the emails were deleted. Unfortunately, he thought there was a decent chance of this happening, but it was worth the risk to find out.

Not wanting to waste any time, he went to *Bitbase* to order another bitcoin. He still had a fraction of a bitcoin left. He'd read how bitcoins used to be worth five times what they were now and also how Shane said bitcoins made a good short-term investment.

Greg was beginning to agree with Shane. He was no investor, but he only presumed the Deep Web would get bigger and better. It was gaining in popularity, despite being really slow and having a lot of broken links. Once it was more refined, it would only explode in growth.

With this thought in mind, he ordered two, even though he only needed three quarters of one to order the hack. The remainder was just convenient, in case he wanted to order something else.

Once those were in his *Bitbase* account, he made his *Hacking4Hire order*. The form had an "Additional information (optional)" field, and he wondered if he should include something.

But nothing sprang to mind.

He was counting on *Hacking4Hire* to return his money if they either couldn't hack into it or didn't want to since it was a Deep Web email address.

He hit send.

After a sigh of relief, he took a break. He hated staring at a computer all day; it hurt his eyes.

Most days at work, he'd have one or two meetings to break up some of the monotony. He got up and walked around his apartment, noticing that it was in desperate need of a cleaning. There was no way he could let Stacy see the place like this.

Thinking of Stacy, he realized he hadn't talked to her in two days now. During the first couple of weeks that they'd dated, they only talked every few days, but now that things were getting a little more serious, they usually talked every day, even if it was just for a few minutes. Yesterday, their schedules didn't align because she had worked the late shift. He was supposed to call her that morning, but it had completely slipped his mind.

Now he was afraid to call, because then he'd have to explain why he wasn't at work. He could get away with not giving an explanation if he called during lunch hour, but she would definitely know something was out of the ordinary if he called now, since she knew he didn't like making personal calls at work.

He thought it over and decided to wait two hours and call her at lunch. Maybe he'd tell her he was home and maybe he wouldn't. He didn't want to lie to her; he supposed he was just too ashamed to tell the truth. That he'd taken two days off to play the role of detective, as if he were on TV.

Thinking about his next course of action, he remembered he'd wanted to open up a Facebook account and do some more researching on the other victims. There was still a lot of potential for clues there.

He went back to his desk and looked out of the window while he waited for Tor to reconnect. Outside wasn't as quiet as he would have expected during a weekday mid-morning. There were people walking the streets, and several cars drove by. He thought of how, at the moment Jessica was murdered, there had been no witnesses and no other cars driving by. He didn't think it was a conspiracy or anything, just really bad luck.

He navigated to TorDir. He wished that he could bookmark all of these sites, but then he remembered that doing so was a potential security risk. At the very least, he wished the names were easier to remember.

The Deep Web had crazy URLs.

It couldn't just be tordir.onion, instead it was 23hj24kh26j4k.onion. He assumed there was a security reason for doing so, but he wondered if making the URL name obscure really made much of a difference. The people at the FBI were fully capable of copying and pasting.

Before he opened up a new, anonymous Facebook account, he wanted to visit *American Hitmen*. He thought it was essential that he check the site out at least a couple times a day to see if anything had changed.

Unfortunately, it had.

A new victim.

Two, in fact.

The first was Mark Quinn. The photo on the left showed him in a hockey uniform, standing out on the ice while posing for the camera. He was a handsome guy with long, dirty blonde hair. Physically fit. Although, it could have been the pads that made him look buff. To the right, there wasn't a picture of the murder like there were with the previous victims. Instead, it was the same hockey picture that was faded out. Diagonally across the picture, in red letters, was the word "DECEASED." Under it was a caption:

Our first Canadian!

Greg looked at the hockey picture and tried to guess what his crime was. Rape, maybe? Another drug dealer? He felt uncomfortable trying to stereotype him, so he stopped. He reminded himself that this guy didn't deserve to be murdered by some sociopath, no matter what he'd done.

The second new victim was Lawrence McQueen. He was much older, appearing to be in his late 60s. His face was scruffy, and he had a weird stare as he looked at the camera. It would have been comical if it had been seen under different circumstances. Greg guessed it must have been a prior mug shot.

The picture to the right, again, was just a faded out version of the first with the same word across it. The reason on this one...

For an unpunished crime, long overdue.

Greg felt queasy, knowing the people behind the site were still out there killing. And while he was mostly in this to avenge his sister's death, he felt a moral responsibility to prevent future victims.

Detective Maxwell said he'd sent the site to his superiors, but Greg wondered if they were really doing anything about it. If so, they must surely have seen the new victims.

Greg thought that the more postings there were, the easier it had to be to track them down. The FBI could look up gas station transactions or something that would link a person to the time and whereabouts of each murder. He wondered if he should call the detective and inform him of the website's updates but decided against it. Mainly because he didn't want the lecture from Detective Maxwell, telling him to stop snooping around.

With these new victims added, it made Greg want to continue the next step in his research, and that was to open up a new Facebook account and look up each victim.

Doing this on Tor was an exhaustive process. If he had known it would end up taking two hours, with all the starts and stops and Internet issues, he probably wouldn't have done it. Now that he finally had, he had the *American Hitmen* proof page in one tab and Facebook in the other.

He could now search for the victims on Facebook without fear that he was getting spied on. There was no way anyone could trace the searches back to him now.

He began with the two latest victims.

Mark Quinn had a Facebook page, which was easy to find. The one and only result that came up when Greg searched his name was the guy he recognized. By his profile page, it was clear that Mark loved hockey. His likes and interests were mostly hockey-related. His favorite team was the Toronto Maple Leafs. He followed every hockey player on the team, from what it looked like. Mark wasn't a pro, just a rabid fan.

As far as clues that pointed to why he was murdered, Greg wasn't finding any. Many of Mark's posts were also hockey-related. He'd post things like "THREE IN A ROW!!!!!!!!!!!!!!!"

Posts like these always irritated him.

He checked Mark's wall and saw the numerous postings in memoriam to him.

"I've lost a dear friend. Why would someone do this? It's a sick, cruel world."

"Mark, I love you and am going to miss you. Thanks for the good times at Banks High. You were the funniest guy I knew, and the world will not be the same without you."

"Whoever did this will suffer, don't you worry. I can't believe this happened. So sad right now. #Justnotright"

The more that Greg read, the sadder it made him. It reminded him of the similar messages that had been posted on Jessica's wall.

Not wanting to read any more, he searched for Lawrence

McQueen on Facebook. Several results came up, but none of them looked like the old man from the website.

He searched Google for "lawrence mcqueen mug shot." In the images tab, the mug shot he'd seen on the website was posted there. Lawrence had been arrested for vehicular manslaughter.

The story had gained quite a bit of attention in the media, because the prosecutor had dropped all charges.

He was about to read more when his phone rang.

It was Stacy.

He hadn't realized it was 12:30 already. With hesitation, he answered.

"Hey, what's up?"

"Hi Greg. We need to talk."

"Sure, of course." Greg already had a bad feeling about this conversation. He could tell she wasn't in a good mood.

"Where are you right now?" Stacy asked.

"I'm... I'm at work. Why?"

"No reason. I called you last night. This morning, too. Why haven't you been answering your phone?"

"Really?" He checked his phone. "I don't see any missed calls. These damn phones. Ever since I've had a smartphone, I've had way more dropped calls," he said. It was the truth.

"All right, if you say so." She didn't sound convinced.

"What have you been up to?" He tried to switch subjects.

"Nothing. Work last night. I have today off. Are you on lunch break?"

"Yeah."

"Where are you? We could have met up."

"I know; I'm sorry. Shane ordered pizzas for everyone in the research department for helping close a new business."

"Well that was nice of him," she said.

Greg was beginning to think that she was in better spirits now and let his guard down.

"How did work go yesterday?" Stacy asked.

"It was... good. Nothing exciting, really."

"What time did you get back? I heard traffic was bad on I-71 south."

"Yeah, it was," Greg said. "I don't know if there was an accident or what, but it was fifteen miles an hour the whole way back."

"So you were at work all day yesterday?"

Greg was having bad feelings again, but he continued his lie. "Yes, all day. Why?"

"No reason. I'm just trying to figure out why your car was parked at your place when I drove by yesterday afternoon."

There it was.

The truth had come out.

He didn't know what to say. All he could get out was, "Wh... what?"

"I said," pause, "I'm wondering why your car was parked outside when I drove by around three o'clock yesterday."

Greg considered continuing his lie but thought he should cut his losses.

"What... are you spying on me?" *Stupid thing to say.*

"No. I was delivering supplies to Tony's Cafe. I happened to look in the direction of your apartment, and what do I see? Your car, parked in its usual spot. I thought... hmm... isn't that interesting."

"Well why didn't you stop by? Or call me?"

"I *did*. But you didn't answer."

"I told you—— I swear. You can check my phone. There aren't any missed calls."

"Why did you lie to me, Greg? What's going on?"

"Huh? Nothing is going on. I'm sorry. It's just——"

"It's what? What is it that you're home on a Monday for and then have to lie to me about?"

Greg chose his next words carefully. He knew this conversation could end their relationship if he wasn't careful.

"I took the day off because of my sister. I was pretty depressed yesterday." It was partially true, but Greg thought that if he scored some sympathy points, then she might forgive his lie or at least be more accepting of it.

"I'm sorry to hear that. But why would you lie to me about that? I'm here for you, Greg. I thought you knew that."

"I do. I don't know, it's just… I've been talking about her so much. I know girls don't want to hear about guys' emotional baggage. They like men with confidence."

"That's not true at all. I *love* that you cared so much for her. It's one of your great qualities, and it's really sweet. You don't have to be afraid to let your guard down around me."

"I'm sorry. I shouldn't have lied; it won't happen again."

"I hope not. I can put up with a lot of quirks, but honesty is a must for me. You're a better person than that, Greg. I know you are."

"I know," he said, wondering if it came across as arrogant.

"So what sales figure did you have to hit for Shane to buy you pizzas? Will you get a bonus?"

Greg sighed, not realizing that she didn't know he wasn't at work today either. Again, he figured he should cut his losses.

"I didn't go to work today," he said, looking down and feeling defeated. It hurt him so much inside that he'd lied. He never wanted to be in this position with Stacy again.

"Are you serious? Two days in a row? Greg, I think you need counseling."

"I'm not doing counseling. I'm fine."

"You're not *fine*. What have you been doing all day today and yesterday?"

"Actually, I've kept busy. I've been digging into Jessica's investigation. I've found a lot of stuff!"

"Greg, you're kidding, right?"

He didn't know how to respond. Her question made him feel demoralized.

"No, I'm not kidding."

"You're not an investigator, Greg. They've already looked into her case."

"They didn't, though! They stopped looking once I showed them the website. The killer is right here, for everyone to see. I ——or at least someone——need to put the pieces together."

"Yeah, but... it's dangerous. I mean, these are sociopath serial killers, right? Do you want to get yourself killed?"

"Of course not! I'm not going to, Stacy. Once I uncover enough evidence, I'll show Detective Maxwell and let him take it from there. He's already said he'd check in on me from time to time and revisit the case."

"Still, I don't think it's healthy to take two days off of work for this. Promise me you'll think about getting counseling."

"I'll think about it. I don't think I need it... but I'll think about it."

"Okay. Look, I have to go. I just wanted to check up on you because you didn't call this morning. Will you call me later?"

"Sure," Greg said. "Stacy?"

"Yeah?"

"I'm really sorry about lying to you. I hope you'll forgive me. I'm going to be better to you."

"You're fine, Greg. You don't need to be better. You just need to be honest."

"Okay."

"Okay. Talk to you tonight. Miss you."

"Miss you, too."

Greg hung up the phone, feeling horrible. If he would have just been honest, she would have been much more understanding. Now, he'd put a serious blip in their relationship. He'd have to be even more careful when he brought up the subject of Jessica. Because now it wasn't just her putting up with his baggage, but bringing up Jessica would be a reminder of the huge lie he'd told her.

Greg fixed himself a sandwich and took a break from his investigative work. He felt guilty not researching Jessica's murder. Stacy had made him feel stupid for doing it, and he resented her a little for it. It was the first time he'd ever had a negative feeling toward her.

Yes, he lied. So maybe it was because she was in a bad mood that she said some of the things she did. Counseling? What a waste of time *that* would be.

He had some making up to do with her.

After lunch, he watched an episode of *Prison Break*. He thought that he could get used to this lifestyle, staying at home all day. He envied the people that got to work from home. Not having to get ready every morning or dealing with rush hour. You could just wake up, work in your underwear, and not have to deal with the endless distractions and meetings that took place in the corporate world.

He did summon the courage to get back on his computer to check his Anonymail email. He was very curious to see if they'd hacked into the account yet. If they did, he'd have no problem going back to his research.

There weren't any new emails, though. Greg was pretty disappointed, as he expected them to have replied to him by now. He'd have to wait a little while longer to find out.

He decided to explore the Deep Web some more. He remembered he'd accomplished what he wanted by getting *American Hitmen* to respond back to his message. While he had wanted them to say more, he at least got their manicsocio009 username. Greg went to TorDir to see if the username had been used anywhere else in forums.

Thinking about it, he was glad that the name was as unique as it was. Not too many people would pick a username like manicsocio009. At least, he didn't think so. If any other forum had someone with that username, Greg thought it was likely to be Jessica's killer.

On TorDir, there were a lot of places where people could communicate. Topics ranged from hacking, legal issues, and drug questions. None of these disturbed Greg as much as the ones about child porn. Seeing what people were talking about and posting, Greg had never felt as guilty using the Deep Web as he did now. Drug use and trying to make money was one thing, but the people involved with kids were disgusting, and he thought that they should be behind bars forever.

He spent the next thirty or forty minutes visiting forums, searching for "manicsocio009" to see if any results came up.

None did.

Deep down, he knew it was a long shot, but he had still hoped that he'd find something. Seeing another one of his ideas fail caused Greg to lose hope. He didn't have many good ideas to begin with, so when one of them turned up nothing, it was a great morale blow.

Thinking that Jessica's murderer was still out there provided endless motivation, but Greg wondered if the day would ever come when he'd have to give up and accept that he'd never meet the killer face-to-face. Leave it to fate, as his mother said.

After giving up on manicsocio009, he checked his email again, but it offered nothing new. He couldn't wait for the response, to see if they could hack into the email account. He needed for that plan to work. Unlike yesterday, where he felt like he'd made progress, today had brought him nothing but setbacks and an unhappy girlfriend. He regretted taking another day off of work. Even though he kept telling himself that there were bound to be setbacks, the reality of it was hard to face.

He thought about his most promising opportunities. The hacking attempt into manicsocio009's email was a good one, obviously. But that was out of his control for now. Greg decided his next best chance was to get ahold of Jessica's phone so that he could log into her account.

He grabbed his phone and thought for a moment about what he was going to say. Then he called his father. It rang four times before the man answered.

"Hello."

"Hey Dad, it's Greg."

"Hey…" He sounded surprised. "What's going on? Is something wrong?"

"No, everything is fine. I just had a quick question. Did you ever get around to canceling Jessica's phone?" Greg felt awkward bringing up the subject of Jessica, which usually only brought depression and crying to those in the conversation.

"I did not. I called the phone company, but they didn't have her phone on record. I eventually found out that her work supplied the phones, so I called them." He sighed. "Turned out to be a headache trying to get through to them… was on hold for twenty minutes. Eventually I spoke with someone in accounting who said they were going to take care of it."

Without hesitation, Greg asked, "And how long ago was

that?"

"I dunno, a couple weeks ago, maybe. Why are you asking?"

"No reason. I was just curious." Greg knew his dad wouldn't press him for answers, unlike his mom who would have demanded he provide a good reason for asking such things. "Do you have her phone still, at the house?"

"Hmm, I'm not sure, to be honest. I know the detective looked through it and didn't find anything. I think we still have it in her room somewhere."

"Cool. I wouldn't mind going through her stuff. Grab all of her movies and music. I'm wondering if there's anything else I'd like to take back with me."

"Sure, yeah, of course. How are you doing, by the way? Holdin' up all right?"

"Yeah, it's been hard. The past couple days haven't been great, but I'm hanging in there. You?"

"Same. Your mother… I worry about her. At night she sometimes sits in the living room, no book, no TV, nothing. Just sits. When I try to talk to her, she just wants me to leave her alone."

Greg didn't know what to say; he felt awful. He could picture his mom doing this, too. She wasn't wired like he or his father were; she kept most of her feelings to herself.

"I'm sorry, Dad. Maybe I'll come by soon."

"We'd love that. You know you're always welcome."

"I know. All right, thanks. Talk with you later."

"Okay, take care of yourself."

"I will."

After he hung up, Greg was unsure if the news of the phone was a good thing or bad. On the one hand, it wasn't official that her number had been canceled. However, chances were that it had been.

He planned on going there sometime at the end of the week so he could find out for sure.

He went back to Anonymail to check for any new emails, but again, there weren't any.

He opened a new tab to complete his next task: conducting further research on all of the previous victims. While he'd done this earlier and hadn't gotten far, he was desperate for anything that would spark his investigation. He went to log into his Facebook account. However, he must have made a typing error, because it gave him a "wrong password" message.

As soon as he read the message, he fell back into his chair. He wasn't sure how or why the idea came to him, but he had to try it. He leaned forward again and erased what was in the username field. He typed in Jessica's email address, which he knew was Jessica's Facebook login. They had both registered with Facebook through their college email addresses because they were some of the first people to sign up, back when Facebook was slowly rolling it out to colleges.

Under the password field, he tried the password that *Hacking4Hire* had provided. If Jessica had been anything like him, she'd use the same password for almost everything. He pushed enter and waited for Tor to load.

When her news feed popped up on the screen, Greg burst with excitement. The notification bar at the top said that she had 196 new notifications. There were also 12 new direct messages and 3 friend requests.

More people had written on her wall than he expected.

The notifications didn't concern him; it would be too painful to read the condolences. What he *was* interested in were the private messages. Maybe he'd never get to her email, where the likely critical information was, but perhaps he'd find something of interest here.

When he opened up to her messages, he saw that she'd used Facebook's messaging feature a lot. Part of him felt guilty for snooping through her private business.

Curiosity, and the fact that he knew his sister wouldn't mind under these circumstances, made him continue.

It wasn't long before he knew he'd struck some critical information.

He'd just uncovered his first breakthrough of the day, and it was a good one.

Chapter 17

The first conversation that he opened up was between Jessica and Stacy. In Facebook, with one click, he could see all of the conversations they'd had together, sorted by date.

Jessica had sent Stacy a picture of him sitting on the couch at their condo in Myrtle Beach. His shirt was off.

Jessica: *Here's a better picture of my brother. He's a super nice guy. I think you two would really hit it off.*

Stacy: *Great, yeah, he's cute! Send him my number. As for the job application, that is SO nice of you. You really don't have to, and I understand if you can't. Your company sounds neat!*
Getting through this last semester is going to be a challenge, but I'm excited to enter the workforce. I've been a farm girl for far too long. :)

Greg was starting to feel uncomfortable reading through their conversation now. If he didn't admit to her that he'd read this, it was just another form of lying, and he'd done too much of that lately.

He closed out of their messages and clicked to the next thread. It was from James, the man Jessica had almost married until he decided to move to Africa. The first message he read was dated three months before:

Hey Jessica! We got Internet installed at our camp, and I am checking Facebook for the first time in years. It was nothing but pictures of us together, and it got me thinking about you. How are you? What have you been up to lately?

I've been stationed at the Sumami camp for a couple years now. The people here are wonderful. I'd love to have you down here to see it, but I know that isn't your thing. I'd love to keep in touch, though, and hope you respond back. Hope things are going well.

Jessica replied a week later. Greg had a lot of things going through his mind. He knew that Jessica had probably read the message the same day that it had been sent. She checked Facebook at least once a day. He also wondered why she hadn't mentioned to him that James had spoken to her. Was it because she was too afraid to hear what he would say? Greg knew he would have told her to ignore him and to move on since it would never work out. Still, he wished Jessica would have brought it up and given him the opportunity to talk about it with her. She messaged back:

Good to hear from you! I'm glad that things are going well. I'm still in Columbus, working as a Director of Marketing at Adriar Pharmaceuticals. I've been here ever since I got out of college. Things have escalated here, and I've received several promotions. It brings a lot of challenges, but as you know from school, I like to work hard. Maybe too hard. :-(

Do you ever come home? How are your parents? If you'll be back in

Ohio, maybe we can catch up? It would be great to see you. Let me know.

James responded the same day:

Yep, I come home once or twice a year. Usually Christmas and also for the AFTA conference, which I have to present to donors, telling them what we've been doing so that we can keep getting funded. Every year it gets tougher and tougher. I'm not sure that we'll get the money to do it for the rest of the year. The conference is in March, and it's in Columbus. We should definitely meet up. It would be absolutely wonderful to see you.

I really hope everything is going well with you. I know we went our separate ways, but it would mean a lot, Jess, if we could still be friends. I love you and will always love you. We just have different long-term goals.

Jessica only took one day to respond:

Great, let me know when you're getting close to coming, and we'll figure out a date to meet. As for your funding, maybe that's something we can talk about. My company is looking to get involved with overseas charity work. They certainly have the budget for it! I think something like what you're doing in Africa would really catch their interest, and I have enough clout here that they'd strongly consider a donation if I asked. I'll look up the AFTA conference and get someone to go to it. Maybe I'll come, too (if you don't mind me being there). I'd love hearing you present! I know you're uber-passionate about this, and it would be nice to hear all that you've accomplished there.

James responded with a shorter message:

* * *

Sounds good! I'll let you know the dates when I find out more about this year's conference. You certainly don't have to make any donations if you don't want to. Your generosity for considering, though, is much appreciated.

Two weeks later, James sent another message:

The AFTA Conference will be March 29-30. I'll be home a couple days before that if you want to grab coffee or something.

Greg saw the dates and his heart sank. Jessica had been murdered a week later. He was anxious to read the rest of their conversation:

James: *I tried your phone, but evidently you have a different number now. Did you still want to meet up for lunch somewhere?*
Jessica: *Yes, sorry. My company gave me a phone, and I just use it now. I'll call you tonight when I get home.*

Two days later:

James: *Again, it was great seeing you! We should get together one more time before I head back to Africa. Maybe after the conference?*
Jessica: *Sounds great. See you tomorrow. We can make plans then.*

The next message was March 31st, the day Jessica was murdered:

James: *I've had a lot of time to think about what happened. The more I do, the more I stand by what I said when we were together. How could you do something like that to me, Jessica? It's just not like you. You've changed, and I have to admit, it hasn't been for the better. Where's the sweet, caring, honest woman I fell in love with and almost married? The woman that would jump in front of a bus to help someone. The woman that once said she was incapable of telling a lie. I know she's in there somewhere.*

I'm sure you don't care about my opinion, but I'm going to give it anyway. You need to leave that company. You should have done it a long time ago, but seeing as you haven't yet, there's no time like the present. Quit now before it's too late. Before they can change you more than they already have. It's going to bring you nothing but trouble, and I don't want to see anything happen to you.

If you never want to speak with me again, I understand. But Jessica, just know it doesn't have to be that way. You can still reach me anytime you wish. You have my number now.

Hope to talk to you soon.

Greg read and re-read the last message dozens of times. Every sentence, every word dissected to uncover its meaning. There was too much information missing.

He read the previous messages for clues, but that made things even stranger. Everything was going smoothly. It sounded like they'd had lunch together. Their later messages implied that it had gone well. There were no issues until the night of the conference, and then *BAM*, everything had turned to shit.

Greg could only speculate. His most logical conclusion was that Jessica had decided not to fund James's work in Africa. Based on the messages, that was the only conclusion that Greg could come up with.

After all, everything had been fine when they first communicated. Jessica said she'd come to the conference and likely fund it. Then afterward, James was upset and told her to quit her job. It didn't get more logical than that.

Problem was, Greg knew James. Up to the point when he and Jessica had split up, Greg considered James to be the brother he'd never had. They'd gone to lots of sporting events together. Buckeyes football and basketball, Cleveland Browns, Cavaliers. They'd even gone to a Columbus Blue Jackets hockey game, and they didn't even like hockey.

James wasn't a good golfer, but he went with Greg and his father every chance he could. James really made the effort to get Jessica's family to like him.

With all that Greg knew about James, he didn't seem the type to whine and pout because someone wouldn't fund his little project. James was the type to hide his feelings and keep his hurt on the inside.

Greg wondered if maybe he didn't know James as well as he thought. Perhaps James was the type of person who could behave one way in front of one person and then become a completely different person behind closed doors. He wondered if James even knew that Jessica had been murdered.

Greg knew his sister better than anyone else and didn't think she'd changed as much as James had said. Then he thought about the line underneath the picture from the crimes scene:

Deceased, for crimes of dishonesty.

He kept repeating it over and over in his mind.
Dishonesty.
Jessica.
At first, Greg thought it was impossible that she'd ever lied to him.
But she never mentioned that she had reunited with James

———never said a peep about it. And she never mentioned that she'd been promoted to VP of Marketing, something Greg thought she'd want to share.

Maybe it was Jessica that Greg didn't know well. Perhaps James was doing the right thing by suggesting that she leave Adriar Pharmaceuticals and go back to being the person she once was.

Greg was unsure of a lot of things at this point.

But one thing he was sure of.

He needed to talk to James.

Chapter 18

Greg looked through the rest of Jessica's Facebook messages, but there was nothing else of interest.

Her conversation with James was by far the biggest find.

Something big was said or done at the conference, and he was going to find out what that was.

Greg thought it was best to stay on Tor while doing his research, even though it was slow. He began by searching for James' camp in Africa. The top results were nothing close to related to James. Google was spitting back random news results related to Africa. Greg skimmed over them, and even searched within the article for the word "Sumami," but there was nothing.

It wasn't long before Greg gave up on finding anything about Sumami, so he decided to search James' name. There were many men named James Cooper, but none of them were the James that he knew. He even narrowed his search down by using "James Cooper Africa" and "James Cooper Sumami," but neither helped. Greg tried "James Cooper Columbus Ohio" and was able to find his Facebook page, but that was all that Greg could find in his online research for the man.

Greg found himself with two options, possibly three. He

could send James a Facebook message from his account or he could pretend to be Jessica and message him from her account.

His third option was to gain access to Jessica's phone and see if she'd added James' number to it before they'd had their little spat.

Greg wasn't quite ready to be bold and make a call to James. He'd try Facebook first.

He thought about every possible thing that he could say. Any way to get James to tell him what happened that night at the conference. The more Greg thought about it, the more he concluded that the truth (or mostly the truth) was his best option.

He opened up his regular browser and signed into his Facebook account, thinking that logging in through Tor wasn't a bright idea, as Tor could easily trace his digital footprint. When he was into his account, he wondered if James was even his Facebook friend. It had been a long time since James used Facebook, and Greg didn't log on often. He searched his name and found that they were still friends.

He went to his profile page and read his latest updates. There were several pictures from the camp. Greg's first reaction was amazement. If this was the place he was staying, how on Earth did they get Internet access?

Sumami was a tiny village with grass huts. In the center of the huts was a campfire.

Scrolling through pictures, every person there was black aside from James. His profile photo was a group photo of him surrounded by about forty Africans. Greg smiled at how much he stood out, a very white man in the center of so many very dark people.

There was an album of photos that were taken in a classroom, which was no bigger than the size of a small living room. There were no desks. A teacher, a middle-aged woman wearing a tan dress and sandals, stood at a chalkboard while ten kids of various ages sat on the ground, looking up at what she was teaching.

Another group of photos showed smiling children and families. Their clothes looked ragged and worn out, as if there was barely any cloth left. They looked poorer than poor. Seeing them gave Greg a newfound respect for James. He was a brave man, growing up in America and choosing to move to a place like this. Again, he didn't know how a place like that had Internet access. Perhaps there was a more developed town nearby.

Greg clicked the message button, which opened a new screen. He stared at the screen with his fingers hovering over the keyboard. He had no clue what to say, other than to tell the truth, so he began typing without much thought:

Hey James, it's Greg Anderson, Jessica's sister. I was scrolling through my Facebook friends today and came across your name and remembered that you were in Africa. It looks quite interesting there. Based on all Jessica told me, you must love it.

Speaking of Jessica, I don't know if you've heard the news or not, but Jessica was murdered about a month ago. Not sure if you have a phone out there, but my number is still 555-682-4711 if you want to talk. We can also set up a time to Skype. Or you can return this message if you have any questions or want to learn more. Either way, let me know when you get this message. I just wanted to make sure you knew if you hadn't heard already.

It wasn't the best message in the world, but Greg tried writing it as if he hadn't just read the man's private conversation with his sister. He wrote it like the nice brother, reaching out to Jessica's former friends.

Now, it was a waiting game. The ball was in two other very important people's courts——James and *Hacking4Hire*.

He watched some TV for a couple hours, his mind preoccupied with what he'd discovered.

Knowing he needed to patch things up with Stacy, Greg decided to call to see if she had dinner plans. He knew doing so would look sappy and desperate, but he didn't mind. He wanted her to know he cared for her.

He grabbed his phone and dialed. It rang once, twice, three times.

She didn't pick up.

Greg's momentary joy from his discovery dissipated. It was possible that she hadn't been around her phone, but Greg was convinced that it wasn't true. He imagined her staring at it, deciding whether or not to answer, and putting it down in frustration.

He could surprise her and show up at her place. He'd only been there a few times, and never for long. She always seemed to prefer hanging out at his place.

He decided to do it.

He'd even buy her flowers, which was something he'd only done one time for Carrie.

Stacy was currently living there by herself. The only issue with the surprise visit was the lack of parking. He'd have to find the nearest empty spot and pray he didn't get towed. It was that or having to walk six blocks while carrying flowers, which he didn't feel like doing as a twenty-nine year old man on a college campus on a random Tuesday evening in May.

He got dressed and walked out the door.

His car was parked in its usual spot by the road. It was convenient; except he now knew that it was a way for girlfriends to know if he was home or not.

He went down to the nearby Kroger, where he usually bought his groceries. They always had flowers in the front. It had always depressed him, seeing them the few months after he and Carrie broke up.

He grabbed a pretty bouquet of flowers——the prettiest and most elegant ones they had. She was worth it. This girl had been everything to him for the past month and a half. He didn't even look at the price until he was at the checkout counter. The bouquet he'd purchased for Carrie had been twenty dollars, and he'd felt like he was blowing money. This bouquet was over twice that amount, but he felt it would be worth it to get another. Anything that would help to patch up their relationship was worth the investment.

Greg drove to Stacy's apartment with the flowers sitting in the passenger seat.

He wiped his sweaty palms on his shirt.

He liked to avoid confrontation but knew he'd have to face Stacy at some point. He figured he might as well get it over with now, before it lingered too much in his mind.

There was a parking spot near the front of her place. Stacy's old, dinged-up car wasn't anywhere to be seen.

He grabbed the flowers and got out of his car. His mind raced as he tried to decide what he would say and how he would say it. He imagined her seeing the flowers and immediately forgetting the lie. That's what he hoped, anyway. But if Stacy was anything like Carrie, she'd hold a grudge for the rest of her life.

He got up to the door, took a deep breath, and knocked. He put the flowers behind his back, thinking he'd at least say hello before presenting them to her. He wanted to see the look on her face when she saw them. Greg waited and was about to knock on the door again when it swung open.

Standing at the door was a man in his mid-twenties. He had no shirt on——only red gym shorts. He was very fit, complete with big pecs and a six-pack. He could be on a fitness magazine.
   "Sup," the man said.
   "Hey, sorry. I think I have the wrong place."
   "Who you lookin' for, bro?"
   "My girlfriend, Stacy."
   "Oh," the man said, surprised. "No, you got the right place."
   Greg didn't know what to say. He looked at the guy, trying to get a read on his face.
   He exuded confidence.
   Greg caught the man's biceps out of the corner of his eye and realized that they were as big as his own thighs.
   He finally uttered, "I'm confused. Who are you?" He tried to make it sound tough, but it didn't come across that way.
   "Name's Jimmy," he said, holding out his hand.
   Greg shook it and felt his tremendous strength.
   "Greg."
   While Jimmy locked eyes on Greg, Greg looked down, hoping Jimmy wouldn't break his hand.
   "Is Stacy here?"
   "No, she went out. Can I help you with something?"
   "Are you her roommate or something?"
   "Me? No, just a friend."
   "Oh, well, do you know when she'll be back?"
   "Not sure, bro. You just missed her. She said she'd be out, didn't say where she was going or when she'd get back."
   "Okay, thanks for your time."
   Greg turned around, trying to hide the flowers from Jimmy's view. He'd never felt more disheartened than he did now. He wanted to rush out of there and hide somewhere.

"Whatcha got there?" Jimmy asked.

Greg considered ignoring him. But he turned around and showed him the flowers.

"Nice! Are those for Stacy?"

"Yeah. They were."

"You want me to take 'em and give 'em to her?"

"Uhh…" Greg didn't know what to do, only that he wanted out of there. "Sure," he said, handing him to the man.

"These are pretty! What did you say your name was again?"

"Greg."

"Greg, I'll make sure she gets 'em."

"Thanks," he said, not meaning it.

"No problem. You take care now."

Greg turned around, this time walking faster than he had before. When he opened his car door and turned around, he hoped Jimmy wasn't still standing there. He wasn't.

He got in his car, thinking about how he should call Stacy and confront her about Jimmy, but he really didn't feel like talking to her.

Why was a guy who looked like a fitness model staying at her place? And why did he have his shirt off? He wished he'd probed Jimmy with more direct questions, but it had caught him so off guard that he hadn't been thinking clearly.

He didn't know what to do now. His belly growled, answering the question for him.

He also needed a drink after that.

B-dubs was having their Tuesday discount wings.

It was an easy decision.

He sat at the bar, eating twenty wings and drinking by himself. Eating alone at sports bars wasn't as bad as other places because there were plenty of TVs to watch. It was right in the thick of the NBA playoffs, so there was plenty to keep his mind off of all his problems. Still, his run-in with Jimmy and his problems with Stacy lingered in the back of his mind. Not to mention the things he had going on with finding Jessica's murderer.

He'd already decided that he wasn't going to check his email when he got home. He didn't need the added stress. He wasn't going to call or text Stacy, either. All of that could wait until tomorrow.

Three beers were a lot for Greg. He'd be over the limit if he didn't slow down.

He stayed there for another hour and a half to sober up. It was 8:45, and he was starting to get tired. It had just occurred to him that he'd have to go to work tomorrow.

He finally made it home, pulling his car into his normal spot.

Going up the stairs, he took his keys out of his pocket. He was so tired; he knew he'd fall asleep as soon as his head hit the pillow.

The hallway was always dark at night.

It was something that Greg heard his neighbors complain a lot about.

It never bothered him much, because usually he was asleep by then. He could barely see his doorknob when he went to insert the key.

As he did and turned the doorknob, it felt strange.

The door opened way too easily.

It was only when he flicked on the light that he realized the door had already been open.

When he looked around his apartment, it all seemed to be in order, but Greg was scared.

Was there someone in here?

He closed the door behind him and got out his phone. He

was ready to call 911 at a moment's notice. It was ludicrous, but he grabbed a butcher's knife from the kitchen. He then walked into his bedroom to inspect it. No one was there, and again, nothing was out of place.

He thrust the closet door open, ready to attack. He then checked underneath his bed. Everything was in order but he was still on guard. The bathroom was clear, too.

He then went back out into the main living room. He sighed with relief but still wondered how and why his apartment door had been open. Had he forgotten to close it? To his knowledge, he'd never done such a thing before.

But then he saw it.

He looked over at his desk by the window.

The laptop, which always sat there plugged into the wall, was gone.

And there was a message on his desk.

Chapter 19

Written on an index card in red crayon and a child's handwriting, the message was left where his computer had been:

Stay out of our business or you're dead. - AH

Greg didn't need Sherlock Holmes to figure out who AH was.

American Hitmen had been inside his apartment.

The thought made him so scared that he wanted to throw up. So many questions ran through his mind. For starters, what did they know? How did they know? He'd sent them a threat, but he'd disguised his identity as best as he could.

How did they know it was him?

He thought about it more. There had to be a way for them to link his actions. "Stay out of our business" clearly meant that they knew he was spying on them.

Then it came to him.

The most likely way they could have figured him out——*Hacking4Hire*.

Greg had put in two orders. The first was to hack his sister's account. The second was to hack the *American Hitmen* address. If they had somehow paid off *Hacking4Hire* (or were, in fact, the same people), then it would be easy to figure out that it was him.

Greg wondered what would have happened if he'd been in his apartment when they came?

He'd surely be dead now.

Everything felt very real. He was no longer hidden behind his computer where he was safe. The darkness of the Deep Web was meeting him in real life.

Detective Maxwell had warned him to be careful, and Greg hadn't listened. Stacy, the only other person that knew what he was doing, had said the same.

Now he knew he'd better listen to them.

He wondered what they'd learn by taking his laptop. Everything he'd done was posted anonymously. Greg hoped they couldn't get into his history and other personal information. None of his work stuff was on there, not that he really cared if Vinditech's information got out.

As for personal files, he'd stored lots of pictures on it, but he had backups of them in multiple places so that he wouldn't lose those. He never saved any of his passwords, but that didn't mean his bank accounts were safe. And, with services like *Hacking4Hire,* Greg knew that if someone really wanted access to his account, it was simply a matter of hiring the right people. There was nothing he could do if they really wanted into his accounts.

They didn't need his computer to do that.

He'd been tired when he got home, but now he was more alert than ever. He had to decide what to do next. He thought about calling Detective Maxwell. Maybe seeing the note would spur him to get the case picked back up. After all, there could be fingerprints or some other way of detecting who had left the note. Greg thought the child's handwriting was done as a disguise so they couldn't tell who wrote it. For all Greg knew, though, they may have tortured some kid into writing it.

He reminded himself of whom he was dealing with.

Detective Maxwell would also be interested to know about the two additional murder victims. That should have gotten someone's attention at the police force, but Greg very much doubted that it had.

Detective Maxwell's name was under his contacts. Greg knew he'd be there within half an hour if he dialed.

But he couldn't bring himself to do it. For one, he didn't want to hear the detective nag him about getting involved. It was also past nine on a Tuesday evening. It was a lame excuse, but by the time he came over and Greg told him about the stolen laptop and everything he'd found so far, it could be midnight before Greg finally got to bed.

His final reason for not calling was that he didn't have a laptop to show him all that he'd found. Greg wanted the detective to see what he'd uncovered and get his thoughts on what should happen next. He hoped the detective would say Greg had done a great job and that the case would surely be re-opened. But that was being very optimistic.

He was having doubts about how much more involvement he should have in finding Jessica's murderer. Was it worth dying for, ensuring the people paid for their crimes? Or would he be better off letting it go and doing as his mom said, letting fate and karma take care of it for him?

That, he didn't feel he *could* do.

Not yet, anyway.

He wasn't a believer in fate and felt that *American Hitmen* would continue what they were doing, killing people that didn't deserve to be so unfairly treated. Eventually, they might get caught, but Greg felt it needed to be sooner rather than later, and he wanted to be the one to do it.

More than anything else at the moment, he wanted access to the Deep Web. Did he have any new emails from *Hacking4Hire*? Had they given him up to *American Hitmen*?

He had to find out.

He did have Internet on his phone, at least. The Facebook app reminded him of his message to James.

When it loaded and the red notification alert popped up to indicate a new message, he got excited. It was, indeed, from James:

Hey Greg,

First off, it's good to hear from you! It's been such a long time, my friend. As for what you said…

No, I hadn't heard about Jessica yet. I just can't believe it. This past hour, I've been sitting here in silence, thinking about it and looking up what I could online.

So she was murdered? In cold-blood, walking on the street? Have you heard, or do you know any more than that? I'm very interested to hear, because it just doesn't make sense why someone would do such a thing. I could go on, but I'd like to hear what you know first. Did they already find the killer?? If not, do you suspect anyone?

It's probably best if you message me on here for now. I'd love to talk over the phone and catch up, but as you know, I'm in the heart of Africa where phone service is less than ideal. It's been so long since I've had the luxuries of a first-world country for an extended period, I've forgotten how much easier life is with them.

Please let me know more details. I'll eagerly await your message. I can check Facebook once a day when I go get supplies, which is usually around

4 PM your time in Columbus.
Thanks, and hope you're all right. I'm so sorry.

- James

Greg thought the note sounded authentic. As if he really didn't know what happened. Another voice inside his mind said that maybe he was so curious to know what Greg knew because he'd had some sort of involvement in it.

After reading the message a few more times, Greg decided he could reserve judgment for later. For now, his one goal was to get more information on what happened the night of the fundraiser. What had happened that night that made James feel that Jessica ought to quit her high-paying job at Adriar Pharmaceuticals?

He thought about how he should respond to James' message. If he really only checked his Facebook once a day, then Greg could wait until the morning to respond. He wanted to respond now, because it would help him sleep. But he hated typing long messages on his phone. It seemed he could never find the right words to say.

He decided it was best to wait until tomorrow. It would give his subconscious some time to think things over. It would also give him something to do tomorrow at work, because he knew his mind would be preoccupied.

Greg double locked his door, which was the only point of entry aside from the window. Still, he made sure that the window was locked, too.

He then double-checked each and every potential hiding spot in the apartment.

There wasn't anyone there.

Lying in bed, there were so many things running through his head. His head would explode if he continued to allow his mind to wander. Instead, he thought about buying a new computer. He was about due for one anyway. Jessica had insisted that he get a Mac, but he didn't think he could bring himself to do it. They were too expensive, and he wasn't sure if Tor worked on it. He figured it probably did, but having to learn something new wasn't something he wanted to deal with now. He decided he'd go get a new PC after work.

Then, after an hour of tossing and turning, he fell asleep.

When Greg woke up the next day, his first instinct was to go to his computer and check his email. He'd almost suppressed the memory of his apartment being broken into.

He'd woken up at his usual time, five o'clock. He went through his normal routine, watching SportsCenter and eating cereal. He absolutely hated the thought of going to work, especially since there were two full days of work he'd have to catch up on, because he knew no one at work had the decency to pick up the slack. It didn't upset him; he would do the same to them.

He was out the door at 8:00 and right on schedule. Traffic was normal. The weather was fine. It felt like a Monday after a long holiday. Greg kept telling himself that he only had to get through three more days. It was the only thing getting him through the dread of going to work.

When he got there, he greeted people passing by, as usual. Most of the people he said hi to probably hadn't even realized he'd been gone the past couple of days.

Bob knew, and he'd given Greg a quick checklist of things to get caught up on. There were a lot of things to do, as Greg had expected, and he figured he might have to stay a little late to finish, because the sales team presented tomorrow.

It was an important presentation. If he hadn't shown up, he wondered how it would have gotten done.

He settled in and began working. The work wasn't as dreadful as he'd expected, as it gave him something to take his mind off of everything. He still had his reply to James' message composing in the back of his mind.

Right as he was got into a good flow, he felt a hard slap on his back. Greg jumped more than he would have, had he not just had his apartment broken into.

"Easy there, sweetie britches. It's just me," Shane said.

"Damn, you scared me."

"I noticed. So where ya been? I've been wanting to talk to you."

"Sorry. Haven't been feeling well the past couple days."

"Bullshit! Don't lie. What's been going on? You lookin' for another job or something? Been doin' interviews?" Shane said. "Hey, you didn't apply to Suntech, did you? Those fucks. You don't want to work there. Trust me. Buncha queers runnin' that place."

"No, I haven't done any job searching."

"So what have you been up to, then?"

Greg hesitated. He'd never shied away from opening up to Shane, because he usually didn't have much excitement to talk about.

This time was different.

In a low voice, he said, "I took a couple days off to try and figure out who did this to Jessica."

"No shit!" Shane said, louder than Greg would have liked. "You figure anything out?"

"Well, let's just say, my apartment was broken into last night."

"Damn, dude. You all right?"

"Yeah, I'm fine. It just scared me. They took my laptop."

"That sucks, man. Hey, you need to be careful. So you find out who did it?"

"Well, no. But I found a lot. Wanna see?"

They went into Shane's office and closed the door. Greg went right to Shane's computer.

When he opened Tor, Shane said, "Whoa. Are you dealin' with drug dealers or somethin'?"

"I wish. It's far worse."

Greg didn't say anything as he navigated his way through TorDir and onto the *American Hitmen* site. Shane looked over his shoulder, surprisingly quiet by his standards.

He got to the proof page and then let Shane sit down.

"After you showed Tor to me, I downloaded it onto my computer. I was just curious, looking around and what not, when I came across this."

Shane continued in silence, his face glued to the screen.

Greg was anxious for Shane to scroll down and see the picture of his sister, but Shane was paying extra careful attention to what he was seeing. Greg knew that Shane was really into it, too, because again, he wasn't saying anything.

He finally scrolled down. Still not enough to show Jessica's picture, but enough to see the victim right above her. Shane covered his mouth with his hand and shook his head. Greg then remembered how shocked he had been the first time he saw this page. He got to see what his reaction was like on the face of another person.

Shane finally spoke. "This is pretty fucked up, man. Makin' me uncomfortable."

Unable to take it any longer, Greg said, "You haven't gotten to the part I wanted to show you. Scroll down a little more."

He did and saw Jessica's picture on the screen. He flung himself back in the chair. "Oh shit, dude. That's Jessica, right?"

"It is."

"Oh fuck, man. Shit. Wow."

Greg couldn't help but crack a small smile as he watched Shane pulling his hair. He'd never guessed anything could shock Shane like this. It reconfirmed that this discovery was a big deal.

"You showed this to the police?"

"Yep, but they didn't do shit about it. They said it wasn't verifiable in court or something like that. So they sent it to their superiors somewhere to look into, but that was about it."

"Dude, I can't believe this. What is this site anyway?"

Greg took control of the mouse and went back to the main page. "These people are sociopath murders. They take free requests through this form and then select whoever they feel deserves to die the most."

"So why did they choose Jessica? What was she so 'dishonest' about that made them want to kill her over all the rapists and pedophiles of the world?"

"Beats me. All I know is that I contacted these people and got their email address. Then I hired someone to try and hack into their account."

Greg couldn't believe he was opening up so much about the whole ordeal. He'd never planned on telling Shane or anyone else, except Detective Maxwell, about all the details he'd found. It felt good, though, letting everything out and not keeping everything so secret.

"Damn, bro. I can't believe you had all of this in ya. Who did you hire? Did they hack into it?"

"Actually—" Greg paused, "I was going to get an update last night until I found out my laptop was stolen."

Shane jumped out of the seat. With a smirk on his face, he motioned for Greg to sit down.

Greg was flattered that, for a change, he was the one with something interesting going on. Usually it was Shane who had all of the exciting things happening.

Greg settled in and opened a new tab. Shane's excitement, which had just seemed almost comical, suddenly became serious and real.

He went through the process of searching for TorDir. He still couldn't remember the exact URL since it was a random collection of numbers and letters. Shane sat on his knees beside Greg, both hands on his mouth, watching the computer screen intently.

Greg took a deep breath; he was beginning to get really nervous. He found the Anonymail link and clicked it. The login screen came up, and Greg froze. He had forgotten what his email and password were.

"What's the matter?"

Greg didn't say anything. He hadn't written it down anywhere, for fear that it could be evidence used against him if discovered. He was kind of glad he'd done that, because the people that broke into his apartment surely would have taken it. He thought hard. He tried to picture the address in his mind. The email he'd sent to himself to test its functionality. Typing it into the form field. Then it came to him.

"Nothing. Just forgot what email I used for a moment there. Didn't want to use any of my usual names in case they tried to track me."

"Good thinking. I never would have even thought of that."

Greg entered his information and hit the login button. Both Shane and Greg inched a little closer to the screen, waiting for it to load.

When it did, all of his previous messages were still there. Greg had been worried that the *American Hitmen* folks finding a way into his account and deleting everything. But they hadn't.

It took Greg a moment to realize that he had a new message. He recognized it from address. It was the *American Hitmen* folks.

The subject line was :-(

Greg hesitated, considering asking Shane to leave so he could read it first. He decided, though, that Shane had already seen plenty, so what did it matter? Also, Greg wasn't sure Shane would have left if he asked him to.

He opened the email and was surprised to see that a couple paragraphs had been written.

Dear Greg (yes, we know your name),

It's time you stop fucking with us and stay out of our way. We know you hired someone to hack into our account. Next time you do that, you may want to hire someone we're not already friends with.

Consider this your last warning. Should you continue looking for us, we'll be forced to do something that we don't like doing: killing innocent people. We'll do it if we have to, but that decision is yours to make.

Sincerely,
American Hitmen

P.S. We're typing this from your piece of shit computer. Why don't you take some of those bitcoins you have and buy a nice, new stolen computer?

Greg regretted letting Shane read the email with him. He wanted to be alone now to think about the death threat and what he should do. Shane eased the tension.

"Dude." Shane laughed as he said it. "You're fuckin' with some serious loony tunes!" He gave Greg a hard hit on the shoulder.

Greg gave a forced smile, but inside, he was terrified.

"What are you going to do now?" Shane said.

"I don't know." Greg then read the email again and took a picture of the message with his phone.

"Whad'ya do that for?"

"I want evidence of the email, but I don't want to forward it to my Google address. A wise man once told me not to trust that company."

"Good thinking. Yeah, fuck them. And fuck these *American Hitmen* guys, too. You want my help? I've got your back, bro. I'm not a killer, but if it comes down to saving my good pal, well, I'll do what I gotta do."

"Thanks, I appreciate it."

Greg knew the polite thing to say would be "thanks, but no thanks," but he couldn't bring himself to say it.

Truth was, he needed help.

Wanted help.

He'd just gotten started and had already almost gotten himself killed. He pictured himself sitting on the couch, the front door bursting open, and getting shot. How was he supposed to sleep now, knowing that they knew where he lived? The answer was he couldn't.

He closed the tab with Anonymail, and the *American Hitmen* site came back onto the screen. Without much thought, he scrolled down to the bottom of the page. Shane hadn't seen all of the victims, and Greg was curious if any more were added.

When he got to the bottom, he couldn't believe what he saw.

On the left, there was a picture of himself.

Underneath it, the words "Better stop, or you're next."

Deep Web

Chapter 20

Greg closed Tor and walked out of Shane's office without uttering a word. He rushed to the nearest bathroom, went to one of the empty stalls, and sat down.

Nervous sweat soaked through his business suit.

As far as he knew, he was the only one in the bathroom. He felt an intense pain in his chest.

Seeing his picture on the site had him scared for his life. But he'd asked for this. He'd provoked them and was trying to discover their identity. Now, they'd hit him with a punch of their own. He foolishly hadn't been expecting it.

But they had, and he needed to man up.

If it were a normal day, he'd stay in the bathroom longer to unwind. Today, though, he had three days' worth of work to get done. There was a presentation that needed researched, and there was no way he could put it off. Of all days to have something like that happen, why did it have to be today?

He stepped out of the stall and looked at himself in the bathroom mirror. He hated the person he saw. It was a dressed-up corporate man who'd gone nowhere during his first five years in the workforce. He was accomplishing nothing in his life. Had just lost his sister. And was now being forced to give up the biggest lead he'd found to date.

He walked out of the bathroom, feeling as bad as when he'd entered.

He got back to his desk and buried himself in his work. All he needed to do was finish the presentation. The other items Bob had given him could wait until tomorrow. He'd have to lie and say they were done. Bob wouldn't have any way of knowing that they weren't. That plan eased some of Greg's stress, but he still had the presentation to do, which would take him the rest of the day.

He worked through lunch, something he'd never done before. He was making incredible progress and knew that if he kept going, he may get it all wrapped up much sooner than he'd expected. If he took a break now, he'd never get back into the flow that he was in.

He was getting through the last twenty percent of the slides when an intruder came up behind him. Greg figured it would be Bob, but it was Shane.

"Sup. How's that presentation coming along?"

"Good. What's up?"

"Nothing. Just wanted to see how you were doing."

"I'm fine. I really just want to get this thing finished up so that I won't have to work overtime."

"I see. Hey, I was talking to some of the sales guys at lunch. If there's anything you need, man, don't hesitate to ask."

"Did you tell them about what I showed you at lunch?"

"Well——"

"Shane! Dude, that stuff is private. Top secret information."

"Relax. I only told them you found your sister's picture online. I didn't say anything about the emails and stuff you got. I'm sorry, man. I had to tell someone. This is crazy shit you've gotten into."

"Please, please don't say anything else to anyone."

"All right, all right," Shane said, waving his hands in surrender. "Seriously, though. If you need anything, anything at all, let me know."

"I appreciate it."

They bumped fists, and Shane walked away.

Greg was upset that Shane had told others about this, but he knew it was only because Shane had a big heart and wanted to help.

He couldn't be too mad at him for that.

Greg got back to work and wrapped up the rest of the presentation. It was far from his best work, and he'd cut several corners to get it done, but he read through it and thought it was more than satisfactory.

He grinned at his accomplishment. This was something that usually would have taken him three days to complete. But instead, he got it all done in less than one. If Bob asked, Greg had already thought to lie and say he'd done all the research while he was at home sick. He also wouldn't tell Bob that it was finished until the second he walked out the door.

It was three in the afternoon, so he still had a couple hours left. Greg decided to go back to the bathroom so he could be alone with his thoughts.

It wasn't the first time he'd gone to the bathroom just to get away. It was his way of taking a break without appearing lazy in front of Bob or other management that walked by. He found himself using the stall any time he was depressed. Before, it was about work, but for the past month, it was usually about Jessica.

As he sat there, he remembered that he needed to respond to James. He'd said he checked his Facebook once a day at 4. He needed to send something soon; otherwise, he'd waste a full day.

He hated typing on tiny keyboards, which was why he normally used the voice command to send messages.

Hey James,
No, they don't know who killed Jessica. The police have given up on the case. It'll only be reopened if they get new information. The detective told me that they've investigated every lead but have come up with nothing.
Just curious, when was the last time you saw Jessica? Did you two ever keep in touch after you broke up? I never asked her, because I didn't want to upset her by bringing your name up. Hope you understand that, but I was/am curious.
Also, do you ever make it home? It looks like you love it there, but I didn't know if you ever came home or traveled elsewhere for vacations or something.
Anyway, just let me know. It's good to be able to talk with you after these past few years. I was disappointed when you and Jessica split up, because I thought you were a really great guy for her.

Look forward to hearing back,
Greg

He read his message over a few times. He wished he could be on his computer, where it was much easier to edit and perfect the message. But it was too late now. Besides, he wasn't as confident as Shane when it came to using the Internet for personal reasons. Everyone in the company knew that the computers were hooked up to the company network, which meant that IT could look up anyone's history whenever they wanted to. Greg thought they'd easily be able to tell that Shane was using Tor, although, they may not know where he went after he signed into it. It was one thing for Shane to do it; he was a top-notch salesman and indispensable to the company. Greg, on the other hand, was easily replaceable.

His message answered all of James' questions. Greg figured James would have liked a more detailed response, but he strategically was being vague about what he knew.

Greg's questions were asked to accomplish one thing:

To make James admit he'd been in Columbus and had met with Jessica.

If he could do that, then he could hammer him with other questions about what happened between them. He made a couple tweaks and brushed up his sentences before sending. If James had been honest about his schedule, he'd hopefully get a response back soon.

The last thing he wanted to do while he was in there was message his mom. While he wasn't about to do any more snooping into *American Hitmen* or use *Hacking4Hire* ever again, he was still very curious about Jessica's email account. On the slim chance that her phone still worked, he could gain access and potentially get some new answers.

Also, he was short a laptop. He was going to see if they had Jessica's old one. He wasn't going to tell them his apartment had been broken into; he didn't want to worry them. But it would be nice to get a new laptop without having to pay for one.

He messaged his mom, asking if he could come over for dinner. Greg stared at his phone waiting for her response. She responded back with "Of course!" and he was in.

***

He was starving when he left the bathroom, so he grabbed a Three Musketeers bar and potato chips from the vending machine. He imagined Jessica watching over him and shaking her head at the junk food.

He took his time getting back to his desk. His plan was to pretend to work for the rest of the day, but after looking at the checklist of items that Bob had sent him, one of the tasks was pretty simple, so he got to work on it. It was a good distraction that prevented him from checking Facebook every five minutes to see if James had responded. Greg stuffed his phone in his desk to help keep his mind off of the temptation.

Before he knew it, it was five o'clock, and he could call it a day and spend the next hour driving through rush hour traffic to his parents' house.

The ride over wasn't as bad as Greg expected. Evidently, the outer belt going south to his parents' wasn't as bad as the internal roads he had to take every day back to his apartment.

When he got there, his dad was on the couch watching TV while his mom was in the kitchen making dinner.

"Smells like mom's favorite pasta," Greg said.

"Of course, did you expect anything less?" his mom asked.

After some quick small talk, Greg's mom told him that dinner would be ready in twenty minutes. It was the perfect opportunity to break away and go upstairs.

He always liked going up to his old room when he was home. Most of his stuff was gone, but the memories of growing up were still there.

Today, he skipped over his room and went directly to Jessica's. Her room was much different, with several boxes of stuff everywhere. It was yet another reminder of what had happened. How the world had been turned upside down for not just Greg but his parents, too.

He didn't have much time, so he went through boxes looking for her phone, computer, and anything else of interest. The first few boxes were filled with shoes and clothes.

Greg moved to the boxes on the floor. The first one he opened made him tear up almost instantly. On top was a framed picture of Jessica and him at the beach. The border of the frame said "Sibs." He'd never seen it before but assumed this box contained her things from work. There was another framed picture of the whole family. And one with her sorority sisters from college. Then, at the bottom, not in a frame, was a picture of her and who Greg recognized as Daniel Kavern, the CEO of her company.

They were standing together, dressed in formal business clothes, at a conference. Greg really focused in on the picture and at the expressions on their face. He didn't like seeing them together. Not one bit. Again, he didn't know why, but there was something about Daniel Kavern that he just didn't like.

The next box he opened contained the jackpot. The entire thing was filled with Jessica's tech gadgets. At the top were various charging cords, neatly rolled up and twist-tied together. Jessica's phone was there, sitting in its case.

He picked it up and saw that it was turned off. He held down the power button but nothing happened.

It didn't surprise him. The battery had likely died, and the phone needed at least some juice before it would even turn on. He shuffled through the box until he found the cord. He plugged it into the electric outlet that was beside him and continued going through the box.

He picked up a small, black box, about the size of a men's wallet. Greg wasn't sure what it was. He read the back and saw the label: "Expansion Portable Drive." He then saw the storage size——1TB——and understood that it was an external hard drive.

Interesting.

There was a lot of potential for the content it contained.

At the bottom of the box was a gray laptop case. He reached in and pulled out the silver Macbook Air. He couldn't believe how light the thing was. He didn't pick his laptop up often, but he knew it weighed at least three or four times more than the Apple laptop.

He opened the lid and pushed the power button, but again, it didn't turn on. So he shuffled through the box again and plugged the correct cord into the wall.

While he waited for the devices to charge, he looked through the rest of the boxes.

He opened up her closet and saw all of her formal business clothes. He took out one of the jackets and checked the pockets. Nothing.

He went through the pockets of all the hanging clothes. Near the end was a jacket that looked like the jacket she was wearing in the picture with Daniel. He reached inside and felt his hand hit something. It was paper of some kind. Greg pulled it out, eager to see what it was. It was the pamphlet for James' AFTA Conference.

It was the jacket she was wearing the night she was with James!

He flipped through the pamphlet. It was everything that he'd assumed, based on their conversations with each other and what he'd researched online. It was a basic fundraising event where multiple charities presented their particular causes in the hopes of getting funding.

He took the jacket out and placed it on her bed. He checked

the other pockets, but there was nothing else inside. Greg took a step back, soaking in one of the last things she ever wore. It reminded him that he was waiting on a Facebook message from James. He likely would have responded by now.

He pulled out his phone, but just as he was about to log onto Facebook, he looked up and saw his dad standing at the door.

"Whatcha doin' there, son?"

"Jesus!" Greg shouted.

"Sorry, didn't mean to scare you."

"I've just been looking through Jessica's stuff, seeing if I could use any of it."

"Of course, take what you need. We still haven't decided what were going to do with it. I see you found her electronic stuff."

"Yeah... think I'll take that back with me."

"Sure, go for it. Why do you have this here?" He was referring to the jacket on the bed.

"I found this in one of the pockets. She must have worn this the night before she was murdered." Greg showed his dad the pamphlet. "Did you know she attended this event?"

"Hmm," his dad said, looking through it. "No, I did not. Interesting to know, though. Might want to let the police know about it. You think maybe someone at the event may have done this to Jess?"

"I don't know," Greg said. "Could have been. It says one of the presenters is James." Greg pointed to the familiar name on the back page.

"Really?" Greg's dad said, surprised. "James would never do something like that to Jessica; he was a fine young man."

"Maybe... but it does seem odd that he happened to be in the country the night before she was murdered, speaking at an event that it looked like Jessica attended."

"Doesn't seem that strange."

"Well… maybe it isn't."

Greg felt the uncomfortable stare from this father.

"I do remember the detective saying the smallest breakthroughs can lead to solving a case, though." He handed the pamphlet back to Greg. "Little things like this could piece that mystery back together."

"Indeed it could," Greg said.

"Come on. Dinner's ready."

"Okay."

"Do me a favor. Don't tell your mother about this."

"I won't. I know she doesn't want to hear anything about the investigation."

"No, she certainly does not. I don't know why you want all of her electronic junk, but when she asks, I'd suggest you think of a good reason. I'd never condone lying, Greg, but——" He paused for a moment, looking at Greg. "Sometimes it's best if your mother doesn't know everything." He gave Greg a wink and smiled.

Greg laughed.

"All right, Dad. Thanks."

They went downstairs, where mom's famous pasta was waiting for them.

Chapter 21

After dinner, Greg ran back upstairs to Jessica's room. He'd managed to work into the dinner conversation that he needed Jessica's laptop because "...work has some new software that only worked on Macs."

It was the perfect excuse.

He didn't have an excuse for taking the phone. He just slipped it into the box and hoped that his mom didn't ask questions. And she didn't.

Greg was afraid to go back to his apartment. It was, after all, the location of a theft and an attempted murder, had he been there.

But he figured that if the sociopaths really wanted to find him, then they wouldn't have any trouble figuring out where his parents lived, so he was just as unsafe there.

He could stay at a hotel, but it would only keep him safe temporarily. He was getting short on funds, too. He might as well face his fear and go back to his apartment while hoping for the best.

He checked Facebook on his phone, but there were no notifications. He viewed his messages anyway, hoping there was a glitch. When he scrolled to the bottom of his conversation with James, though, there were no new messages.

He re-read what James had said about when he'd get in touch. It re-confirmed that he'd said he only had Internet access at "4 PM EST". Greg's message has been delivered at 3:10 PM EST. He figured James might have gotten excited and left earlier, before Greg had sent his message. Greg had wanted to send it earlier, but discovering that he had become the newest poster boy on the *American Hitmen* site had caused a delay.

He put the laptop and charger into the box. He could play with it later. As for the phone, that couldn't wait. He held the power button down and watched it boot up. If the phone worked, he'd be able to use the phone verification to access her emails.

Jessica didn't like calling people on the phone. The police had questioned everyone she'd spoken to, and they all checked out okay. At least, according to Detective Maxwell.

Once the smartphone loaded, Greg waited for the signal to appear, but it never did. Instead, "No Service" appeared in the corner.

"Damn it," he muttered to himself. He thought that the phone would have been provided the perfect solution when it came to conducting investigative work that didn't involve anything that *American Hitmen* would be aware of.

Instead, it was yet another chance that he was missing out on.

Still, he put the phone and charger into the box and closed the lid.

He carried the box downstairs and put it in the trunk of his car while his mom was still in the kitchen cleaning.

Greg stayed to chat for another thirty minutes. His mom asked him how he and Stacy were, and he said fine.

He didn't know what the truth was. She could be on top of Jimmy right now, as far as he knew.

He kissed them goodbye, eager now to get home and see if there was anything on Jessica's laptop. He needed something good to happen, because today had been filled with nothing but disappointment and death threats.

On the way home, he got a phone call. It range several times before he was able to grab it from his pocket.

He checked and saw that it was a local number that he didn't recognize. It wasn't from Utah, which was where most of the telemarketer calls he received were based.

Greg never answered calls from numbers that didn't belong to his list of contacts, but he made an exception this time.

He had a feeling that this call was important.

He touched the screen to accept the call, but right as he did, they hung up.

"Damn it!"

He had the entire ride home to wonder who it had been. Every local that he knew would be in his contacts.

When he got home, it was getting dark. He was feeling nervous about being back in his apartment. He regretted not staying at a hotel. *Face your fears*. He got the box of Jessica's stuff out of his trunk and went upstairs.

When he got to his floor, the hallway was again dark. With his free hand, he tried the door and found it locked. It was relieving, but it didn't necessarily mean that they hadn't come back and waited for him inside. He opened the door and flicked on the light. His heart picked up as he looked into his quiet, empty apartment.

He put the box down on the counter and inspected the house again. He wouldn't be able to think straight until he knew he was alone.

He'd gone through everything and was finishing up checking the bathroom when he heard a noise come from the living room. It was his phone. He *had* received a voice message.

He pushed play, anxious to hear who it was from:

"Greg Anderson?" an unfamiliar male voice began. "This is Daniel Kavern, CEO of Adriar Pharmaceuticals, and former boss of your sister, Jessica. I have some business I'd like to discuss with you, which I'd rather not do over the phone. If you can, please meet me tomorrow at 10 AM at my office. Just give the attendant your name and tell her that you're here to see me. Thanks. I'll see you tomorrow."

Greg smiled. Daniel Kavern, who he suspected had information critical to the case, had called *him*. He didn't need to have another run-in with the security guard. He could have waited it out.

There were two big questions floating through Greg's mind: *What* did Daniel want to tell him, and why *now*? Greg tried to put himself in Daniel's shoes. A big, successful CEO who, a month before, found out one of his employees had been murdered. He stayed quiet, never talking to the family. But now, on a random weekday, more than a month after the murder, he found the phone number for her brother and asked to meet him.

It didn't make sense.

He played back the message again, hearing the *"I have some business I'd like to discuss with you, which I'd rather not do over the phone."*

Greg deduced that something had happened recently;

otherwise, Daniel Kavern would have no reason to call.

He never considered whether he should go or not.

The moment he heard the message, he knew he was going. What he'd tell Bob, he didn't know, but he didn't care.

Even if Bob fired him.

It wouldn't be the worst thing in the world. He could find out who murdered his sister much faster if he dedicated all of his time to the investigation. And the sooner he found out, the sooner he could move on with this life.

He still couldn't believe that Daniel freakin' Kavern had called him. What an unexpected turn of events. There was no way he'd be able to sleep with thoughts of the meeting looming in his mind. Every scenario played through his head.

How much should he tell Daniel?

What parts should he leave out?

It would depend on how the conversation went and the reason that Daniel wanted him there.

Greg reminded himself again of James's words to Jessica. He didn't like her company and told her to leave. Greg had never told Jessica to her face, but he hadn't liked that she had to keep her work so secret. So, in a way, he was on James' side and wished she'd left, too.

Before the meeting, he would need to come up with a list of questions for Daniel, starting with what exactly they did there.

Thinking of James, Greg checked his phone again, hoping to have a message waiting for him, but there was nothing. He must have missed him. By that time, in Africa, it was the middle of the night. Greg figured he should stop wasting his time by expecting a reply at the late hour; it wasn't going to happen.

He decided to call into work again. He knew it would be more realistic to phone in sick the morning of, but he also knew his chances of Bob answering were much lower at night. His colleagues knew that Bob didn't like to bring his work home. He was a good, wholesome Christian man who believed in family values and not working too hard.

Greg grabbed his phone and dialed. It rang once. Twice. He was rehearsing the message in his head. Short and sweet.

"Hello."

Greg paused, not knowing what to say.

"Hello." Bob's voice said again.

"Hey… Bob! It's me, Greg."

"Hey Greg, what can I do for you?" Bob said, a hint of surprise in his voice.

"I just wanted to let you know I won't be in the office tomorrow. I've got a doctor's appointment tomorrow morning. I might be able to come in the afternoon if you need me to, but if it's all right, I'd rather just take a whole day."

"Greg—", Bob said, "how's come you didn't tell me about this sooner?"

"Sorry, my doctor is hard to get into. They just called and said that an opening came up."

"I see. Well, what time is your appointment?"

"Ten."

"Okay, I was going to tell you in the morning, but we've got another pitch for some investors on Thursday morning. I'd really love to have you on it. We're low on resources with Dave and Johnny being out. Do you think you could put in some evening hours to get it done?"

The last thing Greg wanted to do was work in the evening, but what choice did he have?

"Sure, I'll do my best."

"Thanks," Bob said, relieved. "I really need some of your best work on this. This quarter isn't looking too great right now. We're probably not going to hit our numbers."

"That sucks," Greg said, trying to make it sound like he cared. "I'll do my best to help get things turned around." Again, he didn't really feel that way. He'd been in the corporate world long enough to know some of the bullshit that had to be said to make the bosses happy.

"Good, glad to hear it! See you tomorrow afternoon. Hope your doctor's visit goes well."

"Thanks. See ya."

Greg hung up, making a mental note to never call Bob in the evening again. He had managed to get the morning off, so he was set to attend his appointment with Daniel. He had a few hours of prep work to do, so he grabbed Jessica's laptop out of the box.

He turned it on from his kitchen counter and was surprised at how quickly it booted up.

A popup came up, which gave Greg a sinking feeling in his stomach.

It was password protected.

He tried *Tw!nbr0gr3g.*

Password failed. Please try again.

"Shit!" He hadn't expected an issue like this to come up. He thought about what some of the other passwords might be. He tried every Greg Anderson combination he could think of, but none of them worked.

He worried that he would only be allowed a certain amount of attempts. He figured there probably was, but that was a risk he'd have to take.

He needed to get inside this computer.

He then thought about all the other possible password combinations. Nicknames she'd had. For a while in middle school, kids called her "Tissue," because during a three-hour test, she had the worst cold ever and blew her nose every five minutes. Her desk had been covered in tissues, and the name stuck longer than it should have.

Greg tried several combination possibilities, but none of them worked. He then remembered that her volleyball number had been four and her soccer number was two, so he tried all the previous passwords with two and four appended to them.

He guessed for an entire hour, trying different things from her life.

Nothing was working. He had to stop himself, thinking there had to be a better way to get into it. There was some way to gain access; he knew that. If someone could hack into an email address so easily, surely getting through the password protection of a computer was doable, too.

He could research that tomorrow when he was at work.

With nothing else to do, he checked his phone yet again. James still hadn't replied. It didn't make sense. He'd been so enthused after hearing from Greg, and he'd been close to Jessica. As close as two people could get.

James not responding seemed suspicious. Was he still deciding what he would and wouldn't tell Greg about that night? If so, Greg would get that information out of him one way or another. If he had to fly all the way to Africa to find out what had happened between them the night before her murder, he'd do it.

With nothing better to do, he watched some mindless TV. He wanted to talk with Stacy but felt as though the ball was clearly in her court. He'd given her flowers. That deserved a phone call, he thought. Unless…

Unless Jimmy hadn't given them to her.

Of course! Why would he? If he was sleeping with her, he'd hardly have the desire to hand the girl flowers from her poor, pathetic boyfriend.

Greg picked up the phone and called her. He knew she wasn't working, so there was no reason for her not to answer. It rang five times before her voicemail came on. He wanted to leave a message but knew he'd regret whatever he said.

He tried again.

Carrie had been like that——calling over and over again until he picked up. He remembered checking his phone once and seeing sixteen missed calls from her. She was one lunatic of a woman. Whoever ended up stuck with her would have their hands full.

As it rang, he hoped Jimmy wouldn't pick up. He just wasn't in the mood.

After three rings, she answered.

"Hey." It was quick, brief. The kind of greeting that a girl gave when she was mad.

"Hey," Greg said sincerely.

There was nothing but silence. A phone conversation that was already at a standstill after the opening greeting.

Those were never good.

Stacy broke the silence, as she always did, "Thank you for the flowers."

Her gratitude should have made Greg happy, but instead, he was upset that she hadn't called immediately to thank him.

"No prob."

Again, more silence. Their relationship was at a critical point. The moment, those seconds in time, could be the deciding factor between a breakup and a long, happy life together.

Greg couldn't hold back his frustration any more. "I don't understand why *you* are upset."

"Me? You lied to me, Greg."

"Yeah, well, it wasn't even a big lie. So I stayed home and

didn't tell you. Big whoop."

"It's not what you lied about; it's that you did. I thought you weren't like that, Greg."

"Yeah, well, I'm going through a lot right now. I've got fucking death threats coming my way. I'm not exactly in the right frame of mind."

"Death threats? What are you talking about? Who's threatening you?"

Greg hadn't meant to say it. He'd forgotten that Stacy didn't have this key piece of information. "The people that killed Jessica. They're coming after me."

"How do you know that?"

"Oh, I don't know, they broke into my place last night and stole my laptop. Then today, I saw that they posted my picture on their website and said I was next. Little things like that," he said sarcastically. Again, he couldn't believe he was spilling all this information to her. He hadn't planned on telling her any of it, because he knew how she felt about his criminal investigation work.

"Greg, are you serious? Did you call the police?"

"Yeah, I'm serious. And no, I didn't. They aren't going to do anything about it."

"What are you talking about? They broke into your place. Stolen property, death threat online. I think that warrants attention. I don't care how busy they are."

"You don't get it, Stacy. I get the feeling that the chief wants nothing to do with this case. He's an old fart, after all. The thought of dealing with a case the involves something from the 21st century probably confuses him to no end."

"But you said that Detective Maxwell guy offered to help."

"Yeah, well I'm starting to lose faith in him, too. He told me he has too many things on his plate."

"That doesn't matter. If he knew what had happened, he might be able to help. You need to call him. Come over to my place and then call him."

"I'm not going to do that. I don't want to put you in danger. Finding Jessica's murderer is something I have to do. No one else is going to help. I'm going to find them or die trying. There's no other way to put it."

"I don't want anything to happen to you, though."

"Why do you care? You know, it hasn't been brought up yet, but do you want to tell me who that Jimmy guy is?"

"Jimmy?"

"Yeah, the shirtless, buff model that answered your door when I came over."

"I didn't realize he was there."

"What do you mean you didn't realize he was there? How do you think the flowers got into your apartment?"

"I never lock my door. You didn't know that?"

"No."

"You haven't noticed that I never get my keys out when we go inside?"

"No, I haven't. Can we get to the point?"

"Jimmy is a friend, that's all."

"A friend? Really?" Greg started laughing. "And I'm supposed to believe that?"

"Yeah, you are."

"And why is that?"

"I don't know. Because you trust me."

"Right. Look, we've been together over a month, Stacy, and I feel like I hardly even know you. You never tell me anything about yourself."

"I'm sorry? I'm not a person that likes talking about her childhood. I grew up on a farm. I milked cows and raised chickens——not exactly every guy's dream girl."

"You know that I love that about you. I like that you grew up on a farm. It makes you unique. What I don't know is who Jimmy is and why he hangs out at your place. Just tell me if you two are sleeping together. That's all I want to know."

"No, we're not. I'd never do that to you, Greg. Never."

"And again, how or why am I supposed to believe——"

"Because he's GAY! All right? Gay! He's my gay friend, Jimmy, who I've lived next door to for two years now. We hang out. He likes to come over and eat my food. I like to talk to him about how much grad school sucks and my periods. He makes me laugh at all of his big, gay problems. It's a win-win for us both. There. Are you happy?"

Greg had never felt like more of a jerk in his life. He had no reason not to trust Stacy, and he wished he'd thought about that for even a second before coming out and accusing her. She'd never forgive him for that. He'd taken what began as a minor screw-up——lying to her——and made it ten times worse.

"I——" he began. "I'm sorry."

"It's fine," Stacy said.

It didn't sound like she was fine.

"I really am sorry. I've been stupid. I'm just so stressed right now."

"You have been stupid, but it's all right," Stacy said. "Greg, I think it'd be best if we take a little break. It'll give us some time to cool off and think things over."

"Yeah, maybe we should," Greg said, thinking that a "break" was just her polite way of telling him that they were finished. With that thought in mind, he thought he'd better extract as much information out of her as he could before it was too late. "Can I ask you something? Something unrelated."

"Sure."

"This job that Jessica was going to get you. What all did it involve?"

"She wouldn't tell me, said it was a secret but that it was a good opportunity."

"Do you know much about the company she worked at?"

"No, not really. Only that they sell pharmaceuticals or something like that. I wasn't really sure that I wanted the job, but I felt obligated to at least go to the interview since she was going to set it up."

"I see."

"Why are you asking me this?"

"Because I'm meeting with the CEO tomorrow. I don't know much about the company, either. Was hoping you did."

"You're taking another day off?" she asked, bewildered.

"Yeah, I am. I'm going to find out who did this, and I have a hunch that Daniel, their CEO, knows something."

"Well, good luck to you," Stacy said insincerely.

"Thanks."

"I'll see you, Greg. Take care of yourself."

"All right, see ya." And they hung up the phone.

Greg wondered if that was the last time that he'd speak to Stacy. He thought about the week and how his researching had resulted in a serious death threat. And now, he'd taken all of his frustration out on Stacy and likely ended a potentially great long-term relationship.

This had already been a costly endeavor, and he'd only gotten started.

The right thing to do was to go to work tomorrow and tell Bob he'd canceled his appointment. To forget about his meeting with Daniel and go back to a regular life.

If he did that and forgot about Jessica's murderer for a while, then maybe he could make things right with Stacy.

That was the smart play.

The right one.

He couldn't bring himself to do it, though. He felt like he was getting really close to finding out who had ordered the hit, and he was unrolling the mask behind *American Hitmen*.

Tomorrow was a big day; he could feel it.

And how right he was.

Chapter 22

Greg woke up in the middle of the night.

He'd heard a sound, a loud creak that normally he wouldn't think twice about, but not after a day where he'd received a death threat.

Now, even the tiniest sound in the apartment kicked Greg's flight-or-fight response into gear.

In the morning, he was tired, but that was something three cups of coffee could fix. He only drank coffee in emergency situations, where he was too tired to think but had a busy day ahead. Today was one of those days.

Before his coffee, he poured his cereal and watched his SportsCenter. He wasn't paying any attention to the TV but having it on helped calm him down.

He grabbed his phone, not thinking much as he opened up Facebook until he saw the red message notification. He perked up, opening it to see that James had finally sent him a reply. Before reading it, he scrolled down and saw that it was a really long message.

Hey Greg,

Sorry I'm late in getting back to you. An emergency situation went down at the camp, and I had to take care of it.

As to your questions, yes, I have met with Jessica recently. It looks like the night before she was murdered, too. In pains me to say it, but it's the truth.

Just to give you a little background, the Sumami camp where I work is funded by investors. We present annually at locations in the U.S. to make our pitch, explain what we're doing and why we should continue to receive funding. This year's event was in Columbus.

So I hit up Jessica on Facebook, and we met for lunch when I got in. Everything was great. Looks-wise, she hadn't changed a bit. Her personality seemed mostly the same, except maybe a little more serious and business-oriented. Which was fine; that's to be expected, I guess.

She told me she'd been keeping up with my work and had spoken with her boss, who was the CEO, and convinced him to have the company make a donation. I wasn't expecting any of this from her. And I didn't want to get my hopes up too much, but by the way she was talking, it sounded like a done deal.

Then, the night of the conference, she introduced me to her boss, and we chatted for a few minutes beforehand. I did my presentation. All was fine and normal until the networking event afterwards. I approached a couple of my past investors, and they seemed eerily quiet around me, like they didn't want to speak with me. Finally, after mingling with another reliable investor, I asked him outright what was going on and why everyone was acting strange.

That's when he handed me a brochure. It wasn't the official brochure; it was something that I hadn't seen before. It was a charitable organization analysis, a ten-page document that featured all kinds of statistics, charts, and that sort of thing. The analysis was sponsored by Jessica's company. I read through it as fast as I could and saw that, according to their analysis, we ranked dead last in nearly every category. The most important international NGO categories, our ratings were dismal.

All of this, if it had been factual, wouldn't have bothered me. If other organizations were doing better work, then I'd sleep easy, knowing that the right causes were getting funding.

Problem was, the report was a complete lie. I'd done the numbers a dozen times. I've never done any shady practices to get funding, but according to their analysis, we'd basically been using all of the funding on ourselves.

By the time I discovered the brochure, Jessica and her business partner had left. I did everything I could to reach out to her, but she ignored my calls. I even found out from your parents where she lived and stopped by, but she wasn't home. I didn't speak to Jessica again and still have no idea why her company did that.

This past month has been very tough. Without our funding, we may not make it another two months, and the people here desperately need our support. I can't stop thinking about that night. I called her repeatedly and sent her Facebook messages, but I never get a response. Now I guess know why.

I realize this might make me sound guilty, considering what happened, but I assure you Greg, I had nothing to do with Jessica's murder, if that's what you are thinking. I'd never do something like that to anyone, no matter how angry I was with them.

If you can make sense of any of this, please let me know. And if there's any way I can help or if you have any thoughts to share, I'd love to hear them.

Thanks,
James

Greg's first impression was that it sounded very authentic. He hadn't told James that he'd read through all of his Facebook messages to Jessica. Everything from his story fell in line with what he'd told his sister on Facebook.

If James was, in fact, telling the truth, then he was completely and utterly shocked by Jessica's actions.

Why would she do such a thing?

Why would she stab James in the back like that and provide false information about him?

She'd been upset that they split; that was understandable. But Jessica wasn't the jealous, bitter type. From what Greg knew about her, she'd never do something like that. Someone else had to have been pulling the strings. There was one person that it was likely to be, and Greg had a meeting with him in a little more than three hours.

Greg dressed up this time. He wasn't going to go there looking like a slacker again.

The parking lot was again busy, and he parked in the same empty spot by the pond. As he walked to the front entrance, all he could think about was the security guard. He wasn't too concerned about going face-to-face with Daniel, the CEO multi-millionaire. It was the potential confrontation with the guard that had him worried. Did Daniel really set up a meeting? And if so, was the meeting on the guard's list? If either of those weren't true, then Greg didn't want to know how the guard would handle his second visit.

He opened the door and walked in. The guard, the same one as before, was there to greet him.

"Can I do something for you, sir?"

"Yes, I have a meeting with Daniel Kavern at ten."

The guard stared at Greg, as if he was trying to detect any signs of nervousness or lying. Greg was plenty nervous. But lying, he was not.

He looked down at his clipboard, moving his finger across the front page. He then flipped to another page, again moving his finger. When he moved on to the third page, Greg was beginning to doubt that Daniel had added him to the list.

"Ahh, here it is. Ten. Daniel Kavern's office. Reason for meeting undisclosed."

Greg was relieved. He felt like half the battle was already won. Now it was time to meet Daniel.

"Check in at the front desk," the guard said.

Greg took a step forward towards the woman at the reception desk; it was a different woman, a brunette around his age.

As he did, the guard grabbed his bicep.

"Hey, don't I know you from somewhere?"

"Me… umm… I was here before. I didn't have an appointment so you sent me away."

"Right, oh yeah. I take it you took my advice?" he said with a grin.

Greg laughed. "Yeah, I guess so."

"Good." He slapped Greg on the back. "Enjoy your visit."

Greg walked up to front desk, a newfound confidence in his steps.

"Hi, I'm here to see Daniel Kavern," he said, standing taller than he usually did. He thought the fact that he was meeting with the CEO might impress this woman.

She looked at the paper calendar that was in front of her. "Right, got it right here. What you'll want to do is head down that hallway." She pointed with a pen in her hand. "There will be an elevator. Another guard will be standing there, you'll need to hand him this." She began writing something down on a yellow slip of paper.

Greg felt like he was in middle school again, getting a hall pass so that he could use the bathroom.

She handed it to him. "He'll tell you what to do from there."

"Thank you. I appreciate it," Greg said as he gave her a wink.

As he walked around the corner, he looked down at the note. There were lines designated for things like names, times, and reasons for appointments, but the woman hadn't filled any of them out. Instead, in big letters, she had written "CJ" and "DK1." Greg presumed that D and K were Daniel's initials. He didn't know what the number value meant. Probably code for something.

When he turned the corner, he saw a towering black man, with a commanding posture and crossed arms, standing in front of an elevator. The hallway was small, and again, it didn't seem to fit make sense, given the huge scale of the building. Greg was nervous as he walked up to the man.

"Hi. I'm supposed to give you this."

The guard took it, and Greg noticed the scowl on his face. He decided that the guards weren't big on making a friendly first impression.

He pushed the elevator button behind him. While he waited for the door to open, he said, "You're here to see Daniel Kavern? Is this correct?"

"Yes, it is."

"Reason for visit?"

"Uhh, he invited me. Said he wanted to speak with me about something."

"He did not indicate what that something was?"

"No, sir." Greg thought about mentioning that his sister used to work there, but he decided it was best to say as little as possible.

Fortunately, the elevator opened, and the guard motioned for him to enter. Greg stepped in, and the guard joined him. He watched as the man took a key from his pocket and inserted it into a keyhole before pushing the button for the top floor, level 20.

The door closed, and they began to go up. Greg was uncomfortable with being enclosed in a tight space with the man; he had the largest biceps that he'd ever seen in person. Greg felt as though this man could break him in half, if he wanted to, without much effort.

The door opened seconds later, and Greg wondered if they'd made a stop along the way. However, he quickly noticed the number "20" outside of the elevator door. The elevator was just that fast.

When he stepped out, he immediately observed that the place was immaculate. Glass windows surrounded the entire floor. He remembered that, from the outside, they were so darkly tinted that it was impossible to see inside. But from on the inside, he could barely detect any tint and natural light flooded in. It was much different than his office, which had no windows and, instead, was filled with artificial florescent lighting.

He only had a moment to peek to the left, where there were several high-standing cubicles. He didn't see a single person when he looked over. He didn't have any more time for inspection, though, because the guard was leading him to the right. He saw a narrow hallway, which led to a large wooden door. The door stuck out because everything else he could see on the floor was made from glass or metal.

"Mr. Kavern's office is the door in front of you. Please proceed."

Greg looked up at the guard, who was looking back down at him, expressionless. Greg wondered if the man could see the terror in his eyes; it matched what he was feeling on the inside. The guard waited by the elevator and watched as Greg made his way towards the door.

Greg took a few deep breaths, trying to help himself calm down. This was the moment that he'd been waiting for. The moment that he hoped and believed would lead to finding Jessica's murderer.

On the outside of the door, a gold rectangular sign that read, "Daniel Kavern, CEO" in thin, black letters. It looked trendy and professional.

He knocked on the door and waited.

"Come in," a man shouted from inside.

Greg took one last deep breath and entered.

Chapter 23

Daniel's office had huge windows that made up three sides of the room. On the right side of the space were four leather chairs that had been positioned around a small table; it was a place where important people could smoke their cigars and have important business discussions.

At the end of the room, opposite from where Greg was standing, there was a massive desk. It had the dark, polished wood that one would expect an important CEO to have.

Standing behind the desk, watching Greg observe the office, was Daniel Kavern.

He looked older than he had in most of the pictures Greg had seen of him; it made sense, considering a lot of the articles that Greg had read online were from ten or fifteen years prior.

Daniel smiled at him and adjusted his light green tie. He then said, "Well, hello. Greg, I presume?"

"Yes."

"Good of you to come. You seem to be taking an interest in the office. Do you like?"

"It's quite nice. The view is incredible."

It was.

Downtown Columbus could be seen in the distance. The

heart of downtown, where all of the tallest buildings were, was less than a mile away.

Daniel walked around his desk to shake Greg's hand. They both walked over to the window for a better look.

"Many moons ago, I used to work in that office over there. The tallest one, with the antenna sticking from the top," Daniel said, pointing. "I was just a teenager. I thought it was so cool, working in a big building like that. I met some really great mentors there. People I'm very grateful to have met."

Greg looked at Daniel, curious as to why he was sharing such information and why he was being so friendly.

"If you don't mind me asking, what is it that you do, Greg?"

"I work for Vinditech as a market researcher."

"Oh, really? Nice! Do you like it?"

"Yeah, it's all right," Greg lied.

"We could always use more analysts. Let me know if you're ever in need of a job."

"Umm, thanks." He was surprised by the offer, considering they'd just met.

"Please, come over and have a seat. I'm sure you have plenty of questions floating through your head, starting with why I requested that you come here. Did you take time from work?"

"Yeah."

"I appreciate that. I have to apologize; I'm on a very tight schedule lately. This was the only time I had available, and I wanted to get in touch sooner rather than later."

"No problem."

"I want to start by saying that I'm deeply sorry about your sister. She was a fine woman. A hard worker. I can't begin to tell you how deeply missed she is here."

Greg didn't know how to respond, so he kept quiet. He wanted to ask, "So why didn't anyone come to her viewing?"

but he stopped himself.

"I called you here because I was told by one of the guards that you'd come here wanting to see me. Is this correct?"

"Yes."

"Before I go on to my business, I thought I'd give you the opportunity to speak and tell me what you wanted to discuss with me."

Greg didn't want to be the first to talk. He still didn't know what to think of Daniel.

When Greg had pictured this conversation in his mind, he'd seen himself angry and confident, throwing accusation after accusation at Daniel and forcing him to confess to all that he'd done.

Now that it was a reality, Greg was scared to say anything.

And he'd forgotten to write down a list of questions.

"I did," Greg began, stalling to think of a good first question. "Umm, can you tell me a little about this company? I'm afraid my sister never really said much."

Daniel smiled. "That doesn't surprise me. Yes, a lot of the work we do here has to be kept from the public. It's not something that I necessarily like or agree with, but the core of our business is research and development. We innovate and provide pharmaceutical solutions that enhance people's lives using advanced science and technologies. In layman's terms, we create a lot of the pills that you see commercials for on TV."

"The ones that spend 95% of the commercial talking about the side effects?"

Daniel laughed. "Yes, that's one way to look at it."

Greg felt like Daniel was reciting a dialogue that he'd given a million times. It was obviously polished and carefully worded.

He switched gears.

"What I don't understand is this: I know you two were at the

AFTA Conference the night before she died. One of her old boyfriends, James, was there presenting. I've already spoken to him, and he said he was expecting Jessica to seriously consider sponsoring the work he's been doing in Africa. They'd met up a couple days prior and talked, and he thought things had gone well. However, the night of the event, he said you showed up and——"

Daniel slapped his hand against his forehead and began to shake his head. "Oh my. I'm afraid I've made a terrible mistake. Did James say how the Sumami Camp was doing?"

"Yeah, he said that it likely wouldn't be another two months before they ran out of funding. Whatever you and Jessica did, it successfully destroyed the project that he's worked hard on for four years, helping families over there."

"After what happened to Jessica on the day after the event, taking care of James and his project slipped my mind.

"The truth is, we did put together that research. We'd pointed out some inconsistencies with James' work. However, we did that intentionally, because we were hoping to deter others so that we could be the be the sole investors in the work he was doing."

His logic made no sense to Greg, so he was glad when Daniel continued.

"You probably don't understand how some of this stuff works. When an endeavor gets donation funding, a lot of the success is credited to the supporters. Some folks can be very demanding, wanting to know every detail of what the venture is doing and what every dollar is going towards. Others are more understanding, knowing they're doing their best but that some inefficiency is inevitable.

"Jessica did her research, and from also talking a little with James, knew he'd had some difficulty with getting funding from the right people.

"There are rules and regulations that you must go through to remain a non-profit. I'd already stationed off funding, which would help to expand and potentially even double what he was doing out there.

"She'd planned on letting him know why we'd done what we did before he left to go back. Now, I know this sounds sneaky and manipulative. But this is some of the red tape you have to go through to get some of these things done."

Daniel grabbed a planner that was on his desk and jotted something in it. He exhaled. "Thanks for reminding me of that. Do you have any other questions?"

Greg was unsure if he believed Daniel's story. It made no sense that Daniel would need to go through such elaborate measures to fund James' mission. At the very least, he could have let James in on the plan and not leave him there to worry.

Greg supposed that if he heard from James that his African mission had been funded, he'd have an easier time believing Daniel's story.

"So tell me about Jessica. The way you knew her," Greg said.

"Well, what can I say? I know that she started here right out of college, as you probably already know. I'll be honest; I didn't know her well until this past year or so. We're a big company, you see. So I have managers in charge of hiring lower-level positions. Her first couple of years, I remember seeing a few presentations come across my desk that I thought were incredible. I kept seeing her name pop up over and over, and I heard from the managers that she was a rock star. Very hard-working. Intelligent. I finally called her up here to chat and was immediately impressed. She had so many great ideas, and I felt like she had huge potential and could make a very important executive here one day. I wanted to make sure she didn't leave here for a better opportunity.

"So I kept a close eye out, making sure she continued to get promoted. I'd take the long way to where I was going so that I could brush past her desk. We'd chat for a bit. She was always so upbeat and positive. Everyone else I talked to seemed to love her. Well, everyone except——" Daniel paused.

"Who?" Greg asked, trying to sound moderately disinterested.

"Kevin Cole. He was our previous VP of Marketing. The corporate world is a finicky place, Greg. As an executive, you first love someone in your department 'cause they're making you look great. But for some people, like Kevin, a line gets crossed, and they start to fear for their job. He'd started to make some offhanded remarks about Jessica, saying that she wasn't as perfect and wonderful as everyone thought she was."

"What happened to Kevin? Where is he now?" Greg interrupted.

"Well, funny you should mention that. He ended up quitting. I think he saw the inevitable and began searching his network for other opportunities. For a man in his position, it's not difficult to find a job. But like any job, it looks better to leave willingly and seek greener pastures than to get fired. He found a VP opportunity at another place, a little smaller than here but probably with the same pay.

"Between you and me, I was kind of glad that Kevin did what he did. He was right in being worried, because your sister really was becoming the best person for the job. Once he left, I didn't hesitate to hire her. She was doing a great job, too, until, well, you know."

Daniel took a sip from the white coffee mug beside him. He smacked his lips as he set it back down. "But Greg," he continued, "I don't believe that Kevin had anything to do with

Jessica's murderer. No, no. He most certainly did not. I can attest to where he was the night of her murder."

"Oh yeah. And where is that?"

"He was over at Mitchell's, the seafood and steak place downtown. Know the one?"

Greg nodded.

"I was there with friends and bumped into him. I can testify that he was there from 7 to 11, which from what I read in the papers, was when Jessica's murder happened."

Greg wasn't holding back now. "Yeah, but that doesn't mean he didn't hire someone to do it for him."

"True. True. It doesn't. But Greg, I've known the man for ten years. Worked alongside him every day. He wasn't that kind of person, not at all. To be honest, he didn't even seem that unhappy when he left here. I think he was beginning to think of leaving, anyway. Jessica just accelerated his plans a bit. I'll also say that he was very accommodating to her during his last few weeks here. He and Jessica seemed to be on very good terms, and he went out of his way to help with the transition."

Greg told himself that he'd be the judge of whether or not Kevin Cole was innocent.

For now, it gave him one more thing to look into.

"I think that's given you an idea about my involvement in Jessica's life. Is there anything else you'd like to know?"

"You haven't really told me much about your relationship. What were you two like together?"

Daniel hesitated; he seemed uncomfortable with the question. "I don't know what you're getting at. If you're trying to find out if Jessica and I had some sort of intimate relationship, I'll close that door right now. I'm happily married with two kids. Jessica and I were always strictly professional."

"No, that's not what I meant," Greg lied. "The week leading

up to her murder, did anything seem off to you?"

Daniel checked his watch before answering. "As I mentioned, she'd been working towards the AFTA conference and getting that put together. Besides that, I'd been doing a lot of work on the development side. I must admit that I'm more of an engineer than a CEO. I like building and creating things. I'd put a lot of focus there, so I was very busy and only talked with Jessica here and there until the night of the conference."

Greg was dissatisfied with the answer and wanted to press him for more details, but he couldn't think of a way to word his question before Daniel spoke again.

"Anything else, before I move on to why I brought you here?"

Greg was feeling defeated again. He'd gotten a little more insight and was going to check out Kevin as soon as he got to a computer, but as a whole, the meeting had been a bust. He didn't believe every word that Daniel had told him, but he also didn't think that Daniel Kavern had anything to do with her murder.

He had no motive whatsoever. There was "a snowball's chance in hell"——as his mother sometimes said——that he had been involved.

"No, I don't think so."

"Good. I only have ten minutes before my next meeting, so I'll have to make it quicker than I intended." Daniel reached into a drawer in his desk and pulled out a manila folder, which he laid out on his desk.

Greg leaned forward in his chair and watched as Daniel pushed a sheet of paper toward him.

"Let me ask you something, Greg. Do you know a girl by the name of Stacy Melendez?"

Greg put on his best poker face, which was pretty lousy. He pretended that he hadn't heard Daniel's question as he looked over what was in front of him. It was a resume. Stacy's resume. It looked pretty standard to Greg. It had her name and her current apartment address at the top.

Nothing special there.

Objective: Internship, under the direct supervision of Miss Jessica Anderson. Learn corporate marketing, advanced data analysis, and other marketing initiatives in order to learn and grow.

Greg skimmed over her prior job history. He noticed that all the "farm girl" stuff had been left out, aside from her position as a clerk at Seeman's. Beneath that, it said she'd done an internship for Wallace and Associates for a summer as a marketing assistant. Then, the following summer, there had been a similar position at Callace Pharmaceuticals. She'd never mentioned those before; but then again, she'd hardly mentioned anything from her past to him.

When he got done reading it, he looked up and saw that Daniel was giving him an impatient stare.

"Well?"

"I'm sorry, what did you ask?"

"Do you know her?"

"Who?"

"Stacy Melendez," Daniel said, annoyed.

"Oh, actually, yes. Jessica had mentioned her to me before, the night before she died." He didn't know what he was going to say, but his plan was to be as vague as possible.

Daniel handed Greg another piece of paper. It was a record from a juvenile detention center. It said that Stacy Melendez had been a detainee of Hopes School of Correction for four years. He did the math based on her age; she had been there from the age of fourteen to eighteen.

"After Jessica died, I browsed through the records, just to see if there was anything out of the ordinary that I could hand to the police to help with their investigation. I didn't find much, but I found this a little puzzling. Jessica was getting ready to hire this woman for an internship, even though there was red flag after red flag. As an adolescent, she did some time for theft." Daniel slid another paper across his desk. "More recently, she graduated to drug dealing."

Greg looked it over. Two years ago, she had been caught with half a pound of marijuana, selling it on the corner of Pearl St. and 18th Avenue.

Greg knew the spot. It was right off of campus. He wasn't in that area much, but when he thought about it, he remembered that it wasn't too far from where Stacy was living.

According to the paper, she'd been on probation, which had ended at the start of the year.

"Judging by your face, I get the feeling you know Stacy more than you lead on."

Greg was caught.

There was no way he could convince Daniel otherwise.

"You're right. We've been seeing each other for a few weeks now."

"Interesting. Really?"

They both sat there in silence. Greg had no idea what to say, so he just read through the papers again. He'd always found it strange that Stacy never wanted to talk about her past.

Now he knew why.

On top of it all, he now knew she was a liar, a drug dealer, and a thief. He thought about his laptop that had been stolen. He hadn't given her a key to his apartment, but he had a few copies scattered throughout his apartment. He could check to see if any were missing when he got home, but the problem was, he didn't know how many copies he had or where he'd last placed them. Was it three? Four? He wasn't sure.

"I didn't mean to dump all of this news on you, Greg. In fact, I swear I didn't know you two were dating. I brought you here because I was hoping you could provide some insight. I just can't grasp why Jessica would hire someone like this. Sure, her grades have been decent, but we get a lot of highly qualified candidates that want to work here. I looked through the resumes of some of the other candidates. Better grades. More experience. Quality references. Not to mention spotless records. No one in their right mind would have chosen Stacy over some of these folks. I only ask, Greg, because I'm very, very curious as to why she'd do such a thing."

"I'm not sure. The night she was murdered, she came over to my house. She said she'd met Stacy a few weeks prior and, basically, that they'd become fast friends. She said she'd mentioned me and wanted to set us up on a date. Stacy was for it. To be honest, after seeing her picture, I thought she was out of my league. I promised Jessica, though, that I'd call her. Well, on the night Jessica died. I probably would have let the whole Stacy thing go, but she showed up at Jessica's funeral and we started talking and hit things off. I asked her on a date, and until quite recently, we'd been going out."

"Oh, so you know this girl pretty well, then. I'm guessing she's a much better person then her prior history indicates?"

"She's great," Greg said, unsure if he believed it now. "At least, I *think* so. She's always been very secretive about her past, and I guess now I know why."

Daniel laughed, easing some of the tension that had been building in the room. "Yeah, I guess you do." He paused. "It can be frustrating at times. There are so many things I'd like to ask your sister. Things I never had the chance to do. I'm sure you feel the same way. I can't imagine what you're going through."

"Yes, it's been very hard."

"Tragic. Just tragic," Daniel said. "Just out of curiosity, have you heard anything more about the investigation?"

"Not much, the police have shelved the case for now."

"I heard. That's public knowledge. What I meant to say is: have *you* heard anything more?"

Greg looked Daniel in the eye, wondering if he should spill all of the secrets that he'd discovered. Daniel seemed highly intelligent. Of course he was. He was the CEO of a huge corporation. If Daniel had been interested in finding out the truth, he could use the access he had to resources much more elaborate than Greg's. Problem was, he was unsure if Daniel *was* interested.

He wanted to ask, but then he remembered that Daniel had somewhere to be in less than five minutes. It would take at least an hour to give him a proper summary of all that he'd uncovered.

"I haven't heard much."

The hopeful look on Daniel's face faded. "Very well." He stood up. "I'll walk you out. If there's anything I can do for you, please let me know."

"I will."

They walked out of his office and down the hallway. When they got to the elevator, Daniel swiped a card that allowed him to summon the car. While they waited for it to arrive, Greg peeked over to see if anyone was working. It was so quiet. Unlike his office, which was a constant jumble of keyboard-clicking and phone conversations.

"Looking for someone?" Daniel said.

"Me? No, just admiring your office. It's so quiet here compared to my work."

"Yes, this floor is finance. They don't require a lot of noise."

"I see," Greg said. He wanted to explore the place and was about to ask when the elevator opened. Daniel motioned for him to enter.

Greg did, and Daniel pushed the button to take him to the ground floor. Daniel stood outside the elevator, holding his hand over the doors to prevent them from closing.

"Thanks for stopping by to chat," Daniel said. "Again, if there's anything I can do to help you out, just let me know."

Greg wanted to ask if he wanted to help him investigate. But he couldn't bring himself to say it.

"Will do."

The elevator closed, and Greg thought about what he'd gotten out of that meeting, other than the deep, dark secrets of his girlfriend's past. And Kevin Cole to look into.

Wasn't that enough?

Chapter 24

The last thing in the world that he wanted to do was go to work, but if he skipped today, he'd surely get fired.

He stopped at Wendy's first for lunch. Sitting at his desk with a double cheeseburger and fries, he thought back to the conversation he'd just had.

First off, he thought it was pretty cool that he'd just talked with Daniel Kavern. There were a lot of people that would kill for thirty minutes of his time. He'd meant to ask him how he'd become so successful, but the mood of the conversation didn't allow the question.

As he sunk his teeth into his burger, there was a familiar hard slap on his back.

"Hey, fucker, whatcha doin'?"

Greg turned around and saw Shane, with Brian and Kyle, standing behind him, grinning. It was nice to see that they weren't high for a change.

"Na' munch," he said with a full mouth.

"We're going to Hooters. You interested?"

Greg held up his burger, as if it was obvious that he didn't want to go.

"Yeah, I see that. You could put the thing down, though, and come with us. Don't you like seein' some nice titties while you eat?"

"I've got my computer right here."

Shane laughed. "True, true. All right, we'll see ya. You golfing with us Sunday?"

Greg gave them a thumbs-up.

"All right, cool, see ya then." He slapped him on the back again. That one hurt. Brian and Kyle thought it was hilarious. If one of them ever did that, he'd punch them right in the face.

As they walked away, Greg asked, "Hey, mind if I use your computer?"

"What for?"

"You know—" Greg didn't want to say out loud that he wanted on the Deep Web.

Shane tossed him his office keys and walked away without saying a word.

Greg looked through the research project that he needed to complete for Bob. The one he'd said Greg needed to work evening hours for.

It was simple. It'd take him two hours at the absolute most.

Greg finished his lunch, taking his time. He hadn't seen Bob all day and figured he must be booked with back-to-back meetings.

He grabbed Shane's keys and headed to the office. No one saw him enter. Not that anyone would care.

He turned on Shane's computer and was glad to see that it wasn't password protected. Greg thought it could be fun, though, if it had been. He could probably guess it by entering in random derogatory phrases.

Greg opened up Tor. He wanted to start by researching Stacy and didn't want any of his activities traced. Not even by the IT department.

Once he was connected, he checked Anonymail, but there weren't any new messages. Then he went to *American Hitmen* and saw that the sociopathic pieces of shit were still collecting submissions.

He went to the proof page, intending to check for any new victims. He saw the familiar face of Charles Taft, the alleged pedophile. Then Trixie the prostitute. Then Andy the drug dealer. He knew whose picture was next, and he couldn't bear to look at it yet.

He procrastinated by looking through Shane's desk. He opened the bottom-right drawer and shook his head laughing.

The latest issue of *Playboy* was sitting on top. The cover featured the girl from *Sizzle*. He hadn't seen the show, but there was no denying that the main female character was really hot, so he checked it out.

The rest of the drawer was filled with snacks. Beef jerky. A huge bag of Skittles. Peanuts.

After his porn fix, he tossed the magazine back in the drawer and returned to the task at hand, scrolling to his sister's picture. He stared at the picture of her at the beach. He'd learned so much about her since she'd been murdered.

She was as much of a mystery to him as the people who'd killed her were.

He hated thinking that, after she had been murdered, the guilty party had returned home and stalked her Facebook, found a pretty picture of her, and copied it to their site. They must have had no remorse for their deed. This thought motivated him to keep going. To keep pushing for additional clues. He couldn't rely on fate to punish them for what they'd done. They may never get caught unless Greg did something.

They'd keep on killing.

He scrolled to the bottom, hoping that they had taken his

picture down, but they hadn't. It was still there.

He didn't care to look at it anymore, so he went to the picture of Jessica's crime scene. He looked at it closely, trying to see it from a fresh perspective. There was so much going on, so many people there. They said that pictures were worth a thousand words, but Greg could have easily put a few thousand words to the image. The emotions that had run through him on that night were still sharp. He could still feel her warm blood on his hands. The hint of coffee on Captain Sloan's breath. The energy from the crowd and the adrenaline pumping through him. It was something he'd never forget, no matter how much he wished he could.

He figured out that he could make the original image larger if he opened the image URL in a new tab. He had learned this trick after stealing a few images from the Internet to use in several of his presentations.

Seeing the larger image gave him the fresh perspective he was looking for. The faces now had more clarity. He started from the left, taking his time as he went through them.

He still remembered the lady that was crying. Seeing her face made more of the memories flood back. He didn't remember the people next to her but knew he'd most likely shoved them out of the way as he tried to see what was going on. In the center of the group, most of the people had their backs turned towards the camera, so they were of little use. He still took his time, seeing if somehow the back of a head brought a clue.

He knew he'd have to be meticulous if he was going to find Jessica's murderer.

There had to be some clue he hadn't seen yet.

Then, as if it had been blown up for his eyes to see, he found what he'd been hoping for.

He wondered how he hadn't noticed it before.

It was so obvious. Right there in his face.

He went to the other tab, where he could see the smaller image. It was there, too. Just a little harder to see.

There was no denying it.

It was him.

Stacy's supposedly gay friend was in the crowd.

Jimmy.

He was staring right at the camera, as if he knew the person taking the picture.

Chapter 25

Greg tried to calm himself down.

His mind was racing.

He paced back and forth for a good five minutes before he sat back down. He couldn't believe that Jimmy was in that picture.

He'd only interacted with the guy once, in a conversation that didn't last very long. His body wasn't in the picture, only his face. If it wasn't Jimmy, then it was his identical twin.

Maybe Greg was over-analyzing, but the expression on Jimmy's face said a lot. It contained hints of surprise and joy.

Two emotions that no one should ever have at a murder scene.

Greg clicked back to the smaller picture, scolding himself for missing it the first time. It was definitely visible, albeit less distinguished, in the small version.

He was determined to have a little talk with Jimmy. And sooner rather than later.

Before then, Greg remembered something else that he needed to check out. Something he'd been dying to find out since the moment he'd laid eyes on it: Jessica's external hard drive.

Since he didn't have a functional computer at home, he'd have to do it at the office or wait until he bought a new computer. He couldn't do it from his own desk. External hard drives were strictly forbidden. The IT department had made that abundantly clear.

In Shane's office, though, they'd never know what he was doing. He could take his time and not worry that anyone was seeing what he was doing.

He took it out of his bag and plugged it into Shane's computer. Greg had never used an external hard drive like this before but figured it couldn't be too hard to figure out.

He clicked the "Computer" icon, which brought up what he was hoping for. It provided a list of the hard drives on the computer, the DVD drive (as if anyone used those anymore), and then there it was: E:Jessica's_External_Hard_Drive. He double-clicked it.

Excitement built.

But then disappointment ensued.

"Please enter your password."

Greg slammed his fist on the table.

"Damn it!"

He closed his eyes and took a deep breath. "Relax, you can figure it out," he muttered to himself. But he couldn't figure out her laptop password. Why would this be any different?

He started from the beginning, trying the only password that he knew she had used: *Tw!nbr0gr3g.*

Sure enough, it worked!

There were two folders: "Daniel" and "Wedding."

Wedding? What the hell did that mean?

Greg initially figured that Jessica was in an upcoming wedding party. He was curious, so he clicked it first.

The folder had a collection of images: wedding dresses,

flower bouquets, centerpieces, a Word document full of church venues. Everything you'd expect to see in the possession of a woman who was planning her own wedding.

Greg wondered if she'd started the collection when she'd been with James. That had to be it.

He went back and clicked on the Daniel folder, where things really started to get bizarre.

There was a huge assortment of pictures of Daniel Kavern. Some looked like they'd been taken from the Internet, professional images Greg had seen before from his own research. There was every picture he'd ever seen of Daniel and more in the folder.

But that wasn't the weird part.

There were also several pictures of Jessica and Daniel together. Some were from business events. Others were more casual, taken at what looked like a fun company outing. He opened up a picture to enlarge it. They were laughing. Jessica had one arm around Daniel's back and the other hand gently places at his side. There were a lot of pictures from this day, all which had Daniel in them.

Daniel cooking burgers.

Daniel playing volleyball.

Daniel playing cornhole.

Daniel eating burgers.

Jessica had a major crush on a married man.

But it got weirder still.

Inside of the Daniel folder was another folder entitled "AFTA," the name of the conference that James had returned to attend. He was expecting to see some pictures from the conference, maybe a few of James presenting. That would have been normal.

But instead, he saw pictures from a plush hotel room.

Pictures of Daniel with his shirt off. Then pictures of Daniel with his pants off. He wore a sly grin in all of them.

Then there were pictures of Jessica lying on the hotel bed, wearing racy lingerie. She was smiling right back at the camera.

Greg got a quick glance at the rest of the pictures before clicking back. Fortunately, the pictures had stopped with both of them clothed, but he still felt as if he'd seen way more of his sister than he ever wanted to.

From what he *had* seen, it was clear what was going on. Jessica and Daniel had more than just a working relationship.

Much more.

Daniel was married with two kids. He'd been a little too defensive when Greg had implied that they might have had something going on.

Now he knew why.

Greg had checked Daniel off the list of suspected people, but now he had a new name to add: Daniel's wife, or someone else who had found out about Daniel's infidelity and was really pissed about it. *Really* pissed. Enough so that they wanted Jessica dead. He didn't know anything about Daniel's wife, but she clearly had the motive.

He thought again about the caption below Jessica's picture: "crimes of dishonesty." Technically, cheating on a spouse fell under the "dishonesty" category.

There may be more to the dishonesty thing that he hadn't figured out yet, but this was the biggest motive that Greg had found thus far. With a puzzle piece like this, he realized his sister wasn't the sweet, innocent girl that he thought he knew. Instead, she had secrets and information that she neglected to tell him. Never once had she mentioned that she was such a high-ranking person at Adriar. Had she been promoted because of her work ethic, or had she been promoted because she was sleeping with the CEO? If Jessica had been alive and he had asked that, she would have slapped him hard in the face. Maybe it was a good thing that he hadn't found out about the affair until now.

He opened up a slideshow that Jessica had created. It was a collection of pictures of Daniel, surrounded with clip art of hearts and flowers. Very girly. A side of Jessica that Greg had never known.

All of this racked his brain. There were so many new leads to explore.

The affair would be something that Detective Maxwell would be interested to know about. Before Greg called him and gave him the news of what he'd learned, he wanted to find out more about his other new lead.

Jimmy.

He called Stacy. Their relationship was rocky, and this probably wouldn't help his case, but he'd already begun to prepare himself for the end and figured that he might as well extract all he could out of her while there was still time.

"Hello."

"Hey, Stacy. What's up?"

"Not much."

"What are you doing?"

"Just taking it easy. Gotta leave for work in a few hours."

"Cool." As he said it, Greg heard a clang coming from the phone. "What was that?"

"What was what?"

"That sound. Did you drop something?"

"Oh, no. Jimmy's here. He's doing the dishes."

"Oh," Greg said. "Hey, speaking of Jimmy, what apartment did you say he lived at?"

"I thought we went over this." She lowered her voice. "You

don't have any reason to be jealous of him."

Greg laughed in an attempt to ease her resistance. "Relax! I'm not going to do anything. Actually, I just wanted to stop by and apologize to him. I think I was a little rude when we spoke, and I just wanted to tell him I was sorry."

"Apology accepted. I'll say it on his behalf."

"Come on, Stacy, just let me talk to him. If he's a good friend of yours, I want him to be a good friend of mine, too."

Silence took over the line, making Greg wonder what was going on. He looked at his phone to see if she'd hung up, but she hadn't.

"Hello," Greg finally said, but there was no answer. Something had to have happened to their connection. He was about to hang up and call back when she finally spoke.

"You there?"

"Yeah."

"1G. That's his apartment. He should be there today if you come after work."

"Thanks! I really appreciate it."

"So why did you call?"

Greg was the silent one now. He'd called so he could get what he'd already received. The conversation couldn't have gone better, but he had to make it sound like he'd called for something else.

"Huh?"

"You didn't call me to ask for his apartment number, did you? Did you have anything else you wanted to say?"

"Yeah, I called to apologize again. I hate that I lied and kept things from you." He held back his sarcasm as best as he could. "I don't want something like that to come between us again. I promise I'll be honest and tell you everything from now on. Okay?"

"Okay."

"And if there's anything you ever want to tell me, please do. We should be open and honest with each other." He felt like he was pushing his luck now.

"Okay."

He was hoping she'd say a little more than that, but he thought he better quit while he was ahead. "All right, I'll call you in the morning?"

"Okay."

"Bye."

"Bye."

Glad that the conversation was over and that he'd gotten what he needed, a smile spread across his face.

Greg popped in and out of Shane's office over the course of the rest of the day. He'd learned after talking with Steve, a fellow coworker, that Bob had gone to Cleveland for business. Bob would never know if Greg wasn't at his desk much.

He did complete the project that Bob wanted done. It only took him an hour and a half, but he easily could say that it took him the entire afternoon. He went out of his way to make it look like it took a lot of time. Adding screenshots. Stock photos. It only took seconds to do but somehow made it look significantly more extravagant.

He ducked out of the office at 4:30, making sure to lock Shane's office up and leave the keys on his own desk, where Shane could find them. Greg would never have been brave enough to leave so early if Bob had been there, but he noticed a few of his other colleagues were leaving early, too, so he joined them.

He made sure to take the external hard drive with him. As far as Greg was concerned, that hard drive was like carrying around a million dollars. It could be the key, solid proof of a motive.

Before he left, he'd also saved the blown up picture of Jessica's crime scene, the one with Jimmy in it, along with all the other pictures from the *American Hitmen* site. He couldn't count on the site being online forever, especially with how Deep Web sites seemed to come and go. He'd been lucky that it hadn't broken or moved already.

He'd expected traffic to be lighter since he was ahead of rush hour, but it wasn't the case. There were still plenty of cars on the road, and traffic was at a stall.

He was heading straight over to Stacy's apartment complex, where he could confront Jimmy about the picture. Greg thought about it; it was likely that Jimmy knew who he was, if he and Stacy really were best buds. She had to have mentioned that she was dating a guy whose sister had been murdered, and he should've been able to piece it together from there.

Greg began cursing at the stop-and-go traffic. He'd always had road rage. He knew downtown Columbus well and decided to get off the highway and take back roads, which proved to be a good idea. The route was only five or ten minutes slower than the highway under normal conditions, but today it saved him at least twenty minutes.

He got to Stacy's complex and walked up to 1G.

Outside the door, he thought of how he was going to begin the conversation. He decided to keep it as friendly as possible. He also needed to first apologize, even though he didn't mean it, because Stacy had no doubt told him the reason for his visit.

Before anyone had a chance to walk by and see how stupid he looked standing by a random door, he knocked. He'd have to wing the whole conversation and hope for the best.

Jimmy opened the door.

"Hey, wassup? Greg, right?"

"Yep."

"Come on inside. Stacy said you had something you wanted to talk to me about."

Greg was about to say yes but kept quiet as he entered.

Jimmy's place was very tidy. There was a leopard print rug. Two paintings on the walls that could have been from a museum. A black coffee table with a glass top.

"Have a seat." Jimmy motioned for him to sit on one of the two leather couches. "Can I get you anything? Something to drink?"

"Whaddaya got?"

"I'm a martini guy myself."

Martinis? He is gay, Greg thought. "You have any beer?"

"Beer?" Jimmy gritted his teeth. "No, sorry. Martinis and Vodka, I'm afraid."

Greg didn't know much about mixed drinks. He usualy drank Jack and Coke or beer. He was unsure of what people even mixed vodka with and didn't want to sound stupid. He also reminded himself that there was a chance Jimmy was a murderer and would poison him if he made him a drink.

"You know what? I'm fine."

"You sure? It's really no trouble at all."

"Yeah, really. I appreciate it."

"All right," Jimmy said as he flopped onto the couch. "So what can I do ya for?"

"Well," Greg said, "first I wanted to apologize for how I was acting before. If you can understand things from my viewpoint, I knock on my girlfriend's door and a shirtless guy answers."

Jimmy laughed. "Yeah, I suppose that would make me a little defensive, too. If I went by Terence's place and another man answered, I'd probably break his neck."

Greg gave a fake laugh. Jimmy said it with a certainty that was unsettling.

"I'm not one to hold a grudge, so we can move on," Jimmy said. "Besides, I didn't really think you were that rude, given the circumstances."

"I appreciate that," Greg said. "So how long have you known Stacy?"

"Couple years now. We hit it off right away, ya know? Heard a new girl was moving in, so I brought over some cheese and wine, a little apartment-warming gift. I still remember that day; we drank the bottle and a couple more that night. Ate the cheese, too. We hit it off right away. Great girl, Stacy, you should hold onto that one."

"Yeah, I'm trying. I can't get her to open up about her childhood, though. It's like… she just doesn't ever want to talk about it."

Jimmy studied Greg. "Hmm, interesting."

"Does she talk to you?"

"Yeah, well, like I said, we got along really well from the start. Communication has never been an issue with us."

"I know it's something I should hear from her, but… did she ever, you know, talk about what she did when she was younger?"

"Hmm." He hesitated. "I don't think I should say anything she'd be upset by. I will say that she's had a few rough patches. Haven't we all, though? But she seems to be in a good place now."

"What kind of rough patches?" Greg was always persistent. That was something he and his sister had in common. They got it from their mother.

"I'll just say that she got caught up with the wrong crowd. I really shouldn't say much more than that."

"Come on, man. Help me out. I've been having some real girl issues lately."

"They're a complicated breed, my friend. Most problems I see you straight men make is not listening to them. You have to really connect and be empathetic to their needs."

"I am listening to her, or at least I'm trying to."

"Well, try harder. She has to know that you really care about her and that it's not always about your problems."

Greg could tell that he and Stacy had talked about him before, and Jimmy knew a lot about their relationship. "I know that. I've been bad, I realize. It's just that I had something really tragic happen to me a little over a month ago. Stacy has been great, really helping me pick up the pieces. It's only been the last week or so that we've had a few arguments."

"She understands that. You just need to put more effort into what's going on in her life. I mean, not to sound conceited, but you didn't even know about me until recently."

"She never told me!" Greg said, flustered.

"You never asked!"

Greg let the realization sink in. Jimmy was right, as much as he didn't want to accept it.

"Perhaps if you would have asked about what she does when she's home and not with you, it might have come up."

"I suppose. I don't know; I'm not very good at relationships, I guess. I've only dated two girls for more than a month."

"That's not surprising, if you don't mind me saying. You need some lessons on how they function."

"I've tried to get them from my sister. Problem is, she thought more like a guy it seems," Greg said. He'd always thought this to be the case, but then he remembered the photo album with Daniel and realized that she did have a feminine side buried somewhere inside her.

Jimmy shrugged, as if Greg still wasn't getting the point.

He was annoying Jimmy, and he couldn't let that happen. He needed to find out what he'd been doing at Jessica's murder scene.

"You know, I wouldn't mind that drink now," Greg said. "A martini sounds excellent."

Jimmy immediately perked back up. "Sure, any preference? I've got—"

"Whatever you think is best for a rookie martini drinker."

"All right, coming right up."

They'd each gone through two martinis. It took Greg everything he had not to spit out his first sip. He hated the dry taste. Now that he was on drink three, it was more tolerable but still not something he'd regularly drink.

He and Jimmy opened up more. Greg stopped talking about Stacy and Jessica, and allowed Jimmy to talk about himself. Jimmy's orientation was never brought up. Greg needed a few more martinis before he had the courage to hear those stories. He didn't really like Jimmy but could see why Stacy might. Girls loved gay guys, for some reason. Perhaps because it gave them hope that a male could also be sensitive and caring. But Greg could never talk and listen the way Jimmy did.

Jimmy talked about the J. Crew store he worked at. He also talked about how he went to Capitol and majored in art.

Greg didn't care, but he asked if Jimmy had painted the pictures on the wall. He said he had. This really got Jimmy jazzed up. They walked over to the paintings, and Greg listened to Jimmy talk about how the Renaissance era had inspired the paintings. Greg was taking Jimmy's advice and really trying to listen to him. It was so hard to pretend to care; it wasn't in his nature to do so.

Jimmy seemed to be in really good spirits, though. The martinis were certainly a factor in that, but Greg thought he was in a good position to get Jimmy to unlock some secrets. He needed to somehow work the conversation back to Jessica.

"I painted this my senior year. I'd love to do this full time, but there's rent to pay and the arts don't exactly provide a stable income. I'm not blessed with stable parents. I'm living entirely on my own."

"You seem like a really nice guy. I'm sure if you chased your dream and went broke, someone would take you in."

"I suppose. I'd feel bad to intrude, though."

Greg thought Jimmy wouldn't hesitate to stop by Stacy's apartment any time he felt.

They walked back over to the couch, where Greg sat down.

"Another martini?"

"Sure," Greg said. He wondered if he'd be able to drive home. He wasn't going to drink any more but had said yes to be polite. Jimmy, on the other hand, was eager for more, which Greg didn't mind. Jimmy had been hesitant before about talking to him about Stacy, but now Greg thought he'd be willing to tell him almost anything.

Jimmy handed him another full martini.

"Cheers," Jimmy said before downing half his glass.

"So enough about me. Let's talk about you. Stacy told me about your sister. I want you to know how deeply, deeply sorry I am."

"Thanks, yeah, it's been kind of rough."

"I just feel awful. Awful, awful, awful." Jimmy put both hands over his heart.

His personality had taken a one-eighty from the alpha-male he'd been yesterday at Stacy's apartment.

He was sensitive, gay Jimmy now.

Greg was feeling the effects of the alcohol, too, and felt he had the courage to ask Jimmy what he'd wanted to since the moment he opened the door.

"Speaking of my sister, Jimmy. I was hoping to ask you about something I found. You don't happen to have a computer, do you?"

"Yeah, of course. Wait right here and I'll get it."

Chapter 26

Jimmy grabbed his Macbook and gave it to Greg. He didn't know if he could set up Tor on a Mac, but he was about to find out.

"You don't mind if I install some software on here, do you?" Greg asked.

"By all means, feel free," Jimmy said.

Greg thought that Jimmy would have been more reluctant an hour ago, but now he was carefree and up for anything.

Greg sat on the couch with the computer on his lap and went to the Tor site. As he began the download, he pretended to listen to Jimmy talk about the life of a J. Crew employee and the lunatic customers he dealt with on a daily basis.

"So this guy takes five shirts into the dressing room to try on, and he comes out with zero. As he walks away, he's got his jacket fully zipped up, and he looks way bulkier than he was before. I go in to clear the room out and there aren't any clothes there. He tried to walk out wearing five stolen shirts!"

Greg, who was barely listening, asked, "Don't you have an alarm system or something?"

"Ha! Like employees really pay any attention to that. Have you ever gone to a store where you hear the alarm goes off?

Have you ever seen any employees run after them?

Greg shrugged.

"I didn't think so. Truth is, that alarm goes off so many damn times during the day, mostly for non-theft reasons, you sorta ignore it after awhile.

"This guy, though, I confronted. I asked him to unzip his jacket, and he refused. I told him he better put those shirts back or I was going to call the cops, so he did. I wouldn't have; I was bluffing about that. It isn't worth it to hold someone captive while waiting for the police to get there when you barely make more than minimum. But he went back to the dressing room and took the clothes off, and I was hero for a day."

Greg laughed, despite not really finding it funny. Tor had downloaded; he just needed to install it.

"Almost got what I need set up," he told Jimmy. Greg was afraid that Jimmy would notice he wasn't paying attention, but instead, he kept on rambling about another clothing store adventure.

When the browser installed, he opened it up and it connected.

"All right, I think I got what I need here." Greg sat up next to Jimmy. He couldn't believe how light the thing was. Macbook Air. He'd check out how expensive they were later.

Greg began to get nervous, wondering how Jimmy would take the information that he was about to share with him.

"So this is a browser I installed on your computer. A friend told me about it and how you can access sites that you can't normally get to." He went through the whole Deep Web spiel, just to give Jimmy some background info, and explained all the bad things that a person could get to on it. Then, he went to TorDir, explaining everything he was doing with each step.

Greg glanced over at Jimmy for a reaction. He was laser

focused on the computer screen, martini glass in hand. Greg was unsure what was going on in his head. He kept going, though.

"Once I found this directory for all of the sites, I then found this site at the bottom called *American Hitmen*. It's exactly what you think it is." Greg clicked it and skimmed through the homepage while giving a summary of what it said. He then scrolled back up and went to the Proof page.

This was the moment.

The part where he showed Jimmy his face in the picture.

As the page was loading, Greg peeked over at the front door. He was planning for the worst-case scenario: Jimmy attacking him (if it turned out that he was guilty). Greg knew that, in a fight, he didn't stand a chance against Jimmy, who had twice the muscle mass. He figured he could jump over the couch and get through the door before Jimmy could catch up to him. As long as Greg could get outside and start running, he'd be safe.

In Greg's mind, it was a likely scenario. He prepared himself for Jimmy's attack. He handed the laptop to Jimmy and inched a few inches away, both so he could duck out of reach and also to get a better view of Jimmy's reaction when he saw it.

"This site provides supposed proof of all the murders they've done. If you scroll down there, you'll see the fourth one on the list is my sister."

Jimmy's head swiveled around to face Greg, shock on his face. Greg had known about this for so long that he'd forgotten that this discovery was new for most people.

"Are you serious?"

"Yep, check it out."

He scrolled down, and when he got to it, his hand covered his face.

"I suppose you may know what I'm going to show you next."

The room got very quiet.

Greg peeked over and saw Jessica's two pictures on the screen. Jimmy inched his face closer to it. Greg could tell that he was much more interested in the picture on the right, the one with both the crime scene and his face in it.

"So, tell me, Jimmy, what were you doing at my sister's crime scene?"

Jimmy was still staring at the picture, inspecting every last detail.

"Jimmy?"

"Sorry, I'm still taking all this in." He couldn't seem to look away from the computer.

"Let's start from the beginning. I presume that's you that I see in the picture, correct?"

"Yes."

"All right," Greg said. "What were you doing there?"

"I was out with Terence. There's a bar a couple blocks away, Tewey's."

Greg knew the place.

It wasn't officially a gay bar, but he'd been there once and noticed that there seemed to be an unusually high number of same-sex couples. Carrie had been the one to say it: "You know this is pretty much a gay bar, right?" He hadn't known. He'd researched different hangouts near his house and hadn't read the reviews on the place.

Jimmy continued, "It was early, and we were planning on staying out late, so we thought we'd take a break for a nine o'clock dinner. Terence isn't very familiar with the area, and I knew what was nearby, so we walked in that direction.

"When we turned the corner, that's when we saw a huge crowd of people. I told Terence to stay there while I went to see what was going on. I didn't see the body, because there were people in the way, but if you were there, you knew what had happened because people kept yelling things like 'Has anyone called the police?' or 'Did anyone see the shooter?' I can put two and two together. So once I figured out what was happening, I ducked out before the police got there, and Terence and I went to Truman's to grab a burger. I looked it up the next morning and saw it had been a girl around my age, but I didn't know her."

"Does Stacy know?" Jimmy didn't answer, and Greg repeated himself. "Did you ever tell Stacy that you were at a crime scene? Because if you told her where it was at, she would have known it was my sister's."

"No, I didn't tell her. Didn't tell anyone. I was afraid that, if anyone knew, I might get into trouble for withholding information from the police, even though I don't know anything. I want you to know that, Greg. I don't know anything!"

Greg didn't think; his emotions were high and he blurted it out. "I think you're lying."

"I'm not, though. I swear!"

It was amazing. Jimmy could snap Greg like he was a toothpick if it came down to it, but Greg was the enforcer here. When it came down to finding out who did this to his sister, he had no time for lies or games.

He tapped hard on the computer screen. "Look at this! You see the goddamn expression on your face, Jimmy? You saw someone you knew, didn't you? You know the person that took the picture!"

Greg really had no idea if Jimmy did or not. But he thought if he said it with confidence then Jimmy might confess.

How right he was.

"All right, all right!" Jimmy screamed. He then began crying.

He waited for Jimmy to collect himself.

"I'm not a bad person, Greg. I want you to know that. I'm just scared. I know what I've done is wrong, but I'm so terrified of what could happen."

"What the fuck are you talking about?" Greg asked, keeping command of the conversation.

"What're you going to do, Greg? Are you going to go to the police when I tell you what I know?"

"Chances are, probably not. But that depends on what you know. In case you haven't figured out yet, I've been doing a lot of digging into my sister's case. I'm going to find out who did this, and I'll keep looking the rest of my life if I have to. And you're going to help me by telling me what you know."

"Okay, I really don't want to be involved in this. You gotta promise me that you won't tell anyone it was me who told you."

"Fine," Greg said, even though he didn't mean it. He knew it would just stall things if he didn't promise.

Jimmy took a deep breath. "All right, here it goes. You're right, I *do* know the guy who took the picture."

"Who is it?"

"I went to school with him. Middle school, maybe one year of high school. I don't know. I can't remember."

"Why not?"

"Because he got expelled. He was always kind of a loner. Well, one day, they supposedly searched his locker and found a gun. That was the rumor, anyway. Probably true, because after that, no one heard from him again. They said he and his family moved. Like I said, he didn't have many friends, so after the few days of buzz, no one seemed to care or talk about it. But I'll tell ya, no one minded that he'd moved away. Not even the teachers."

"What was his name?"

"Steve. Steven Cartwright."

Greg took the computer from Jimmy. He no longer was scared that Jimmy was going to attack him. Greg's heart was racing.

This was the massive breakthrough he was hoping for.

"Tell me more about that night. So you saw him take the picture?"

"Yeah. He was standing in the middle of the street. When I first saw him, he had the camera down at his side. I couldn't place him when he was looking down but noticed that he looked familiar. Then, when he lifted his head, I recognized him. It was weird, because I hadn't seen him in twelve or so years. There he was, all grown up. Well, he hadn't grown much. From a distance, he still looked like he was pretty small, maybe five foot six."

"How sure are you that it was him, though?"

"Really sure. His face is pretty distinct. Not to be mean or anything, but he kinda looks like a weasel. Long nose. Ratty hair. No deformities or anything, but just a real unlikeable face. Might have been part of why he didn't have many friends. He never smiled and always seemed to be in a bad mood. That was another reason."

"Did he recognize you?"

"I've been wondering that off and on over the past month," Jimmy said. "Why? Do you think Steven is the killer?"

Greg didn't answer. He opened a new tab and went to StartPage to a new search.

Jimmy kept going. "I didn't think much about it. I mean, I saw him take the picture. But I didn't know anything about this website you found. If I had, I *absolutely* would have gone to the police. I thought it was weird seeing him there and a little odd that he took a picture, but that was as far as my thinking went."

"I understand," Greg said reassuringly. "Do you think he'd remember you? Like, if I spotted you in the picture later?"

"If I had to bet, yeah, probably. Maybe," Jimmy said. "I really don't know!"

"All right, but you're sure it was him?"

"I already told you, yes! I'm confident of that."

"So he takes the picture. Then what happened?"

"Well, once I saw the flash, I turned away. I didn't want my picture taken. I hid down for a second. When I looked back up, he was gone."

"Gone?"

"Yeah. Couldn't find him. To be honest, I didn't look for him very hard. I didn't want him to see me. I didn't want anyone to know that I'd been there, so I left." Jimmy finished off his martini. "Terence was still on the corner where I'd left him. I told him what had happened. We left there and went to Truman's. As we did, we saw several police cars zooming by. That's it. That's all I know." He looked at Greg, as if pleading for him to believe him.

Greg let out a short breath of air. "Thank you for telling me this."

Jimmy jumped off the couch. "Damn, I need another drink now. You want—— Oh, I see you're still working on the last one."

"I'm fine, thanks."

Jimmy walked into the kitchen while Greg waited for the search results to come up. He peeked over his shoulder a few times, checking to see what Jimmy was doing. Each time he looked, he saw he was, in fact, making his martini. Greg still wanted to make sure that he wasn't grabbing for a knife or anything.

Jimmy came back, his drink in hand, and sat next to Greg.

Greg looked through the top results but wasn't many hits for Steven Cartwright. There was a Steven Cartwright in the Army.

"Do you know if he joined the Army after school?"

Jimmy shrugged his big shoulders. "No idea. I don't know anything about what happened to him after he left."

Greg opened the page up and saw that the Sergeant Steven Cartwright was in his forties and balding.

"I take it that's not him?"

"No, definitely not!"

Greg went back and visited a few more of the top listings, but it didn't take long for him to realize the results weren't getting him anywhere.

"Anything else you can tell me about this guy?"

"That's about it, I swear. Wish I knew more, but like I said, I haven't seen him in over a decade," Jimmy said. "I can't believe that picture was posted online. So how does this secret Internet thing work again? How does someone go about making a website on there?"

"Well, to be honest, I'm not exactly sure. That TorDir site with all the website listings had a few links that went to website-creating sites. I clicked them but didn't find any that were all that good. As far as I know, though, it's just like building a regular site. Again, I'm not entirely sure how to even build a regular site, but it can't be that hard if millions of people are doing it. Why do you ask?"

"I don't know. Just curious as to how likely Steven is to be involved in this."

Greg thought that it was highly likely. The facts were undeniable. If Jimmy was telling the truth, Steven Cartwright took the picture of the crime scene. The owners of *American Hitmen* were top secret about their identity. It wasn't like

Facebook, where anyone could post something to it. No, if a picture was posted on *American Hitmen*, it had to have been by someone involved in murdering Jessica. The content on the site implied that there were multiple people doing the killings.

We're your friends and neighbors. The guys you see at the bar on a Friday night…

Plural.

But whether it was just Steven or multiple people, it didn't matter.

Again, Steven Cartwright took the picture, and it got posted to this site.

Finding Steven Cartwright became Greg's top priority.

Once he found him, he could torture him for answers.

Gain access to his computer and see what the message said for the hit on Jessica.

He may not be able to figure out who it was, but learning the reasons why it had been done could only help him gain closure.

It was the most optimistic he'd felt about his detective work.

He'd gotten most of the puzzle pieces.

He'd started to put them together.

Now, it was time to finish the job.

Chapter 27

"Thanks," Greg said. "This has been *really* helpful."

"Wait, where are you going?" Jimmy said, trying to keep Greg from leaving.

"I've got some things I need to do now. Rest assured, though, I'll make sure you're not involved with this in any way."

"What are you going to say? You're going to tell the police, right?"

Greg thought that Jimmy must be really worried, because thirty minutes ago, he was drunk without a care in the world. Now, the whole Steven Cartwright mess had brought him back to reality.

"I need to… I don't know what I'm going to say. I might not even go to the police. The police don't do shit around here, anyway. Maybe I'll find him myself."

"Whoa, man. Don't do that. Stacy would kill me if anything happened to you."

His comment took Greg off guard.

He wasn't expecting it to mean so much to him. That Stacy would miss him.

He was flattered, and it reminded him of how great she'd been. Yes, she was a liar and a hypocrite, but she was caring, a golf lover, and unbelievable in bed.

"You don't get it, Jimmy! I've gotta find this guy and make him pay for what he did to my sister. He may know who submitted her name in that contact form, too. I want both people to pay, but especially Steve, because I think he's the one that pulled the trigger. Don't you get that? Can't you understand that nothing else matters to me until justice is served?"

Jimmy looked down. Again, Greg couldn't believe that a big guy like Jimmy could be guilt tripped by him.

"Yeah, man, I get it. Just… be careful, all right? I mean, if Steven did do all of these things, then he's one dangerous dude. He's got a gun for sure. What do you have to protect yourself?"

Greg thought Jimmy made an excellent point.

What *was* he going to do when he found out where Steven lived? He couldn't barge in there without some kind of weapon, preferably a gun, which he didn't have.

"I don't suppose *you* have a gun, do you?" Greg asked.

"No, guns aren't for me, man."

"Yeah, me neither." Greg had never even shot a gun. His mom was very opposed to the weapons, so they never had any in the house. Jessica had asked for a BB gun one year for Christmas. Their mom refused to get it.

Greg remembered his parents debating it for weeks. Their mom always won the arguments. Once she was fired up about something, there was no stopping her from getting what she wanted.

Greg thought of anyone he knew that might have a gun. It didn't take him long to run through his list before he thought of a likely candidate.

Shane.

"I'll see you, Jimmy. Thanks again for telling me all that you did. It's been a huge help."

"Wait, come here," Jimmy said.

Greg didn't know what he was planning on doing but was afraid he might attempt to prevent him from leaving. Instead, Jimmy gave Greg a big hug. The guy had superhuman strength, and Greg thought Jimmy might crush him. He could feel his ribs bending.

"Please be careful!"

"I will. Thanks for the martinis. They were excellent!" Greg lied.

"You're welcome. I think I need about three more."

"I think you have a martini problem," Greg said, grinning to show him he was teasing.

"This has just been *so* stressful for me, man."

Greg noticed, for the first time, an inflection in Jimmy's voice as he said the word "so." He grinned slightly at the stereotype.

"Bye," Greg said and walked out the door.

Greg felt the effects of the alcohol and tried to focus himself into a more sober state. He sat in his car and pulled out his phone.

He figured that Shane would be out with Brian and Kyle, probably getting lap dances at Siren's. He had been with them today on sales stuff, and whenever the three of them were together for work, Greg would often get a call later from Shane, asking if he wanted to meet up. It was 8 p.m. now. That was right around the time that Shane usually called.

Greg used the voice command, "Call Shane." The man was his best chance.

"Hello."

"Hey—"

"Greg?"

"Yeah, it's me." He hadn't been nervous when the number was dialing, but now that he heard Shane's voice, he didn't know how to phrase his question.

"What the fuck is up, man? Little weird for you to be calling *me* at this hour. Everything 'ight?"

"Yeah. Are you with Brian and Kyle?"

"No, not tonight. We've got an epic Friday planned. Decided to lay low tonight."

"I see, that's cool. You can't party twice in one week anymore?" Greg didn't know why he asked this; the nerves and alcohol were taking over his mind.

"We can. I dunno, just wanted to sit tight tonight. Gotta pitch at 8:30 tomorrow, too, so just wasn't feeling it."

"Oh, all right. I won't bother you then."

"Whoa, hold on now! I've always got time for my Greggie Weggie Waffle Face. What can I do you for, bro? It's not like you to call me like this," Shane said. "You're not pregnant, are you? I better not be the father."

Greg laughed. It eased a lot of the tension he felt. "No, I've got a question for you, though. You're going to freak out when I ask you, but I really need your help."

"Damn, dude. I gotta hear what this is. If it's not about babies, I can't imagine what else would freak me out."

"It's not about babies," Greg said, laughing again. "Not even close." Greg sighed. The smile faded from his face. He couldn't do it; he was too scared to ask.

"Just give it to me straight. We're cool, no matter what," Shane said.

"Okay. Do you have a gun?"

"As a matter of fact," Shane said, "I do."

"Good. Do you think, maybe, I could borrow it?"

"Well, Greg, I think I'd like to know why you want a gun

first. Usually a lady buys me dinner before I give her the Glock."

"I understand. Are you at home? I can drive over now?"

"Yeah, man. I'm home."

"'Kay, I'll be over in... oh, about fifteen minutes."

"Take your time. I'm not like you with a damn 8:30 bedtime. I'll be up 'till at least midnight."

"Hey, my bedtime is 9:00, thank you very much."

"Whatever. I'll see ya."

"Okay, see ya."

Greg drove to Shane's place. It had taken him fifteen minutes. Exactly as he'd predicted. Shane, of course, lived in a luxury apartment complex. It was downtown, by the river. He was on one of the top floors in a real bachelor pad.

Jimmy would probably love it.

Unlike Stacy's shitty apartment complex, Shane's place actually had visitor parking. There was a security guard at the parking lot gate who handed a ticket to each visitor as they entered. There was some kind of system, Shane had told him, that dictated how often they could have guests. It sounded complicated, but Shane said it worked out somehow. It was always a pain in the ass to find parking in downtown Columbus.

Greg thought about how crazy the night had been. Was he being stupid, getting a gun and going after this Steven Cartwright guy? He didn't even know where the man lived, or if he was even guilty.

He wondered if he should tell Detective Maxwell first. It had been a long time since he'd filled him in on what he was doing. The temptation was growing stronger since the detective had seemed convinced that Greg wouldn't be able to find anything.

Now, he could show him solid evidence of a strong lead. Maybe later. He wanted to see how his conversation went with Shane first.

He found the elevator and headed up. The entire building wasn't simply full of apartments. Greg wasn't sure what most of the other floors were, but he knew that some were for business and only the top five floors were apartments.

When he got to the right floor, he realized that he didn't know Shane's room number, but he knew where it was. For him, it was like driving directions. He never knew road names, but he could remember to turn left after a certain gas station or take the exit after the highway split. Shane's place was to the right, the second one from the end.

He knocked, and Shane answered.

"Hey, good to see ya. Come on in."

Greg hadn't been to Shane's place in about a year. Most of it looked the same. Clean and polished. There was a new stone statue by the door.

"What the hell is this? A gargoyle?" Greg teased.

"Oh, I see. Make fun of me. I've seen your shithole of an apartment. You don't have room to talk," Shane said. "For your information, this is a Chinese fireball dragon. Cost me three grand."

"Where, exactly, does someone get a Chinese fireball dragon?"

"Down at the Chinese fireball dragon store. Duh, motherfucker." Shane grinned. "Are we going to talk about this shit all night or are you gonna tell me why you need a fuckin' gun?"

There was something about being face-to-face with Shane that made him less nervous.

"My bad."

"Have a seat, my friend. Wanna beer or something?"

"No, thanks. I've been drinking martinis with a gay guy for the past couple hours."

Shane laughed, "Get the fuck outta here. Man, what is with you lately? You're like an entirely different person."

"I know. It's been a crazy couple of weeks."

Shane went to the kitchen and grabbed himself a beer. He popped the cap. Then, with a running start, he jumped over the back of the couch and plopped onto it, his beer held high in his right hand.

"Ya see there, Greg? Not a drop spilled," Shane said as he took a swig.

"Impressive."

"So," Shane said, sitting up. "Let's hear it."

"Okay, so I was just talking to this gay guy—"

"Now hold up right there. Who is he and how do you know him?"

"Well... I told him I wouldn't give out his name. He's a friend of Stacy's. I met him yesterday when I went over to her apartment, and he answered the door with his shirt off."

"Oh my god!" Shane yelled, jumping off the couch and pacing back and forth. He was being overly theatrical for comedic effect, and it worked, because Greg knew how ridiculous this must have sounded.

"All right, so you meet a mystery, shirtless gay man at Stacy's apartment. Got it. Carry on"

"Right, so... I meet this guy, and I didn't know he was gay at the time. So I call Stacy later, asking her about him."

"Wise move," Shane muttered.

"She tells me he's just a friend, and I'm not sure I believe her, but that doesn't matter. What *does* is that I have a tiny feeling that I've seen him somewhere before. I don't think much else of it. I go to work today. Well… first, I go Daniel Kavern's office, but that's a whole other story."

"Daniel Kavern? The CEO of Adriar?"

"Yeah. I take it you know him?"

"That guy's a total dick. I've run into him at a couple different networking events. Thinks he's so much better than everybody else because he took advantage of a couple good ideas with his daddy's money. Don't get me wrong, I've got respect for someone who can grow businesses the way he has. It's just a lot easier when you've got all the seed money and your dad's wealth of information."

"I didn't realize he had a rich daddy."

"Yeah, Ken Kavern. He's a hedge fund manager. That guy, I have a lot more respect for. Anyway, continue."

"I go into work in the afternoon, and I don't feel like doing shit——"

"Yeah, it didn't look like you were getting much done with your supersized Double McCheeseburger."

"Hey, it was Wendy's. And no, I wasn't getting anything done. That's when you came by and gave me the key to your office. I went and hopped onto Tor, because I wanted to look some stuff up. That's when I went back to the *American Hitmen* site that I showed you."

"Oh man, was there something new added?"

"No. That's why I was checking. But then I realized that I could blow up the picture from Jessica's crime scene. When I did that, I found something I hadn't seen before."

"What?" Shane was pumped with excitement.

"Fucking Jimmy!" Greg said, mocking Shane.

"Who's Jimmy!?"

"Oh shit!" Greg said, realizing he wasn't supposed to tell anyone his name. "The shirtless guy from Stacy's apartment.

His name is Jimmy."

"Oh, all right," Shane said. "What was *he* doing there?"

"That was what I went over to his place to find out. Stacy told me where he lived. I went over, we had martinis. Anyway, I show him the picture, so there's no way he can deny it. He then tells me he remembers seeing the guy that took the picture. And, even better, he knew the freakin' guy! What are the odds?"

"Dude, you sure this guy isn't lying out of his ass? Sounds like a load of bullshit."

"Well——" Greg said, "I don't know. I guess I didn't consider it. I really don't think he was, though. He was drunk and spilling all his darkest secrets."

"All right, continue."

"Well that's about it," Greg said. "Now I need a gun so I can blow that guy's head off."

Shane sat back down on the couch. He was thinking hard; his tongue was sticking out. He began stroking his chin with his hand. It looked like he was trying to figure out every possible angle and scenario.

"I see what you're saying. If that picture got on the site, then it definitely has to be this guy. What's his name?"

"Steven Cartwright."

"Steven Cartwright. And do you know where Steven lives?"

"Well, I still need to figure that out."

Shane throws his hands up in the air. "Well, what the hell have you been doin'?"

"I Googled his name. Couldn't find anything. I just found out about him a little over an hour ago."

"I take it Google didn't turn anything up?"

"No."

"Do you know where he lives? Like what city, or even the

state? Is he in Ohio?"

"Not sure. Jimmy said he grew up around here. Not sure where, though."

"Cool."

Shane got up and grabbed his laptop. He put it onto the coffee table and waited for it to boot up. Greg got up and sat by him.

While they waited, Greg said, "Man, have you ever used a Macbook? It's crazy how fast those things boot up!"

"Yeah? You know, someone the other day said the same thing." He pulled out his phone and began typing something. Greg was about to peek over when Shane showed him. "This look good?"

Greg recognized the Amazon website; a $1,500 Macbook Pro was on the screen. "Yeah, that's probably good."

"Cool," Shane said.

Greg watched him hit the buy button with one-click. He shook his head. A $1,500 buying decision in a matter of seconds. How nice that must be.

His computer had finally booted up, and he opened up a web browser. He went to whitepages.com.

"I have to use this every now and then to find clients' home addresses to send their wives flowers and other bullshit."

"Hmm, that's pretty smart."

"I'm not as dumb as I look, Greg."

"Yeah, well, I don't think anyone could be as dumb as you look," Greg said, smiling.

Shane gave him the regular hard slap on the back. "You're a funny guy, Greg." He went back to the computer. "What was his name again?"

"Steve Cartwright."

Shane typed the name in and put Columbus, Ohio as the

address.

"I told you, Jimmy said he doesn't live—"

Shane held his hand up. "Patience, my friend." When he hit enter, dozens of Steve Cartwright results came up. However, only one of them listed a Steve Cartwright from Columbus, Ohio. Shane clicked it.

It then said "Steve S Cartwright, Age: 25-29" It had two listed addresses. The first was in Columbus, Ohio. The second was in Lawrence, Indiana.

"Boom!" Shane yelled. "There you go, my friend."

"Wait, are you sure it's him?"

"Pretty sure. You're lucky that Steve Cartwright isn't as common of a name as John Smith, or else we'd have a lot more of a problem finding him." Shane scrolled down. "Looks like this fucker's moved around a bit. But now, he's got a house in ol' Lawrence, Indiana."

Shane went to Google Maps and typed in the address. Greg was surprised to learn that it was only a two-and-a-half hour drive from Columbus. He zoomed in and got a street view of the house. It was small and white; there were no other houses nearby. It had a small backyard, and behind it was nothing but cornfields. It didn't look like he owned the farm, though. Just lived near one.

"There you go, my friend. There's your boy. Take I-70, and you'll be there before you know it."

"Wow, that was a lot easier than I thought it was going to be."

"You leave it to ol' Shane to take care of all your worries. I'm here to help."

Greg was thankful that Shane had found the address. He wasn't completely sure if it was the correct one but thought it was very likely.

He made Shane type his own name in for reassurance. When it listed the exact addresses of the three places he'd lived in his lifetime, along with the college apartment he'd rented for two years, he had much more confidence in the website.

Now it was time to ask the big question, the reason he was here.

"So Shane, are you going to give me your gun?"

Chapter 28

"Look, man, I totally get where you're coming from. I see why you want this fucker to pay. But, have you really thought this through? I mean, is this guy worth it?"

"He killed my sister. He's going to keep killing more people. Yes, I'm sure this is what I want to do."

"Why don't you hand this off to the police? Save yourself the trouble of getting ass raped for the rest of your life."

"If the police handle it, first off, they'll screw it up somehow. I know it. Secondly, I don't want this guy to go to prison. I want him dead. And before he's dead, I want to find out what the hit request on Jessica said. The police are never, ever going to get *that* information out of him. They don't care. They'll find their man, take all the credit, and go half-ass finding their next person."

"All right, I just want to be the voice of reason here." Shane paused, waiting for Greg to laugh, but he didn't. "The guy may very well get the chair. And if he doesn't and spends the rest of his life in jail, that isn't so bad, is it? As for finding the person who sent out the hit…" He got up, pacing again.

"You know I'm right," Greg finally said.

"You just never know, Greg. They may have some way to get

that information out of him. Reduce his sentence or something."

"I don't want a reduced sentence!"

"Okay, okay." Shane held out his hands so that Greg would calm down. "Bad choice of words. I'm just saying… hell, I don't know what I'm saying. Kill the bastard, if you want. I just think a lifetime prison sentence for the guy is better than a lifetime sentence for you."

"I'm not planning on going to jail. You saw his place. It's out in the middle of nowhere. I could get there and shoot him without anyone knowing."

"Again, I remind you, this guy has potentially killed god knows how many people. Or is friends with some motherfuckers that have. There's a good chance he's going to be armed; you can count on that."

"Look, I'm scared. Scared out of my freakin' mind. I have to do this, though. Now, either you're going to help me by giving me your gun or you aren't. Either way, I'm getting a gun."

Shane stared at Greg, then looked down and shook his head. "All right, I'll help you out. You've gotta understand, though, if you get caught, you gotta say you stole it from me."

"I will, don't worry. You're not going to get in trouble for this. I'll take the fall."

"Be right back," Shane said, walking out of the room. A few minutes later, he returned with a black pistol in hand.

Seeing the gun, Greg realized that it was all becoming very real. In his mind, he knew what he wanted to do. But his heart was telling him he didn't have what it took to go through with it. He was too scared, and there were too many unknowns.

"By the look on your face, you've never used one of these things before," Shane said.

Greg's eyes were fixated on the gun; he was barely hearing

Shane speak.

"Hey," Shane said, and Greg moved his head up to look at him.

"I'm gonna ask again: you sure you want to do this?"

Greg nodded his head. "I'm sure. Show me how to use it."

They both went over to the couch and sat down.

"This right here is the safety. Here means safe. Click it over, and the red means it's ready. You've got your chamber here," Shane said as he demonstrated with the gun. "Move this and pull this down, and you can see how many bullets you've got left." Shane then pulled a pair of thin black gloves out of his pocket. "Put these on." While Greg did so, Shane pulled a Ziplock bag of bullets out of his pocket. "Why don't you try loading it?"

Greg took the bag of bullets. The bullet chamber to the gun was already open, so it was easy to put them inside. It reminded Greg of filling up his Pez candy dispenser as a kid. This was a very grown up version of that.

He got all of the bullets in place. Counted twelve total that fit in the chamber. Greg didn't need Shane to explain how to put it back together. He popped it hard with his palm and it clicked into place. Greg felt like a badass.

"Good. Now see if you can reload it."

Greg fidgeted with the chamber. He got it, though, taking it out and putting it back in.

"All right, I think you've got it."

"Good. Now as for aiming." Shane took the gun from Greg and positioned it so that Greg could see how to look down the barrel and line it up. "That's what you'll do if you're looking to shoot something from a distance. If you're up close and personal, just start blasting."

"Do I just keep pressing the trigger for multiple shots, or do I hold the trigger down?"

"Keep pressing. Hold this puppy in two hands. It'll kick back on you more'n you think."

"Okay. Anything else?"

"Yeah, don't fucking do this, Greg. You're making a mistake. You don't know what the hell yer doing and are only going to get yourself killed."

"Thanks for the words of wisdom; I've gotta do it, though."

Shane shrugged his shoulders. "All right. Well, good luck. When are you… ya know… going to?"

"I don't know. I guess right now. No time like the present, right?"

"Sleep on it, man. Think it over. This guy's been on the loose for over a month. It can wait one more night. This is a big decision, Greg. You don't want to rush it without thinking it through."

"I have thought it through. No, I didn't know who the person was until just now, but I've thought a lot about what I'd want to do if I ever figured out who it was. I've thought about it a lot."

"Still, give it one more night. Hell, you'll probably fall asleep at the wheel driving over there. It's already past your bed time, and you've been drinking."

"I don't think I'll have trouble staying awake. Not tonight."

"I know. Don't make me beg, Greg. Take the night off. Call in sick tomorrow. Hell, I'll even lie to Bob and say I saw you and you looked like death. I'll put in a good word for ya."

Greg didn't know where this newfound impatience was coming from. He wanted to chase the lead before it got away.

But Shane was right.

Rushing this wasn't a good idea. It didn't feel right.

"Fine. Tomorrow it's happening, though."

"Unless you talk yourself out of it."

"I won't. But we'll see."
"Yeah, we'll see."

Greg drove home. He was so surprised by Shane's reaction, thinking it wasn't a good idea. This was the same guy that had slept with hookers that he knew had gonorrhea.

He thought tonight may be the best time to go through with doing it.

Emotions were high.

That would either really help or really hurt.

It was ten. The walk to his car was terrifying, having a gun in his bag. He'd asked Shane where he got it. His "you don't even want to know" was enough of an answer to know he'd be in big trouble if he was caught with it. Shane had thoroughly wiped it for fingerprints before letting Greg take it. He'd also insisted that he only touch it with the pair of black gloves he gave him. The same was true for the Ziploc bag of bullets.

When he turned the light on in his apartment, he half-expected Steven to be sitting there on his couch waiting for him. He'd have loved to kill him right then and get it over with, but cleaning up the blood from his living room floor may have caused suspicion.

But there wasn't anyone there waiting for his return. His apartment felt empty, more so than it ever had before.

He brushed his teeth and went through his pre-bed routine. He didn't think there'd be any chance that he'd fall asleep, especially knowing it may be the last night of his entire life.

It was a crazy idea, especially considering that he might drive to Indiana and realize the address was completely wrong.

That Steven either didn't live there or no longer lived there.

Tomorrow could turn out to be a big misunderstanding.

Greg slept well that night.

It was the best night of sleep he'd had in a long time.

Better than any night of sleep since Jessica's death.

It was almost as if Greg's subconscious knew he'd need all the energy that he could muster.

It was going to be a big day.

Chapter 29

Greg woke up at eight-thirty. Any thoughts of postponing the trip to Indiana and going to work instead were out of the question.

He didn't have enough time to get ready and get through traffic.

He decided not to call in sick. He could die today, so what difference would it make?

If Bob fired him, so be it. In moments like this, a person really understood the important things in life, and his dead-end job wasn't one of them.

He began packing all the things he'd need.

The gun and bullets were obvious firsts.

He didn't eat breakfast. Wasn't hungry. But he figured he'd better bring some food in case his appetite came back to him.

Over and over, he played it out in his mind.

Could he really go through with it?

As many reasons as he had against the plan, knowing that he should just call the Detective Maxwell and have him take care of it, he couldn't.

His gut told him to take care of the problem.

Today.

Right now.

He just wanted it to all be over with.

He briefly thought about hiring someone to do it for him, but there were two problems with that. First, he didn't have enough money to do so. Shane did, and he'd probably give it to him, but Greg wasn't one to ask for charity. Especially when the money would be used for something like this. Secondly, he didn't trust any of the other Deep Web hitman sites. *American Hitmen* was the only sight that he knew was legitimate. The others looked like they'd take his money and run.

Finally, he told himself he may or may not do all that he hoped. He wanted to at least drive by the house to see it. Maybe just inspect it for anything suspicious. He could always come back later. A two-and-a-half hour drive wasn't that long. From what he'd seen of assassins on TV, they were always careful and methodical. Rarely did they just show up somewhere and start blasting.

He was now ready. He picked up the book bag that had his gun and food.

As he did, there was a knock on the door.

He set his bag down, wondering if he should grab the gun. Greg decided to check through the peephole first to see who it was. He walked to the door, being careful not to make any sound. Was it Shane? Detective Maxwell? One of his neighbors? Steve?

When he looked, he saw that it was Stacy.

What on Earth is she doing here?

He opened the door.

"Hey," Greg said.

"Can I come in?"

"Uhh, of course." Before he'd finished answering, she was already stepping in. She was in a bad mood; that much was obvious.

Greg closed the door. As soon as the click of the door sounded, Stacy spoke.

"Going somewhere?"

"Umm, yeah. I took a vacation day," Greg lied. He'd promised her he'd never lie to her again, but it came out naturally.

"I see. Where ya headed?"

"Thought I'd go backpacking. Get some fresh air, ya know? Think things over."

"What does one bring to go backpacking?" she asked, reaching down to look into his bag.

"Hey, don't!" he said. He grabbed his pack before she had a chance to look. He knew how glaringly guilty it made him look, but what else was he supposed to do?

"What do you have in there, Greg?"

"It's nothing," he said. "What are you doing here, Stacy?" He tried to turn the attention back to her.

"Nice try. What do you have in here?"

"It's… nothing. Just some snacks and stuff. Now please, answer my question. How did you know I took a vacation day?"

"Well, I didn't. Seeing as you don't go to work much these days, I thought I'd take the chance. I was in the area, so I thought I'd stop by."

"I see. Is that the only reason?"

"No. You went to Jimmy's last night?"

"I did."

"What did you guys talk about?"

"He didn't tell you?"

"He did, but I wanted to hear it from you."

"Stacy, quit with all the games. What do you want from me?

Just say it."

"Fine," she said. She walked over to the couch and sat down. Greg followed her over.

"He told me you might have found out who killed Jessica."

Greg didn't say anything. He didn't know what to say.

"It's okay, Greg. You can trust me."

He wondered what Stacy knew from her conversation with Jimmy, and more importantly, what she *didn't* know.

"I'm sure Jimmy has already told you that he's in the picture that was posted of Jessica's murder scene. Which makes me want to ask you, did you notice Jimmy in the picture when I showed it to you?"

"Absolutely not," she said. "I would have told you, Greg!"

"Okay," he said.

"I haven't gotten to see the picture again. Jimmy couldn't figure out how to get to it. Can you show me?"

"Well, I could. But I don't really have a computer right now."

"Isn't there a Macbook on the table over there?"

"That's Jessica's, but it's password protected."

"Oh."

"As I was saying, I showed the picture to Jimmy. He then told me his story, saying that he just happened to be in the area. He told me, though, that he remembered seeing the person taking the picture. And even better, he happened to know who it was."

"That's great, Greg! But how do you know that he's the one who killed Jessica?"

"Because the picture was posted on the site. Only the hitmen could have access to the site, so if he took the picture, he has to be involved."

"Oh, yeah, I guess that makes sense!"

"So I just need to find out where exactly this guy lives. That's the next step."

Stacy looked at him and said, "Why do I have the feeling that you've already figured out where he lives, and that your 'backpacking trip'"——she used her fingers as quotations——"is really a trip to pay the guy a visit?"

Greg hesitated. "Jimmy didn't know where he lived. He hadn't seen him since middle school. I checked; he wasn't on Facebook. Nothing came up when I Googled his name," Greg said. He was careful to give her factual statements.

"If you're really going backpacking, then can I see your bag?"

"No, Stacy. There's something in here that I don't want you to see. It's as simple as that."

"If you don't show me what's in that bag, then I'm afraid we're going to have to go our separate ways."

Greg considered it.

He knew this moment was going to come.

Why hadn't he taken five seconds to hide the backpack before he answered the door? *Stupid mistake,* he thought.

"It doesn't have to be like this, Stacy. Please trust me."

She got up from the couch. "Fine. I'm sorry you feel this way. But I can't be with someone that I don't trust. And you've given me reason after reason not to trust you."

Stacy got halfway to the door, her back turned to Greg.

"Wait," Greg said. She turned around. "You really want to see what's in the bag?"

She didn't say anything, but her eyes answered for her.

He unzipped the bag and held it out so that she could see the gun.

Both her hands went to her mouth. It was as if he'd showed her a severed head.

"Where did you get that!?"

Greg hesitated. He realized he'd already told her almost

everything. Might as well lay it all out there. "I'm not going to tell you where. Please don't make me do that."

"All right. *Why* do you have it?"

"I found him. I know where he is."

Stacy shook her head. Greg could tell she was upset that he hadn't admitted this before. "Where?"

"Couple hours away. In Indiana."

"So… what? You're just going to go over there and shoot him? I can't let you do it. Why don't you just call the police?"

"I explained this to——" He caught himself. "I've thought about this. I can't wait months for it to go to trial and then to watch him somehow get off for lack of evidence or some bullshit loophole."

"You don't know that will happen. You could find out and see if it does. Kill him then, if he gets off free."

Greg thought about it. "No, because if he got off free, he'd hide from me. Worse, he'd kill me for sure. And I still don't know for sure if it's just him or if he's working with other people."

Jessica shook her head. "You're right. You never should have shown me. Now I'm just as guilty as you if you go there and kill him."

"Then you shouldn't have guilt-tripped me into telling you. But if it makes you feel better, you can just say I never showed you. I won't admit it to anyone."

"Thanks, but that doesn't matter. What if they strap me, or you, to a lie detector? What then?"

Greg didn't have an answer to this. He didn't have an answer to a lot of things.

"I don't want to see you get hurt, Greg. I wouldn't be able to live with myself if something happened. I do care for you, Greg."

"What? No, you don't. Ten seconds ago, you were breaking up with me. You were going to walk out that door and never see me again."

"No, I wasn't. That's the main reason I came over here in the first place: to work things out."

Greg was remembering all of the wonderful times they'd shared together. How she'd helped him pick up a lot of the pieces that had been shattered after Jessica's death. He owed her so much for that.

"I don't know what to do," Stacy said.

"*You* don't have to do anything. Go home. Let me do what I've already made up my mind to do. I'll stay out of your way for awhile, just so there's nothing that can link you to any of this."

"Oh, sure. That makes a lot of sense. Just sit around my room and knit while my boyfriend gets himself killed? No, I'm not about to do that, and if you think I would, Greg, well… you don't know me very well."

"All right, well what do you——"

"I'm going with you."

"What? Absolutely not."

"Why not? You're most certainly going to get yourself killed. Have you even fired a gun before, Greg?"

"No. Have you?"

Stacy didn't answer. Instead, she looked down at her feet, and Greg wondered if that was how he had looked during Stacy's interrogation.

"Well, since we're fessing up about everything, I guess I should admit some things, too."

"Yeah, I wasn't going to bring it up."

"What? I suppose you played detective and discovered some of my past?"

"No, not exactly. Jessica's boss told me."

"When did you speak with——oh, nevermind. Doesn't matter. You probably know I was in and out of juvie. I've stolen more things than I can count. I've been about as far from perfect as a person can get," she said. "But Greg, I've changed. For two years now, I can honestly say I've been honest. I haven't even thought of stealing anything. I'm really trying to put a stable life together."

"Why did you... you know... do those things?"

"Stupidity. My parents had everything laid out for me. Keep working on the farm. Take over the business some day. They wouldn't pay for my schooling. They said there was no need. That's when I decided to try to get some money on the side. Make it out of there on my own. Unfortunately, I decided to take the easy route and steal it instead of working for it. As you probably saw, that didn't get me very far."

"I'm... I'm just trying to understand you, Stacy. On the surface, you're one person, and underneath, you're entirely different."

"I know. But so are you!" she said. "Believe me, I don't want my past to reflect the person I am today. It's something I'll be stuck with my entire life, having to explain it to people."

"It's all right; no one is perfect," Greg said. Inside, he thought he understood why such a remarkable girl was settling for a guy like him. She still didn't have the confidence in herself to go for a guy she truly deserved. "I forgive you for not telling me. I get it, being afraid to admit something like that. You can tell me anything, though," he said, grinning because it was something she'd once said to him.

She smiled back. "I know."

"Call it even? Our web of lies?"

"Even."

"Good," Greg said. He didn't know where to go from there. As always, Stacy was the one to prevent the long, empty silence between them.

"I've got an idea."

"Oh, yeah? What's that?" Greg said.

"I'm coming with you. You can't do it alone, Greg. You'll get yourself killed."

Greg was ready to interrupt, but she held up a finger to stop him.

"Think about it. What's your plan? Knock on his door? He probably recognizes you, Greg. No, not probably. I'm sure he *does* recognize you. If he came to your apartment, I'm sure he's at least seen a picture of you."

Greg thought about it; she had a point. He didn't want to kill the guy without interrogating first, and he couldn't interrogate him without catching him off guard and getting inside his house.

"All right, what do you propose?"

"Well, that all depends on where he lives and if there are multiple points of entry. I'm thinking I can be the one that knocks on his door. It's less likely he'll recognize me."

"You don't know that for sure, though. He could very well know who you are."

"Well, it's a chance I'm willing to take. The one thing we do know is that he *definitely* knows you."

"Then what? What am I going to do?"

"We can figure that out later."

"That's not good enough. I'm not going to let you get yourself killed either. If you ask me, I'd say it's just as likely that he knows who you are. In fact, I'd say it's a certainty."

"Maybe so. Well, we should bring along someone that he doesn't recognize. It would make all of this a lot easier."

"Well, I have someone in mind," Greg said hesitantly.

"Who?"

"Someone that I know always has my back, no matter how much he may disagree with my decision."

"Who!?"

"Shane."

Chapter 30

"I have always wanted to meet him. Especially after all the stories I've heard."

"You're not allowed to sleep with him. Never, ever. Promise me."

She laughed. "I'm not going to. Those guys aren't my type."

"Shane is every girl's type."

"That may be true. I solemnly swear, I will not sleep with him," Stacy said with her hand against her heart. "Now, are you going to call him or what?"

"I don't know. He said he had an important presentation this morning. It started early, though."

"Okay, we'll wait if we have to."

Greg wanted the ordeal over with as soon as possible. He took out his phone, ready to call Shane, when he stopped. "Nah, I can't do this. If I call, I'm getting him even more involved than he needs to be. It's bad enough that I have his gun. If I call him hours before killing someone and they find out that it's me, he's going to be in a world of shit, too."

"Oh, come on," Stacy said, shoving Greg. "Grab your backpack and let's go. Where do you suppose he is now?"

"Well, his presentation was at Axix, which is northeast

Columbus. He'll probably come back to the office around 10:30. After that, it depends on how it went. If it was bad, he'll probably assist one of the other sales guys for the rest of the afternoon. If it went well, he'll probably go to every strip club in a thirty mile radius and then get a massive hotel suite somewhere to throw a party."

"Sounds like we better get to him before he gets to his office."

"Yeah, that's what I was thinking, too."

Greg drove Stacy over to his office. He didn't want to get her involved, but at the same time, he was too scared to do it alone. The fact that she was willing to be with him, risking her life in the process, meant a lot.

They pulled into a parking spot that faced the entrance. From there, they'd be able to tell when Shane pulled in with his red Corvette. Shane went through more new cars in a year than Greg would have in the next twenty. He'd told Greg once that he liked the new car smell more than cheap stripper perfume, and that was saying something.

Greg hadn't really been sure when Shane would arrive, if at all, when he'd told Stacy 10:30. It turned out, though, that his guess was pretty accurate.

Shane pulled in at 10:40. Alone.

When he got out of his car, Greg got out, too, and motioned him over.

"Jesus, Greg. I haven't been able to think straight today. Have you——" he stopped himself when he saw Stacy in the passenger seat. "Hey, I'm Shane." He gave a wave.

"Hi, I'm Stacy."

"Can I talk for you a sec?" Shane asked while they were both standing outside of Greg's car.

"Yeah, of course." Greg motioned to Stacy that he'd be right back. They walked out of earshot.

"So what the fuck is going on, bro? Getting her involved in this? Or does she not have a clue?"

"I was getting ready to leave for Indiana, and she came to my door. Long story short, I told her what was going down. She convinced me to let her in on it. While she was working on a plan, she thought it would be good idea to have you involved, since Steve Cartwright wouldn't have any clue who you were."

"Good. I like this girl. You know I always got your back, bro. So…" he sighed. "Am I in?"

"You're in."

"Gotta ask, though, do you trust this girl? I mean shit, you've only known her, what, a month? This is some heavy shit going down."

"I realize that. Well, to be honest——"

"Your lack of confidence isn't what I was hoping for," Shane interrupted.

"I trust her," Greg said with as much confidence as he could.

"Ahh, man," Shane said, clearly frustrated, "This just doesn't feel right. Something about it. I know you feel the same way."

"I do," Greg admitted. "What do you suppose we do, though?"

"Damned if I know. Mind if I talk to your girl? See if I can get a better understanding of what the hell she's thinking?"

"By all means."

Greg had assumed that he'd be included in the talk, but Shane stopped him.

"You wait here. I'd rather talk one-on-one."

"Oh, all right," Greg said, feeling stupid.

He watched Shane walk over and get in his car. It was just him and Stacy, talking about who knew what. He had a strong impulse to go over to them. He'd give anything to know what they were saying.

Whatever it was, it took awhile. Five minutes passed and Greg could still see their heads bobbing back and forth in conversation. Anxiety was building as Greg looked for something else to direct his attention towards. Finally, he heard the door open, and Shane got out of the car. He nodded for Greg to come over.

"So here's the thing," Shane began. "I'm going to drive separately. I've got a few things to take care of, and besides that, it's a good idea to have another car in case something goes down."

"Umm, all right."

"You two go ahead. I'll meet up with you in an hour or so. I told Stacy to just find a Wal-Mart parking lot or somewhere low-key to camp out for a while. Don't go anywhere in Lawrence. It's best that there isn't any video evidence that we were there. You two just hang tight for an hour or so. Feel free to take two of those minutes for a quickie in the backseat."

Greg didn't laugh. Instead, he found it annoying that Shane was cracking jokes when it came to something as serious as this.

"Where are you going? I'd like to know."

Shane put his hand on Greg's shoulder. "Buddy, relax. I'm coming. I've just got something to do first."

Greg didn't like it, but he let it go. Shane made his way to the Corvette.

"See you in a few," Shane said.

Greg didn't say anything back. Instead, he went to his car.

"So what did you two talk about?" Greg asked.

"Nothing. I think he was trying to figure out if he could trust me."

"Well…"

"Well what?"

"Can he trust you? Can *we* trust you?"

"Of course, Greg. Why would you even ask that?"

"I still don't understand so many things about you. You're a big cloud of mystery to me."

"Well, why don't we talk on the way? We should probably get going, though."

"All right, fine," Greg said. He felt it was going to be a long car ride, for many reasons.

Greg drove while Stacy talked. He knew how to get most of the way there, so they had a distraction-free discussion.

Stacy told him more about her history. How she'd made some really awful decisions at a point in her life when awful decisions are often made. Greg thought about his own past and some of the stupid things he'd done, especially in college. Never theft, but he easily could have been arrested on numerous occasions for driving drunk.

Greg was no saint, and he tried to remember that while he listened to Stacy talk. Hearing her tell her side of the story, it didn't sound nearly as bad as when it was laid out to him on Daniel Kavern's desk. He couldn't believe it then, but Stacy made it sound like a few innocent mistakes.

Greg told her that he forgave her.

When he said it, he was unsure if he really meant it, but he was aware that they could all very well be dead by the end of the day, and that made petty resentments matter much less.

They saw a Wal-Mart ten miles outside of Lawrence. It seemed like the perfect place to stop and wait for Shane. As they sat, Greg began the conversation for once.

"Now, can you tell me why Shane couldn't come with us? And what he's up to?"

"You'll see, Greg, soon enough. I promise."

"Why can't you just tell me now?"

"I probably could. But Shane didn't want me to for some reason, and I promised I wouldn't."

"Whatever," Greg said. He looked out the window, doing anything he could to think of something other than the task at hand.

Blocking out such feelings was proving to be very difficult.

Greg left twice to use the bathroom.

He always got the pre-game dumps before stressful situations.

Shane finally called forty-five minutes later.

"Where you at?"

"A Wal-Mart, just outside of Lawrence."

"Okay, I see it. Be there in a minute."

Shane pulled up next to them in a gray Corolla.

"Get in," he said.

"Whose car is that?" Greg asked.

"Not important," Shane said. "Come on, let's go before someone sees us."

Greg sat in the front seat, Stacy in the back.

Not a word was said until they all saw the faded sign:

Welcome to Lawrence

Shane handed Greg an old Garmin GPS.

"1308 Tarr Cove Drive, Lawrence, Indiana. That's where our little friend lives."

Greg did as he was told but asked, "So what's our plan? You gonna tell us or are you keeping that secret, too?"

He expected some animosity returned, but Shane had never seemed more calm and reserved in his life.

"For now, all we're gonna do is survey the land. Just drive by the place. After that, we can discuss strategy."

They pulled off of the main street. Lawrence was a tiny little town. It reminded Greg of the place that his grandma used to live. A purposefully uneventful town. The kind of location that old people flocked to.

Or, Greg thought, people who really wanted to stay under the radar.

He could already imagine Steven Cartwright living there. No one would disturb him in such a town. He'd drive the ten-minute route to Wal-Mart for groceries, which would be less conspicuous than the IGA in Lawrence, where people would recognize his face if he showed up too often.

Just beyond the main street, the cornfields began. They crowded onto both sides of the road.

The GPS directed them to turn right, onto a narrow road that was just wide enough for two cars to pass each other. Not that it mattered. This road didn't look like it got much use anyway, except for the occasional homeowner on their way to town.

There was a home about every quarter mile. Greg had an unnecessarily firm grip on the GPS unit, and he saw that they were less than a mile from their destination.

There was a stop sign ahead. He didn't need to read the street sign to know what it said.

Tarr Cove Dr.

This was it.

"What is the house number, again?" Stacy asked.

He'd almost forgotten she was in the back seat. He wished that she wasn't.

"1308," Greg and Shane said at the same time.

A quarter mile away.

They passed a two-story white house in desperate need of a paint job.

Shane rolled the Corolla up. "Not it. 1284," he muttered.

Just to the left of the front door, Greg saw the crooked black numbers.

"Next one must be ours," Shane said.

Not far ahead was another house. A tiny home, only one story. It had a small yard surrounding it, around twenty yards wide. Behind it was nothing but cornfields.

Greg turned the GPS unit off and wiped the sweat from his hands onto his pants. He let out a deep breath, but it did nothing to slow his heart rate down.

"Take 'er easy, Greg. You look like you're gonna go into cardiac arrest or somethin'."

Shane took his time, strolling by at about ten miles per hour.

The intensity in the car could be felt by all.

Greg saw the wooden mailbox.

It looked like it had been put up a century before.

On the side, it had shiny, newer-looking black numbers.

1308.

Chapter 31

Shane stopped in front of the house, but only for a second.

There was a red Chevy Cavalier parked outside.

The quaint little white home was nothing special. A one-step porch. One window. The yard had recently been mowed.

Shane sped off. Greg whipped his head back to get one last look. He saw that Stacy was looking back, too.

"So what did you guys think?" Shane asked.

"Small little house. Nothing special," Greg said.

"No dog fence on the outside. That's good," Stacy said. "No side doors. That means, chances are, there's a back door."

"Agreed," Shane said. "Anything else?"

"Nope, not really."

Shane drove the car a mile down the road. A few trees were on both sides and no houses were in sight.

He popped the trunk, and they all looked in.

There were two massive rolls of plastic sheeting. Greg could guess what they were for, and it reminded him again of the realness of the situation.

There was also some rope. And handcuffs.

"Do I need to ask where or why you got all this stuff?"

"Keep your eye on the goal, Greg," Shane said. "Here's what

I'm thinking," he began. "Stacy, you drive us up, and Greg and I will go to the backyard. Hopefully he won't see us, but if he does, we'll be ready." Shane grabbed a pistol out of the trunk and cocked it. "Once we're in the back, we'll give you a thumbs-up or something if we see a backdoor and if the coast is clear. When we do, that's when you pull in. Go up to the front door. Shove your titties in his face or whatever it is you want to do. Enough to distract him so that we can slip in through the back."

"Woah, that wasn't the plan," Greg interjected. "That was the whole reason we brought you here, because you wouldn't be recognized."

"Fuck that. Whether he recognizes her or not doesn't matter. We'll barge in there before he or anyone else has time to do shit."

For the first time, Greg heard a hint of annoyance in his voice. "I don't like that one bit. What if Stacy——"

"Got it," Stacy said confidently.

Greg tugged at his hair. "Just to play devil's advocate here a little bit… what if this isn't even his house? What if an eighty-year-old grandma opens the door?"

"Then Stacy will give some bullshit excuse and leave," Shane said. "But it's going to be our guy. I did some more digging online, and the dude definitely lives here."

"Okay. What then? I want to get as much out of him as we can before, ya know…"

"Of course. We're not gonna open the door and start blasting unless we have to! We'll get all that stuff taken care of once we're inside and have him handcuffed. Then you can do all your twenty questions bullshit. Who knows, you may not even want to kill him. But we can decide all of that later."

"Fine," Greg said.

Shane reached in and handed Greg a thick cotton ski mask.

"I'll tell you when to put it on. But not yet, 'cause we'd look guilty as hell, standing in some dude's backyard with ski masks on," Shane said before turning to Stacy. "Sorry, you'll be the only one whose face is exposed."

"Not a big deal. I understand."

"All right. We ready?"

There were a million things Greg knew that he should probably say, but none of them were coming to him. How the other two had so much confidence, he didn't understand. But he tried to feed off of it as best as he could.

"Ready?" Stacy said.

"Ready."

Stacy drove while Greg and Shane sat in the back. Shane tucked the gun into his pants, and Greg followed suit. He stuffed the ski mask in his back pocket.

She stopped the car a few hundred feet short of the house.

"Let's go," Shane said.

Greg followed Shane's lead. A light jog through the cornfield. The stalks were barely higher than their ankles, so it was easy.

Greg felt like he was in a virtual reality game.

It didn't feel like real life.

They got to the backyard and saw only a shed and a tiny strip of yard. There was a back door, right in the middle. There was one tiny step with a slab of concrete in front.

"Wait here," Shane whispered before tiptoeing over to the corner of the house and giving the thumbs-up to Stacy.

Greg felt the sun beaming down on his face. It felt good. Especially with the occasional chilly breeze.

He could hear Stacy pull into the driveway and turn the car

off. Then the slam of the car door.

Don't do it, Stacy.

Greg wanted the three of them to get back in the car and leave. He couldn't take the stress that his body was going through. He looked down and saw Shane's gun pointed at the ground ahead of them, ready to use at a moment's notice.

Then, there was knock on the door.

"Put your mask on," Shane whispered.

Greg reached into his back pocket and then panicked. He tapped his other pocket and then both side pockets.

"Shit," he whispered.

"What's wrong?"

"My mask? It must have fallen out or something."

"Damn it, Greg!" Shane said, a little louder than he'd intended. "It's a good thing your dick is attached; you'd have lost it years ago." Shane slapped him hard on the chest. Greg looked down and saw that Shane had his own mask in his hand. "Take mine."

"What? No. It's my mistake. I don't want you to get in trouble for——"

The front door creaked open.

Shane and Greg listened closely to the muffled voices.

A man's voice. A short statement. Probably hello.

Then a higher pitched voice.

Stacy's.

She strung together a few sentences, but Greg couldn't tell what she was saying.

The man responded.

Then Stacy said something back.

"Now," Shane whispered.

He put his hand on the doorknob.

As he did, Greg fumbled with the mask. His mouth had

never been so dry.

Shane slowly turned the doorknob.

Greg hadn't considered that it might be locked until that very moment. Fortunately, it wasn't.

Shane pushed it open and walked inside, his gun pointed ahead, as if he knew what he was doing.

Greg hadn't even stepped onto the concrete step when he heard Shane shout.

"Freeze right there, motherfucker!"

Greg's eyes bulged. Everything was happening at lightning-pace.

When he finally got inside, all he could see were Shane's broad shoulders. He had two hands on his gun, pointed toward the door.

"That's it. Keep 'em up. Down on your knees."

When Greg stepped to the side, he saw him.

It was Steve Cartwright.

It had to be.

An ugly guy. Weasel face. Greasy hair.

The scrawny man had his hands up and a look of pure shock. Stacy stepped in and closed the door behind her.

Steve looked closely at Greg's face. Greg wondered if he recognized him but then remembered the mask on his face. He felt stupid, but he was so disoriented that he couldn't think straight.

"Who are you?" Steve asked, looking directly at Greg.

"That's Mary Lou Retten," Shane answered. "Or maybe it's Satan. Doesn't matter who it is, motherfucker. We've got some questions for you. First, you alone here?" Shane turned the gun to the side. "Don't lie to me."

Steve nodded.

"You expecting visitors any time soon?" Shane asked.

"No," Steve said.

"Better not be."

For the first time, Greg saw the computer workstation in the corner of the room. It didn't look like anything special. A wooden desk with a small monitor on top. It was plugged into a laptop that was closed.

After seeing the computer, anger built up inside him, replacing some of the fear.

"Why doesn't one of us go check? Just to make sure," Shane said.

"I'll do it," Stacy said.

She walked over to Greg and reached out her hand. It took him a second to realize that she wanted his gun. It never even occurred to him that he should be the one checking for other people until Stacy had taken his gun and left the room.

Between the three men in the room, nothing was said.

Greg was trying to collect his thoughts and all of the questions that he wanted answered. He was also trying to decide whether he thought Steve was the guy.

He started with the facts that he had, based on Jimmy's story.

Fact: Jimmy had spotted Steve at the crime scene taking a picture.

Fact: Jimmy had said he looked up and saw the flash of the camera.

Fact: A picture had been posted to the American Hitmen site.

Fact: Jimmy said that Steve had been caught bringing a gun to school. And that he didn't have many friends.

Greg thought of all the puzzle pieces fitting together. But then there was a shout in the other room. It was Stacy.

"What? What is it?" Shane said.

"Come and look at this."

Shane looked briefly at Greg before turning back to keep an eye on Steve.

"Go check it out," Shane said.

Greg walked towards her voice, glad to be out of the intensity of the room. He walked down a tiny hallway, his shoulders almost touching the walls on either side.

"Where are you?" Greg said.

"In here," Stacy shouted from a room to his right.

He walked in and saw what was on the floor.

A pistol.

A large stack of hundred dollar bills.

Lots of ammo.

And a semi-automatic.

Chapter 32

"Were these guns just lying here?" Greg asked.
"No, they were under the bed."
"Holy shit," Greg said.

The weapons further solidified Jimmy's story; ol' Steven wasn't such a nice guy. The pistol, the shotgun; those were fine. Every hunter in his hometown had those somewhere in the house. But the semi-automatic? Loads of cash?

That was a different story.

"What do we do?" Greg asked. "I don't want to let these out of my sight, but then again, I don't want to touch them either."

Stacy winced. "Oh crap! I didn't think of that."

"It's okay," Greg said, which wasn't what he was thinking. "Just wipe it down with your shirt or something. I'm going to go tell Shane."

Greg walked back and saw that Shane hadn't moved, still holding the gun at Steven's head.

"What's wrong? What is it?" Shane asked.
"Dude's got a fuckin' semi-automatic under his bed."
"Well, well." Shane smiled. "Whatcha doin' with that, huh?"
They both looked at Steven.

"They're registered. Just exercising my second amendment

rights. Are you going to tell me who the fuck you people are and why you burst into my home and have a gun to my head?"

"Yeah, we'll get to that. Just hold your horses," Shane said.

"What should we do?" Greg asked. "With the guns?"

"Just leave 'em there. He's not going to get to them." He flicked his wrist. "I'll make sure of that."

"I don't know. I got a bad feeling for some reason," Greg said.

Shane peered at Greg's eyes. "Stacy, stay in there. This'll only take a few minutes."

"Okay!"

"Now, where was I?" Shane began. "Here's what's going to happen. The way I see it, you have two choices: the first is to log onto that computer and show us who killed my friend's sister. You do that and maybe we let you live. Option two, you refuse or deny what a piece of shit you really are, and I blow your head off right here. Either way, we go home happy. But it's up to you to decide if you want to live longer than the next five minutes."

Steven had a habit of quickly licking his upper lip. It gave Greg the creeps. He didn't think that Steven was as scared as he should be. Another sign that this might be their guy. But he didn't allow himself to think about it, or else his emotions would get the best of him.

"Look, whatever you think I did, I'm afraid you're mistaken. I won't call the police if you leave right this instant."

Greg couldn't stand to listen to this guy talk. Even his squeaky voice reminded him of a rat. He could see why Jimmy and his classmates hadn't liked him.

He turned away, looking back at the door they'd come in. There was a kitchen table that he hadn't even noticed walking by.

He burst with rage at what he saw on top of it.

It couldn't be.

It was.

His laptop.

"You son of a bitch!" Greg screamed, bewildered. "It was you!"

Greg charged forward, reared back, and cold-cocked Steven's face with his fist. He hadn't even tried to resist.

The punch sent the man backward onto the ground. Greg wanted him to get up. Pleaded for him to.

He heard Shane laughing behind him.

"Ahh, shit! Damn, dude, you got him good."

"Get up!" Greg ordered.

For a few seconds, Steven did nothing. But then he struggled back to his knees. A steady drip of blood came from his right nostril. His upper lip was red and starting to swell from where Greg had hit him.

Greg grabbed a fist full of his shirt.

"You want to tell me what my laptop is doing here? The one that was stolen from my apartment."

The last thing that Greg expected appeared on Steven's face.

A smile.

Greg roared and punched him again, sending him back to the ground.

"Greg!" Stacy shouted.

He had no remorse for what he did.

"Was it *you* who did it? Did you pull the trigger? Or was it one of your friends?"

Steven looked back at him and again just smiled.

The arrogant fuck.

"What does it matter?" Steven said. "What would you like me say to make it all feel better?"

Greg turned away. "I can't do it. I can't look at him. I'll fuckin' kill him."

He stormed to the kitchen. Stacy reached out to comfort him, but he shoved her aside.

She followed him.

He wanted to cry. Knew the tears would come later. But for now, all he wanted to do was squeeze Steven's neck until all his breaths were gone.

Forget what Shane said about the choice of a lifetime in prison. Right now, it was worth it. Several lifetimes' worth, if it meant that Jessica's murderer reached the fate he so rightly deserved.

And not just her death. All the people on that site. No one deserved to have their life taken from them and the crime proudly displayed on the Internet. No one.

He hugged Stacy. Grabbed her tight. He got another whiff of the cherry-scented hair that he loved so much.

Greg didn't know how long they stayed there, holding each other. But he knew he could have been there forever and not have minded a bit.

Shane shouted. "Greg, come in here."

Greg saw that Steven was sitting down at the computer. Shane was behind him, still pressing the gun to his skull.

He pressed a few keys on the keyboard and instantly Tor popped up on the screen.

"What's he doing?" Greg asked.

"He's gonna find out who ordered the hit on your sister," Shane said.

"Yeah, is it bad that I don't even remember?" Steve said. "Poor little Jessica must have had a good reason to die. But let's just see what that reason was."

Shane struck the butt end of the handle hard onto the back

of Steve's head. For a moment, Steve looked dizzy, but he didn't acknowledge any pain and kept on typing.

"Just shut up, motherfucker, and find the email," Shane said.

Greg couldn't believe that all of this was happening. Everything he'd wanted over the past month was unfolding right in front of him. He'd had so many doubts that this moment would ever come.

Steven typed a long string of letters and numbers, followed by the familiar ".onion."

A login screen popped up, where he quickly entered in his information.

It was an email client. The interface reminded him a lot of Anonymail's.

It was flooded with emails. At least twenty per day. The subject line for all of them was "Form Submission Received."

So many cruel, sick assholes in this world.

Steven typed Jessica's name in the search box. After a brief delay, a result came up. Again, the subject was "Form Submission Received."

"Wait," Shane said. "Greg, you sure you want to see this, bro? She's gone, man. Nothing you can do."

"Click the damn email," Greg said.

Steve didn't hesitate.

As it opened, Greg grabbed Steve by the shoulder and forced him out of the chair.

This was it.

He was about to find out what the hit said. The next few seconds would answer the burning questions that had plagued his mind since Jessica's death.

The email popped up on the screen, and he began to read.

Chapter 33

Jessica Anderson of Columbus, Ohio, has to be removed from this planet.

He stopped reading and turned away.

"Guys, can you give me a minute?" Greg asked.

"Yeah, of course," Shane said. He obstructed Stacy's view of the computer screen and led her away. Then he gave Steve a hard push with the butt of his gun.

When they had disappeared into the kitchen, Greg returned to the screen.

He closed his eyes. What was it going to say? Who was involved?

Did Daniel Kavern's wife find out about the affair?

Did Kevin Cole seek revenge after Jessica took his job?

Had James been so mad the night of the AFTA conference that he ordered the hit?

Greg opened up his eyes, just wide enough to read the date. It was on March 7th, a few weeks before her murder. No time of day was given.

He couldn't take it any longer. He started reading.

I love my wife. She's the mother of my beautiful children. But I'm a rich, very powerful man who has his needs and deals with temptation every single day.

I started cheating on her a year ago with Jessica Anderson, a girl that I work with. I made it quite clear to Jessica from the beginning that I wasn't interested in anything but a physical relationship, which she said she was fine with. But over time, she wanted more, and I told her that we should go our separate ways. She didn't take the news well and threatened to tell my wife. While I didn't continue fucking her after that, she did force me to give her a significant promotion, one that she didn't deserve and was unqualified for.

I thought that was enough to make her happy, and she seemed satisfied, but things only got worse from there. She came to me about a month later and told me she was pregnant with my child.

This lying bitch admitted that she'd stopped taking her birth control medication in a desperate attempt to keep me. She begged me to leave my wife and kids, and stay with her.

Now, I'm forced to tell my wife of my wrongdoings, unless you can help. Kill this woman, Jessica Anderson, who's done nothing but lie to me since we've been together. Any woman who is so manipulative in that she'd stop taking the pill so she could have your child deserves to die. Should you do that, I'd be forever grateful.

Greg read it again. Then again. Letting it all sink in.

Then, without conscious thought, he flung the mouse against the wall, shattering it into a dozen pieces.

Daniel fucking Kavern. He'd never liked the guy.

But that wasn't what made him maddest. That wasn't what made him get up from his chair, ready to strangle weasel-faced Steve Cartwright to death.

Jessica had been pregnant when she died.

"You motherfucking son of a bitch," Greg screamed. He got up from the chair, which rolled out of the way. He picked it up with both hands and launched it against the wall over the couch. It put a sizable hole in it before reaching the ground.

He stormed toward the kitchen, but Shane cut him off.

"What is it, bro? What did it say?"

"Get out of my way."

Shane looked terrified but said, "Think about it Greg. There's no turning back if you do this. Trust me, take five minutes and——"

"Get the fuck out of my way, Shane. Now!"

Shane gave him a look of disappointment and concern. But he must have known that, no matter what he said, Greg's mind was made up. He stepped out of the way.

In the kitchen, Steve and Stacy were standing next to each other.

"Stacy, out."

Without hesitation, she ran out of the kitchen.

"You motherfucker," Greg said. "You *knew* she was pregnant, didn't you?" He could hear both Stacy and Shane gasp from the other room.

Steve didn't say anything. In fact, he showed no emotion.

"Was it just you? Or did you have someone else helping you?"

Steve hesitated, but then said, "It's always just been me. You think I'd share my secrets with someone else?"

"So it was you that killed Jessica? You drove by and killed her?"

"Let me think. Was she the one in downtown Columbus? Yeah, I looked her up. Found out where she lived and what she looked like." He told the story as if it was a pleasant childhood memory. "Then, I watched her leave her apartment and walk about a block down. It was daylight then. Too noticeable. So I found a parking spot and waited." He coughed. "Actually that's not true. I went and had dinner. There was a diner across the street nearby. I ate there, watching to see if she'd go back to her apartment, but she didn't. *Then* I went back to my car. Sat there for a few hours until she finally left. I'd almost given up. Really, the plan was to follow her up to her apartment, but I looked around and saw the streets were eerily quiet. I trusted my instincts and decided to do it right from the car. Even if someone was looking, I had a mask and the car had fake plates."

Greg watched him as he told his story. Every word out of his mouth was torture; Greg noticed that he clenched his left fist so tight that his nails dug into his palms, nearly breaking the skin.

"From there, the rest is pretty much history. I drove off and parked the car a few blocks away. Switched the plates. I was a little sloppy in that I didn't throw the gun away. I stuck it under my seat. Walked over to the crime scene. By the time I got there, there was a swarm of people. As was expected. Took a few pictures. Walked back to my car. Drove home. Pretty simple. Almost too simple, actually."

Greg didn't want to hear anymore. He squeezed the handle of the gun a little tighter, ready to fire, when someone spoke behind him.

"Don't, Greg." It was Stacy.

She reached for his hand, the one with the gun pointed at Steve, but he shoved her aside.

"Get away from me, Stacy. It's too late. I'm doing this."

He pointed the gun back at Steve's head and looked into the cold, black eyes, wondering how someone could have no remorse for anything that they'd done.

He tried to imagine the man in front of him, doing something so terrible. He did give off the vibe of danger and evil. There was definitely something twisted.

Greg wanted to end it. End this man's life. He was ready. His finger was on the trigger. He squeezed it a millimeter or two but stopped.

He still couldn't get over the look on Steve's face.

"Are you even scared?" Greg asked.

"What's there to be scared of?" Steve said. "You pull the trigger. The lights go out. That's it."

"Aren't you worried about going to hell?"

Steve laughed. "You don't really believe that fiction, do you? Those are just stories people came up with to try to make everyone behave like good little boys and girls. Fact is: we're on this earth for a little while until we're not. Then that's it."

"Not you, my friend. You're going to burn. You and Saddam. You'll get gang-banged for the rest of eternity by Ted Bundy and Hitler."

"If you say so." Steve sighed. "So, you gonna pull that trigger or what?"

Greg raised the gun up again. His mind was racing, wanting to do it. But then he thought about what Steve had just said. His naive nonsense.

It didn't matter if Steve was right or wrong about the afterlife. No one really knew. What mattered was what *he* believed. And if he felt that dying would cause no pain, then Greg couldn't kill him. He had to have this man suffer.

"If that's how you feel, then maybe it's best that you rot in a jail cell. You may never feel bad for what you did——I doubt you will——but living the rest of your sad, pathetic life getting your ass raped and beaten in prison is exactly what you need."

Greg kept the gun pointed at Steve's chest. *He* believed in hell and was confident that was where Steve was going. He pressed his finger against the trigger, ready to pull it.

A gun fired.

Greg flinched, confused by what had happened. He hadn't pulled the trigger. His ears rang from the noise.

In front of him, Steve's blood and brains were spattered on the cabinet.

After the lifeless body fell to the ground, there was an eerie silence.

Greg got a whiff of the gun smoke.

He turned to his right and saw that Stacy had taken the pistol from Steve's room. She still had it pointed to where Steve had sat moments before.

There was a hint of a smile across her face.

Chapter 34

Shane said what Greg was thinking.

"Holy fucking shit!" followed by "Oh god, oh god, oh god!"

Greg wanted to ask her why she'd done it, but he couldn't get the words out.

He looked at Steve's bloody body on the floor.

"Do you think the neighbors heard the gun?" Shane asked.

The nearest neighbor was a quarter mile away. Growing up in Ohio during deer season, Greg knew that the sound of gunfire could be heard from at least a mile away. But that was outside. He'd never heard a gun go off inside of a house until now.

"I hope not. I don't think so," Greg said.

"We should probably go now, regardless," Shane said.

"We better clean this up. Cover our tracks as best as we can," Greg said.

"Yeah, agreed," Stacy said.

"All right. But let's hurry up. The cops could be here any minute," Shane said.

They put on winter gloves that they found in the closet, and the three of them wiped down anything they thought they'd touched.

Greg was concerned that his hair or sweat may have fallen to the floor, especially around where he'd punched Steve. So Stacy vacuumed the living room and then emptied it out into a trash bag.

The three of them racked their brains, trying to think of other things they needed to do. There was a brief discussion on whether they should do something with Steve's body, but they decided it would be foolish. An unlimited number of things could go wrong.

Shane and Stacy walked out the front door, each holding a trash bag to put in the car. They were going to toss it in the nearest dumpster they could find.

Greg gave one final look at Steve's body. The fucker that had killed his sister. She'd been pregnant, too. The thought was too crushing, so he blocked it out.

Ever since she'd died, this was the moment he'd wanted more than anything. To stand at the corpse of the person responsible. He'd imagined the sense of relief and satisfaction of justice.

But the reality was far bitterer.

At the moment, he actually felt worse.

He went to Steve's computer, which still showed the email account on the screen. He sat down and took one of his gloves off.

He reread the email that Daniel had sent. What a twisted fuck he was, too. He forwarded it to a random Mailinator email address that he'd set up. That seemed like a better choice than his own personal account, so it couldn't get tied back to him. He wanted to make 100% sure he had some evidence of the email. Greg hadn't even had time to process what he was going to do about Daniel Kavern. He needed to ensure he was in the clear after Steve's murder and make it home first.

There were so many emails. So many sick, evil, twisted people in the world. He read a few of the evil rants. The language was so grotesque. He considered saving it somehow. It was the right thing to do. He felt up against the clock, though, knowing they needed to leave soon.

Greg looked through drawers, hoping to find somewhere that Steve kept all of his logins. He then searched for it on his computer, but something told him that Steve didn't keep them anywhere. After all, it would be pretty stupid to go through such great lengths to disguise your identity and then have your information saved for the police to have access to. No, this was Greg's last chance to read through these emails.

He glanced through more emails, but nothing stuck out so he clicked to the sent mail folder. Immediately, he knew he'd discovered something big:

Two emails, both with Daniel Kavern's name in them. He opened up the most recent one and read through the conversation.

First off, thank you for killing Jessica Anderson. I'm glad you agree that she deserved it. But I must confess that I haven't been entirely honest with you. I made it sound as though the message was being written by Jessica's boss, Daniel Kavern, but I'm actually somebody else.

I found out Daniel had been cheating with that little whore three months ago. He finally fessed up to me about it.

He's been a lying, cheating asshole for years. I've turned a blind eye to it, but after this, I can't do it anymore.

To apologize for my previous untruth and to make it worth your while, I'm willing to offer you $100,000 to kill Daniel Kavern. I know that you normally don't take cash, but I'm hoping that you can make an exception. And if that figure is too low, let me know and I'll see what I can do.

I can provide the cash however and wherever you'd like. Please get back to me, if interested. I'm really hoping that you do. You can send a reply email to sj3425@k4lk3ji.onion.

Greg read through the email again. While it didn't specifically say, he thought that it was highly likely that Daniel Kavern's wife had written it. Whoever it was, it wasn't Daniel. Unless he wrote this as a way to try to disguise that he'd sent out the first email.

But Greg didn't think so. The site had already proven that it worked. It was unlikely that Daniel had the balls to request a hit on himself.

No, Greg was certain that Daniel wasn't involved after all.

Which meant that Daniel had been in serious danger. The email request had been sent out a week and a half before. He read through the rest of the conversation:

Springfield, Ohio. Snyder Park. Today. There's a trashcan just to the right of the tennis courts. Drop the money next to it and leave.

That explained the stash of money in Steve's bedroom.

Greg remembered passing Springfield on the way to Indiana. It was about forty-five minutes west of Columbus. Not quite halfway, but a good middle ground. The transaction had obviously gone through. Had Steve made any progress on delivering? Or was he taking the money and running?

Missed on my first opportunity. Never happened before.

What did that mean? Greg wondered what had happened. He wanted to know more but that had been the end of the conversation.

The other emails were sent to different addresses and just

said things like "done" and "okay." They had nothing to do with Daniel. Greg looked for the message that he'd sent, but it wasn't there. Steve must have deleted it.

Shane and Stacy walked back inside.

"Find anything else?" Shane asked.

Greg didn't respond; he was busy scrambling through the computer, looking for anything else he wanted to email himself. He forwarded the conversation he'd just read to his Mailinator email, too. It would drive him crazy, reading and re-reading it, but he'd go even crazier if he tried to remember exactly what it said.

He decided to leave all of the other emails. What was done was done. If Steve really was the only person involved with the *American Hitmen* site, which Greg was unsure of, then there wasn't much else he could do. It would take forever to sift through all of the emails and find the requests for the victims he knew about. And even then, what would he do with them? Send the culprits' names to the victims' families? Greg had already planned on sending anonymous emails to people so that they could find closure, even though some of the victims didn't seem like they had much in the way of a family life. But the police? They weren't doing much with the case, so giving them information would do Greg little good.

But he did want to have another conversation with Detective Maxwell. There was something that Greg *had* to know.

Had Jessica been pregnant?

It was something Greg was sure they would've uncovered in the autopsy. He had to know the truth. And if she had been pregnant, why hadn't the detective told him before?

"Come on. Let's finish up and get out of here," Greg said. He looked at the screen one last time, took a deep breath, and shut down the computer.

Deep Web

Chapter 35

They'd dumped the pistol that Stacy used to kill Steve on their way home. Greg had found it strangely satisfying to discard it in Springfield.

That night, Stacy stayed with Greg while Shane went back to his place. It had been Shane's idea, thinking that it might raise suspicion if they all hung out together. It was better that they stay away from each other for at least a few days.

"What are you thinking right now?" Stacy asked.

She'd caught him staring off at the wall for a lengthy period of time.

"I just can't stop thinking about whether or not Jessica was pregnant. And wondering if it really was Daniel's wife that sent out the hit. And, if so, whether or not Daniel is safe now or if he's still in danger. I just don't know if Steve was telling the truth. It sounded like he was, but how can you take the word of a sociopath like that, you know?"

"Just call Detective Maxwell. You're going to make yourself crazy until you do."

"What am I supposed to say?" Greg asked. "I just can't think of a way to start that conversation without giving myself away."

Stacy shrugged, "I don't know." She snuggled up next to him

on the couch and put her arm around him. "But you're a lot smarter than you give yourself credit for, Greg Anderson."

Greg half smiled, looked into her beautiful eyes, and gave her a kiss. He was exhausted but had a wired energy at the same time. He felt like he was back in college, taking shots of espresso at midnight to cram for an exam.

She was right. He did need to call Maxwell. He felt a moral responsibility to at least drop a hint that Daniel Kavern could be in serious danger. Greg knew he'd feel guilty if something were to happen to the man. He still had no idea what was true and what wasn't from those two emails, but he did know one thing was true. Jessica and Daniel had a relationship together. He'd seen the pictures. Whether it had just been a fling or whether it was something more, Jessica had definitely been interested in the man.

Greg picked up his phone, his hand shaking ever so slightly.

Stacy noticed and leaned up against the other side of the couch, watching Greg's every move.

Greg couldn't take it another second. He was up against the clock and had to clear his conscience. He dialed Maxwell's number.

As the phone rang, Greg gulped. The roof of mouth was dry, and he looked around for a quick drink of water, but there was none.

"Greg, what is it?" Detective Maxwell answered, sounding rushed.

"Is this a bad time?" Greg responded.

"Kind of. Something big just went down."

Greg froze. He immediately jumped to the conclusion that the "something big" was the same something that he was dreading. He was tempted to hang up the phone, but instead managed to eke out, "What… what is it?"

"There's been a high profile murder. Happened this afternoon."

"Oh really? Umm… where at?"

"Muirfield Village."

He knew it was wrong, but relief poured out of Greg. A murder in Ohio was of no concern to him.

"Are you allowed to say who was killed?" Greg asked, not so much interested as wanting to make conversation.

"Technically, I shouldn't say, Greg. But if you flip on the news, I'm sure 10TV is covering it. There are reporters everywhere."

Greg looked over at Stacy and made a flipping motion to indicate that he wanted the TV on. He whispered, "10TV," and she rushed for the remote, a scared look in her eyes.

"What can I do for you, Greg?"

"Oh, it's nothing. It can wait." There was a pause, and he shook his head in disappointment. He had to get answers. "Detective, there is one thing," he said. "Was there anything of interest in Jessica's autopsy report? Perhaps something you forgot to share?"

"Like what?"

"I don't know. I mean, I know that she died from the gunshot wound and all, but anything about her health that stuck out? Something prior to the shooting?"

"Hmm," Maxwell said. "No bruises. No indication of a prior struggle. No cuts or scrapes. Far as I know, she was healthy as a horse." When Greg didn't reply, Maxwell said, "Is there something you need to tell me?"

"No!" Greg said a little too defensively. Then he laughed to cover it up. "It's just, I had this dream last night." He thought for a moment before he continued to blurt out this lie. "I had this dream that Jessica was pregnant. It's not the kind of thing she'd normally keep from me, but——"

"Oh, heavens, no!" Maxwell said. "Something like that would be vital to the case, and I certainly wouldn't have forgotten something like that. In fact, you would have hated me more than you probably already do from all the questions I would have asked you regarding it."

Greg gave a brief chuckle, even though it wasn't particularly funny.

"Anything else, Greg? I do need to get back."

"No, I think that's all." It wasn't. But Greg could sense that Maxwell wasn't so much asking as he was telling him that he couldn't answer anymore of Greg's questions.

"Okay, take care of yourself," Maxwell said.

"You, too," Greg said, hanging up the phone.

As soon as he did, Stacy had it flipped to 10TV.

It showed dozens of police cars outside of a very luxurious house in a really nice neighborhood.

It didn't surprise Greg, as he was already familiar with Muirfield Village, one of the wealthiest areas in Columbus.

What did was surprise him was the headline.

Marla Kavern, wife of Adriar Pharmaceuticals CEO *Daniel Kavern, dead at 43.*

Chapter 36

For the next several days, Greg didn't miss a second of the news coverage. It went national, all of the big names covering it.

Greg knew that what was told in the media and what the police actually knew were probably worlds apart. What had been reported, however, was that Marla and Daniel Kavern had a heated argument in their kitchen. Marla then went into the laundry room and returned with a pistol. Two shots were fired, one connecting with Daniel's left shoulder before he was able to grab her. After the first shot, there had been additional struggling before Marla had shot the gun once more, and the bullet had managed to find its way to her skull.

Cameras from inside the house had captured it all, validating Daniel's story.

A later report came out, unveiling that there had been another threat on Daniel's life a week prior. Details on that weren't provided, and a suspect hadn't been named.

When Greg heard it, a line from that email conversation ran in his mind:

Missed on my first opportunity. Never happened before.

* * *

Steve had been behind the first murder attempt. For Greg, there was little doubt. Even the date that it supposedly happened aligned perfectly.

As for the requests to Steve, Greg was becoming more and more confident that it had been Marla. He would never be 100% certain of it, but the chances that the two emails had been written by anyone other than Marla Kavern were so improbable that it didn't matter.

She'd done it.

Still, there was plenty to keep Greg on edge. He logged onto *Tor* daily to check Indiana news sites for anything on Steve's murder. There had been no reports, and Greg wondered how long Steve's body would rot in that house before anyone discovered it.

Ten days later, he got his answer.

According to the reports, Steve's neighbor, a farm wife in her sixties, was baking cookies and realized she was short a half-cup of sugar. She walked over to his house and rang the doorbell but got no answer. That was when she noticed the rank smell.

She called the police.

The rest was history.

How much the police really knew, Greg was unsure.

He called both Stacy and Shane to let them know. He disguised the conversation as best as he could, in the off chance that someone was listening in on them.

Waiting was the hardest part. Every day, he wondered when the knock on his door would come. He always imagined that it would be two police officers, both male, not the captain or Detective Maxwell. Cops he didn't know, ready to arrest him for Steve's murder.

He'd shut up. Wouldn't say a word. After all, that was what lawyers always told their clients on TV.

If it came down it, he'd take all the blame. Talk with his lawyer and find out what needed to be said or done to ensure that Stacy and Shane were kept out of it.

But that time never came.

Weeks passed and the case went cold. A teenage girl was kidnapped in Lawrence, and everyone in the surrounding area, including the police, seemed fixated on that. Greg thought that Steve's case likely went cold and was filed away somewhere, soon to be forgotten.

The *American Hitmen* site went down, too. Greg had checked it daily and was happy when, a week after Steve's murder, the site had an error message.

There was a little talk about it on other forums. Some people were praising the site. Others questioning if the site had moved. But no one could find it. The last post, by mc89314, said it all:

"probably got arrested, killed, or both. when ya'll do illegal shit like dat, it's gonna come back to you at some point. don't be so surprised when it does."

It made Greg smile. It was just as his mom had said, that karma had a way of coming back around. He hadn't believed it at the time, but now he realized that she was right. And not just with Steve, but with Marla Kavern as well.

But would karma come back to him? Or Stacy and Shane? They had killed someone, after all.

Greg didn't think so. He never saw it as killing Steve but more as saving a countless number of people. Who knew how long his killing spree would have lasted, and how many bodies would have piled up if they hadn't done something? A good lawyer would have somehow convinced a jury to let Steve walk. At least, that's what Greg told himself.

So Greg rested easier with each passing day.

Knowing that her murder was avenged gave him the peace of mind that he needed to move on.

To pick up the pieces of his life.

And to live a life worth living.

Epilogue

Greg never worked another second at Vinditec. He'd learned that life was too precious to waste on a job that he despised.

Growing up, he'd been told over and over again to find a job that he loved. A job that didn't feel like work at all. It had seemed so cliché before. But after all that had happened, he realized just how much truth there was to it.

Shane had pulled a few strings with his connections and found Greg an analyst job at a non-competing company. It even paid nearly twice as much as his former job at Vinditec.

But he turned it down.

He'd rather work for minimum wage, doing work that he felt contributed to society, than to put together another PowerPoint presentation for higher-ups to glance at.

He decided to join the police academy. Looking for Jessica's murderer, he'd spent hours researching. Time seemed to fly by. Sure, he had been more driven for his sister's sake, but he realized that he did enjoy all the little discoveries along the way. It was something that he could see himself doing for the rest of his career, and the police force had obvious room for improvements.

His parents, even his mom, couldn't have been more supportive.

He and Shane still hung out and golfed every Sunday. But they never spoke about what had happened again, not even when they were alone together. As far as Greg knew, Shane had repressed the entire memory, and that was fine by him.

Then there was Stacy.

With as monumental as the Steve incident had been, they formed a special, inevitable bond. It was as if they were inseparable from that point forward.

It was about three months afterward that he realized he couldn't imagine being with anyone but her. The event had been too dramatic, too devastating to go on living with someone else. It would take decades to get over all that had happened.

Stacy was surprised when Greg proposed, as she hadn't been expecting it at all. But her answer was an emphatic yes.

Greg did have lingering doubts about whether they were rushing into it or if he was somehow emotionally forcing her into marriage. But he knew that he loved her, and only time would tell if it was really meant to be.

Every Sunday morning after Steve's death, Greg went alone to Jessica's gravesite.

The first time he went, he'd told her all that had happened. He felt she deserved to know why, and it was his best way of communicating the message.

The second time, he had asked her all of the questions he wanted to know the answers to. Why the secrecy about her job? Why the affair with Daniel Kavern? What was her side of the story about James and the AFTA conference? Things he knew she couldn't answer now, but that he'd want the answers to when his time came and they'd meet again.

Every time he visited after that, he talked about his life. Updating her on what was happening, just as he had so many times over a plate of mom's favorite pasta. He told her about Stacy, about his new career path, and about all that was going on in his life. Even though he was the only one speaking, he could imagine what she would say to him if she were still there.

She'd have been so excited that she'd finally gotten one of her matchmaking attempts right.

He knew she'd be supportive of his decision to enroll in the police academy, too, and that she would've asked a million questions about it.

But it was what she wouldn't say that would matter the most. He knew she would've looked into his eyes and seen that, for the first time since their childhood, he was optimistic about the future.

While there was still a lot of time before the wounds would heal and he'd fully be able to move on, he was happy.

And going to her tombstone was his weekly checkup.

And a reminder that life could be way too short.

That he should never take a single day for granted.

Because no one knows when their time will come.

Afterward

Thanks so much for reading! I hope you enjoyed it. Whether you did or not, I'd love to hear from you. Visit www.ryanwiley.com/contact to send me an email and tell me what you thought. I PROMISE I'll read it and respond back. Seriously, try it. I dare you.

Also, if you're interested in receiving new book updates, as well as monthly updates on what I'm reading and doing, sign up for my email newsletter at ryanwiley.com or like me on Facebook at facebook.com/RyanWileyAuthor.

Finally, indie authors such as myself often struggle to get the word out about our books. We don't have the luxury of large media spend that big publishing companies offer. Instead, we rely on readers like you to help spread the word.

It would mean the world to me if you took a brief moment to post a review on Amazon, Goodreads, or wherever you bought the book from. It doesn't have to be anything elaborate, one or two sentences will do. Just be honest and let other readers know what you thought of the book. :-)

Thanks again!

Until next time,
Ryan Wiley

Printed in Great Britain
by Amazon.co.uk, Ltd.,
Marston Gate.